BRIAN C. AUSTIN

First Printing: 2024
CHICKEN HOUSE PRESS

Library and Archives Canada Cataloguing in Publication
CIP data on file with the National Library and Archives

ISBN trade paperback edition: 978-1-990336-66-9

Bible Quotations are taken from the *HOLY BIBLE*, AUTHORIZED KING JAMES VERSION.

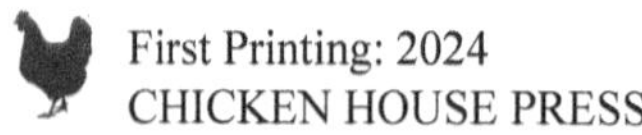 is a facsimile of the lettering used for "Holy Spirit" in *THE GOSPEL OF MARK in the language of the Chipewyan Peoples of Northwestern Canada.* Copyright 1975 Canadian Bible Society. It is used in this manuscript as an approximate translation for *"Great Spirit."*

My Soul And I John Greenleaf Whittier, 1847, Public Domain

"It is Well With My Soul" Horatio G. Spafford, 1876

Hind's Feet on High Places Hannah Hurnard, 1955, The Olive Press UK

"In Flanders Fields" John McCrae, 1915, *Punch* Magazine

Chicken House Press
282906 Normanby/Bentinck Townline
Durham, Ontario, Canada, N0G 1R0

www.chickenhousepress.ca

To **Alanna**
who writes better than her Dad,
but doesn't know it yet.
May your pen and your passion be
powerful tools to touch and change lives.

And to **Doug**
who never quite fit the 'Religious' mold of the family
but who shows compassion for wounded people,
and who deeply respects the God of the Bible,
if not always the god of popular religion.

Author's Note

A word about measurements used in this book. Roland, like so many Canadians of his generation, uses metric measurement. For simplicity, measurements on Canadian roads are in kilometres. Weights are in kilograms throughout, although in a few places pounds are also given. Because international rules apply to aviation, miles, feet, and inches are used for aviation and occasionally for underwater. However, Roland has grown up with metric and uses it exclusively, although once in a while he tries, with limited success, to offer the alternative.

The creation of believable fictional characters borrows heavily from real people. It is a dangerous claim for an author to say *any resemblance to specific persons is accidental.* Yet, the author shapes even the most recognizable characters. They are molded, even as they themselves mold the unfolding story. All characters in this story are products of the author's imagination.

Place names and locations are a blending of fact and fiction. The *Smoky Ridge Hunting Camp* is wholly fictional, although many such rugged, isolated sights exist along the shores of Lake Superior.

The Indigenous Peoples Legend is wholly fictional, although the product of much research.

In excess of 1000 hours of mathematical calculations have gone into the weight, water displacement, and acceleration capabilities of the *EAGLE*. (Because of the many years this book has been in the works, those calculations were made before I owned a computer.) Because of the weight, the calculations were essential to ensure any reader with a moderate understanding of physics would not disdainfully close the book before the tale was well launched. A brief summary of that work is included in the Appendices, sufficient to stimulate the imagination of those who are technically minded, but removed from the body of the manuscript so as not to distract those who are not.

Books that have deeply influenced my fascination with caves include: *The Longest Cave* by Roger W. Brucker & Richard A. Watson, and *Rockwatching* by Michael Gordon. That book has had an old man itching to get farther into some of the caves that can be found here in Ontario, though age is beginning to catch up to me concerning the physical demands of belly crawls through tight holes – since I'm quite anxious to be able to make it back out without someone else having to rescue me. A much more recent publication is *Rising Water* by Marc Aronson, the story of the Cave Rescue in Thai. While that book didn't impact the writing much, it helped reinforce how crazy Roland had to be to do cave diving alone (even just passing through short sumps).

Writing a novel is a task of creative delight, often peppered with agony. People sometimes ask where the idea for a story comes from. The Ram-Wing X-114 featured in a very tattered *Popular Science Magazine* from December 1977[1] is what started the creative juices flowing for this story. Because I wanted the *EAGLE* to be able to dive (and resurface) basic math demanded about 10 times the weight of a similar sized airplane. The flips and loops my much younger imagination at that time longed for quickly proved impossible, so like my main character, I had to settle for a craft that could fly, but just barely. The *EAGLE* proved much more at home skimming the surface or fully submerged.

Thank you for the privilege of sharing this venture that has elements of science fiction and elements of fantasy but is not quite either. I trust you will find as much delight in reading as I have found in writing.

Brian C. Austin

---

[1] *See Appendix A, Image 1*

WHERE EAGLES NEVER FLY

Brian C. Austin

The steps of faith
fall on the seeming void,
and find the rock beneath.

John Greenleaf Whittier

PROLOGUE

The legend tells of a cave, old even then. A painting on the wall shows a man. Beside the man a creature comes out of the water. Many people shelter under the wings from a wild storm.

The reasons have been forgotten for unnumbered years but the shamans teach that when the man is purified in the whirlpool, the lovers will show him a world so new that *Michabo* has not yet painted the sky blue or let an eagle's feather fall to the ground. They teach that the serpent still lurks in the dark waters and hates all sons of *Edáyíné Nezqi*.

CHAPTER ONE

ALONE

ourteen has to be the worst age in the world. At least if your dad does something stupid like getting himself killed. They had all left, but they'd be back, Police and Child Protective Services. What did I need Child Protective Services for? Now that I was alone, I couldn't be trusted to wipe my own backside. Stupid laws!

My head pounded. The people who thought they had to come and *comfort* me had finally left. Flowers wilted on the kitchen table. Remains of casseroles crowded the fridge. The freezer lid barely closed over pastries, squares, and sandwiches. The dishwasher completed its cycle and fell silent. Somebody had even taken the dog. I didn't know who or when. It didn't matter. It was Tacye's dog anyway and only barely tolerated me. The feeling had been mutual, although after the last few days anything that didn't talk all the time would be a relief.

A car drove the gravel road and stirred up dust. Frogs piped shrilly from the pond. Pond? Mud-hole more like, though Dad had called it 'the lake.' "Shut up!" I screamed at the frogs but they ignored me. I had been aching to scream for the last several hours.

I tramped through the empty house, relieved to finally be alone. How many times had someone mouthed: "We're so sorry! If there's anything we can do..."

Yeah. You can do something! My mind would spit the words back. *You can turn the clock back. You can take the guy who did it and drown him in his beer!*

I turned off lights, then stumbled down the stairs to my basement bedroom. Bedroom? I could usually find enough of the bed to sleep there. Shelves overflowed with electronic gadgets I had torn apart and put back together in different ways. A soldering iron lay on old newspapers on the corner of a small table. Magazines made a pile beside a ratty old chair. A chemical smell blended with dirty socks. Dad had sworn I would burn the place down.

I undid the tie that had been strangling me and stripped off the sweaty suit. Dad had bought it for me for Tacye's graduation and wedding, so it even still fit. In the shower I sagged against the wall as warm water sprayed over me. I soaped myself, flushing away sweat. Slumping to the floor of the tub, I hunched down as the water beat on my shoulders.

"Hot water costs money ya know." I could almost hear Dad hollering. I twisted the hot-water tap, shutting it off. I gasped as the icy stream struck me, but sat there, willing myself to endure, to face pain I could control.

Shivering, I finally turned off the water. Forcing myself to stand, I pulled the curtain back and reached for a towel.

A cut on my neck as I shaved pleased me. "Just a little deeper," I muttered. I didn't need to shave. Once a month was more than enough and I had shaved before the graduation ceremony. Tacye was graduating, then getting married in a few weeks. It's a sick joke that she would never get to see her diploma, never see Jenton's eyes when he saw her in her wedding dress. I'd always thought anyone interested in my sister had to be crazy, but now that she was gone...

I lay in bed for a long time and told myself I wouldn't cry. I lied.

I wished I was a writer like Dad had been. Maybe I could have dumped it all on paper. Maybe somebody would even pay for it, a sappy sob story.

I didn't go back to school for a few days but knew Child Protective Services would be in there like smelly socks if I didn't show up soon. It wasn't that they were bad. I knew a couple kids at school whose dads used to beat on them. Child Protection got them out of there, maybe even saved their lives. But my dad never beat on me.

I got some of the left-overs cleaned up from the fridge. Most of them were in those throw-away foil pans, but some glass dishes had names on the bottom. I scrubbed those out. I figured a house full of dirty dishes would be all Child Protection Services needed for an excuse. I didn't want to be here all alone, but I sure didn't want any foster home either. If I could just stall them, I had a birthday coming up in October. 15 didn't sound so young as 14, though 16 was the magic age when they had to butt out. The worst of it was I still had a baby face and that baby pudginess even before I shaved, though at least my voice had changed.

I tramped around the place, snooping through the old barn. It was a big, ugly thing, like half a pipe turned upside down, all rusty. It had been a hanger or something. The guy we bought the place from had an airplane. He sold after he crashed it and smashed himself up. One end was wide open to the wind and sky and looked down over 'the lake.' Somebody had made a road from the barn down to 'the lake' as well. Mostly dirt, but if you looked careful you could see gravel in spots.

It was a perfect place to raise mosquitoes and black-flies. It almost looked like a lake in spring when the water was high, but you could walk most of it in a pair of tall rubber boots this time of year if you didn't get stuck in the mud. There were a few fish but the water wasn't cold enough for them to be good. We often saw deer as well as ducks and geese. I wanted to get a hunting license but Dad wouldn't have a gun on the place.

Did you know you become a nobody when your Dad dies? I somehow didn't have a name anymore. I was Ronald's son, or Tacye's brother. I was never just me, Roland. Roland Jason Handson if you want the whole miserable thing—almost 15—stronger than I looked, but now a nobody, an orphan. Did you know life stinks for orphans?

I got a boring job pumping gas for a couple hours after school. Almost everybody used the self-serve pumps but a few were "too important" to get out of their cars to do that. I tinkered in the garage a bit too, changing oil, doing some of the nothing jobs. The mechanic charged $80 an hour and paid me $19. He was helping me out, the jerk.

I got a kick out of the hybrid cars, though he would hardly let me touch them. But I studied the manuals enough that I could have told you how many amps and volts and ohms and all that other garbage about the batteries, and how quick they could fry your brains if you shorted the wrong wires out.

When I got to the school for the graduation the police were waiting for me. I had bummed a ride with some neighbours and must have gotten out of the house just before the phone started ringing. I don't go in for dope or meth or any of that kind of stuff, so I didn't know what the police wanted. I wish now it had been something like that. I don't remember much about the next few hours but somewhere along the line I got to thinking about the mess Dad called his office and all the papers I'd have to find. There'd be insurance and stuff like that. Ha! Maybe I'd be rich. I guessed there had to be a funeral. What do I know about a funeral?

The drunks who did it had walked away. They weren't even locked up, at least not for more than an hour or two. It had only been six o'clock and they were already stupid drunk. They never let me see Tacye or Dad, but my guess is that she had bled all over her graduation dress. Pretty much nobody ever saw her in it. And the wedding dress in her room just waiting? The stupid saps made sure she'd never wear that too. I wondered what strangling somebody would feel like. I hoped they wouldn't still be so drunk they didn't know when I did it.

It was one of those great big pick-up trucks. I don't usually read the newspaper but the picture was on the front page the next week. It was crumbled in a bit, but the car looked like it had been hit by a freight train.

Tacye had to go to school early so they could tell her how to wear her cap and gown, stuff everybody knew by kindergarten, but now that they were graduating, real adults, they couldn't trust them to get it right.

There was insurance. I found that out a couple days later. And wonder of wonders, Dad had completed his will a few months before the accident. Him and Mom had kicked it around for years before cancer murdered Mom though I hardly remembered any of that.

A couple of people from the church messed in my life so much that it drove me crazy. What songs did I want? Had Dad prepaid for a funeral? Had he named anyone as a guardian? Did he want to be buried or cremated?

How was I supposed to know? For a little bit I hoped Dad and Tacye hadn't gone to heaven. What if the people there were as weird and meddling as the people in our church? I'd never hated a song so much as when they sang "It is Well With My Soul" during the funeral. I had agreed to it but I'd never paid attention to the words when I'd heard it before.

Yeah, I still believed in God, kind of, but I wasn't too impressed that He'd let something like this happen.

The lawyer hung around with his hand out for weeks, but the paperwork finally got done and the house was mine, sort of. Until I was 18 everything was locked up. Dad hadn't figured on getting rubbed out, so hadn't named anyone as guardian. I didn't need a guardian but the law said I couldn't be trusted. Stupid law!

I had no close relatives. Dad only had one brother and he had died. "Crazy!" Dad had always called him. Mom didn't have any brothers or sisters, and I couldn't remember my grandparents. I guess they had died when I was still a baby.

I kicked up a big stink every time they tried to make me move out of the house. One of the 'workers' actually helped keep things slow. So the months crawled by with those lousy court hearings getting recessed and delayed. I was pretty sure I would make it to 16 when Child Protection

Services had to butt out, but all the time the lawyer was there with his hand out. I couldn't get a nickel without him skimming some off the top, though he lied like a sidewalk about how much it hurt him to have to take his fees.

I stumbled on a caving site on the Internet. Because a lot of it was Ontario caves, I got kind of hooked on the idea. I ordered *Rockwatching,* a book written by the site creator, and contacted the author a couple times, but I never told my worker. They were scared about me riding a peddle bike so if I hinted I wanted to go belly-crawling through some hole in the ground they would probably call in the SWAT team. I did manage to get into some of the crevices at Inglis Falls, and the Scenic Caves at Collingwood. Even that took pulling some strings. I bought a good helmet and light and I researched the newest cave mapping technology.

Summer holidays came and went. My 15th birthday came and went. My case-worker remembered two days late and dropped off a card. Cake and gifts? That was a dream.

Bills! There were telephone bills and electricity bills and bills for the internet. I'd get them paid and think I had everything caught up when some other bill would come, taxes, or something else somebody had dreamed up. It was no wonder there was never any money. The lawyer gave me an allowance like I was a 5-year-old. By the time I paid all the bills I was lucky if I could eat. I got more sticky than Dad had ever been about turning off lights.

Dad's last book had finally started to sell. Since Mom died when I was a scrawny runt of 10, Dad had sort of quit living for a long time. Then he got so he would work all hours day or night. That's the weird thing about writers. They hide in a dingy hole of an office and dream their life away, swearing at the computer, then looking over their shoulder hoping nobody hears them. At least Dad did. To actually talk to their kids? That was too much to expect.

I didn't miss him all that much. Not like I should have I guess. But when the first royalty notice came, I thought maybe I'd be a writer.

The lawyer had his hand out again before he found a way to transfer the money into the estate account. It was still going to be months before I could touch it.

It stunk. There had never been money for a holiday. Tacye and I had pushed hard to go to Disney Land, but that never happened. We had always driven old clunkers. Dad could buy all the books he wanted but everything else was too expensive. Oh, he'd thrown a wallet-full toward Tacye's wedding, though it would have been a wonder if he remembered the wedding day. Too bad she hadn't gotten a chance. She deserved that much at least. I wish I had been a bit easier on her. She was just my bossy big sister, a nuisance. I had never thought much about her.

I did buy a cool computer. Dad's computer was okay, but loaded down with book manuscripts. Since the one book was pushing a quarter million in sales, I figured there might be other stuff in there worth saving. I wondered about trying to find some of his writer friends but was afraid they'd be as weird as him, getting all in a tizzy about 'p.o.v,' and 'tense,' and 'voice.' I didn't think I could face that yet. What was 'p.o.v.' anyway? Putrid Old Verbs? I'd hear him giving himself a lecture *because he'd done the same stupid thing again and changed 'p.o.v.' in the middle of a paragraph,* or he'd take a strip off me if he read some essay I had written for school. Whatever it was, he should have gotten a medal for the way he fought it.

I kept pumping gas and I also found a site where I could get all the inside dope on those hybrid cars. I wasn't keen on the totally electric cars, but the batteries were getting better fast, so maybe in a few more years they'd be worth something. I got to looking at the power plants and generators and started thinking in weird ways. I got to spending longer and longer on the computer, designing something I kept in a secret file. Nobody in their right mind wants to look through a teenager's computer but I kept it secret anyway. I say nobody in their right mind. My case-worker seemed to think she had to check what sites I was visiting. She'd get a glazed look when she found hybrid cars, submarines and airplanes, cave exploring, mountain climbing and scuba-diving. There was enough technical stuff to make her go cross-eyed. It was kind of funny watching her. I knew she was looking for skin. That's what every teenage boy is after isn't it? I probably disappointed her. She most likely guessed I was gay. She'd have been dead wrong. Girls looked way too good to me even though I couldn't make myself talk to any of them and I still looked too young for any of them to care about me.

I pretty much quit going to youth group at church. It seemed like every time I went they harped on the way teen boys looked at girls. I was pretty sure most of the stuff I heard in the gym change rooms at school was lies but I didn't think we were all quite as sex crazy as the youth leaders seemed to think. I did go on Sundays, though not very often. I didn't feel much like singing, especially those old songs the grownups sang. And the sermons dragged on and on. Sometimes I wanted to jump up in the middle of the sermon and ask the preacher if he even lived on the same planet I lived on.

When I slept through the alarm one morning, my boss called. He told me I could pick up my cheque, but not to bother coming back. I had enough money to get by and it was a boring job anyway. He shorted me two days, but it wasn't worth fighting over since he was paying spit to start with.

I pretty much lived on the computer for a while after that, though I did keep going to school. I wasn't quite sure why, beyond keeping Child Protection Services off my back.

Nobody called me in the mornings. Nobody made my lunch. My case-worker snooped through the fridge and cupboards whenever she came to make sure I had some *real* food in the house. I always burned the Kraft Dinner boxes so she didn't know how often I ate it. Cooking bored me. Eating my own cooking was awful. The old combination wood and oil furnace was really a pain when I went to school. The oil part of it hadn't worked for years. So it had always burned itself out by the time I got home. Having to buy wood and get it stacked in the basement seemed an awful crazy and dirty way to go.

It was a Saturday night. Like usual I had a hot date with the computer. I didn't have school to get up for so didn't force myself to go to bed. At 2 a.m. I finally pushed back. My eyes burned. As the hum of the computer stilled, the empty silence of the house screamed at me. I screamed back but it didn't make me feel any better. A bunch of papers slid off the printer. They hit the floor with a slap, spread with a hiss, and stirred up all the dust in the room.

Mom wouldn't have approved of the words that sort of snuck out of my mouth. I didn't much approve either but it felt good in a crazy way. It scared me though. I was getting more like Dad than I thought.

The papers uncovered my Bible. I'd only opened it a couple times since the funeral. I didn't know a book could tell you off without making a sound.

I dragged myself back out of bed at 6:15. That was stupid but I wasn't sleeping. I went upstairs in my underwear and got a pot of coffee going.

I pulled a box of dry cereal out. I hated doing dishes, but Child Protection Services always made a report if the sink had dirty stuff left in it.

I had learned to cook enough to get by before Dad and Tacye got killed. If we had lived in town I would probably have eaten out more but I didn't have a car and riding my bike a couple of clicks for something to eat wasn't worth it. Getting groceries with the bike was a pain but the taxi wanted more money than I wanted to give. I would buy frozen mixed vegetables but had to force myself to eat them. I don't know why they added those awful lima beans. Probably some divorce lawyer had shares in the company. It was perfect for getting families fighting at the table. What more could a lawyer want?

I wasn't exactly rolling in money even if there was a fat bank account waiting for some magic date on the calendar, so I always ate the food I cooked. Besides I was going to build the *EAGLE* and it was going to cost more than if I started driving a Lamborghini.

I stomped back downstairs and had a shower. Before I got dressed I pulled the sheets off the bed and stuffed them in the washing machine. When I looked at myself in the mirror I thought somebody else had snuck into the bathroom. The guy looking back had more fuzz on his face than I remembered on me. His cheeks were hollow and his hair was a long tangle.

I shaved. I don't know when I did that last. The face in the mirror looked even more hollow. I stood in Tacye's bedroom door as I buttoned my shirt. I had let some of her school friends pick over her stuff. They'd had a real crying fest and drove me crazy. The room was neater than when she was there. Only a few knickknacks remained.

Upstairs, I stood at the piano and stared at pictures, remembering. I plinked out *Mary Had a Little Lamb* on the black keys. Even Dad had played piano. But not me.

A half hour later I locked my bike and snuck into the back of the church. A few people said hello but I hadn't been there for months. It didn't look like anybody had missed me much. I stood and sat when the others stood and sat but I don't suppose I fooled God. I don't know what the preacher talked about.

Back home again, I caught myself wondering why I'd gone at all. Yeah, I still believed in God. Every once in a while on the times I went, the preacher had said something that clicked. I used to read my Bible all the time, at least a chapter or two most days. I hadn't done that much since the funeral.

I'd totally quit going to youth group. I'd become a nobody. No one at church seemed to care. Maybe they just didn't have a clue what to say. And *if* God cared, I wasn't seeing much to show it.

Dad had a bunch of books by Jules Verne, you know, one of those guys dead and moldy a hundred years ago. I think I had read too many of them.

The ugly old barn had room to do some neat things.

For months I had worked at the computer. You wouldn't believe the things I was planning, though I still had the biggest part of a year to wait before I turned 16. Child Protection Services and the lawyer and a bunch of other people were still messing in my life.

I had gotten pretty good at doing drawings with a computer program. I'd also poked around in Dad's office and found an old computer disk that came from the uncle who had died. I had to fire up Dad's old computer to look at it since my new one didn't have anywhere to plug in the disk. I think it was an accident or something. He'd come up with a power source that everybody seemed blind to. But he had a weird note to Dad on the disk, like he was scared somebody was trying to kill him. It didn't look like Dad had even taken the disk out of the envelope. Not surprising since Dad had talked about him as "that crazy brother of mine."

I checked his specs and drawings over and over. I was pretty sure he was on to something big. I started emailing companies and making phone calls, but my uncle's 'accident' kind of scared me. Maybe he wasn't so crazy. And maybe it *wasn't* an accident.

I started getting prices on parts from people who didn't know I was a 15-year-old orphan kid. They treated it like some big, important business contract and I thought that was pretty cool.

I started checking out small submarines and airplanes too. I got a flight simulator program, and then a submarine simulator program. Most video games bored me, but this was close to magic. It showed a real instrument panel. At times I would forget it was a game and be really flying or diving. I'm not sure when it got to be more than a game, but those drawings started to have prices beside them. The prices would blow your socks off.

I'd never been the life of the party before Dad and Tacye got killed. You'd think I had some catching disease after. One of my teachers talked about me growing up extra fast. She missed it by a mile. I was just growing old.

It's weird how life changes. October 16, my birthday, finally came and went. The bills kept coming. When the tax bill came, I knew they'd probably boot me out in the middle of winter if I didn't pay it, so I got on my bike and peddled down to the municipal office.

It's weird having a bank account with a cool half mil in it. I couldn't spend much of it at a time till I turned 18, but I had learned ways to wiggle around some of the restrictions. I could have gone out and got myself a real hot car, and a motorcycle, and a snowmobile. But I wasn't hanging with the guys and I didn't have a girlfriend. There was nobody to impress.

It's a mess trying to get your driver's license when there's no mom or dad in the picture.

I bought one of those RRSP things and all of a sudden I had people calling trying to tell me how to invest so I'd be a millionaire before I knew it. Maybe it would have been a good idea, but I didn't know who I could trust.

Dad's book with the weird name, *The Crucible and the Fire*, had sold more than a million copies now. The cool part was about $2.15 for each copy sold got sent in a cheque a couple times a year. Bankers are weird when a 16-year-old comes in with a big fat cheque. They want you to come in a limo and wearing a tuxedo or something. If you show up on a peddle-bike in blue jeans, they don't know whether to "Mister" you, shake your hand, or call the police.

Chapter Two

Never So Famous

I had kept to myself after Dad and Tacye got killed, and pretty much now the other kids ignored me. The football coach cornered me a couple of times. I guess he'd seen me throwing weights around in the gym. I was stronger than I looked. But belly crawls through mud-filled caves interested me a whole lot more than butting heads on the football field. A couple of bullies tangled with me, but just once. When they started pushing around one of the other weird kids, a stubby guy with thick glasses who stuttered, I told them to back off. That got all their attention. I didn't even know the kid's name, but one of them backed him up against the lockers while the other one got in my face.

"'Back off,' baby-face says." He sneered at me. "Back off?" He looked up and down the empty halls. "Still in diapers, but you're man enough to make us, I suppose?"

I heard the smack of a hand against skin and a gasp escaping from the stubby kid. I didn't think things through. I just dropped my head and drove it into the belly of the guy in front of me. I backed him across the hall and drove him into the lockers. He was back-peddling fast, so when we hit there was enough of me deep enough in his belly that all his fight was gone before I even got started. The other guy stood there with his mouth hanging open, one hand still squeezing Stubby's arm. I planted my fist in his gut like I was digging a hole to grow a tree in. I grabbed his arm as he went down and reefed it behind him. I didn't plan on breaking it. I didn't plan any of it. And I sure didn't plan on that being the perfect time for a teacher to show up.

I got hauled to the principal's office. The police came. There were questions and reports and more questions and lectures and threats of reform school and lies about "zero tolerance" for violence.

I could think of answers later but not then. I never heard anyone ask how a kid faces two big strong bullies who don't seem to know about zero tolerance. I got a five-day suspension. I don't know what the other guys got. They told me it was none of my business. That's a lie! But adults seem to have the privilege of lying when it suits them.

The newspaper the next week made a big noise about not being able to release the name of *"a kid who'd never grown up, guilty of a brutal and unprovoked assault,"* with one of the victims suffering a broken arm and both being monitored for internal injuries. It deplored the laxness of the justice system that could not or would not lock up young hoodlums.

I'd been put on trial and condemned, and once more labelled a baby. The other two, in trouble for fighting at least once a week, got the 'poor victim' treatment. I'd never been quite so famous even if they didn't print my name. I'd gotten used to it. But the tough guys left me alone after that.

Most of the kids at school knew the truth. I think most of the teachers did too. But the dad of one of the bullies was a big-shot in town and a donor to sports teams and other things. I guess everybody was scared if they told the truth about his kid the money would stop.

It was a strange five days because things quit being a game in the barn. I had all these designs and I knew more about flying than most pilots by now. I don't know why but I started to think I *could* build that thing. Even weirder, I started to think I should. I told myself a hundred times to grow up and dump the idea. If I was that desperate to get rid of all the money I could use it for toilet paper. But I started ordering parts. The whole list was ready with suppliers and prices. Of course prices had gone up, but trucks started delivering strange packages to the barn.

Cave stuff continued to fascinate me, so I ordered a mobile LiDAR mapping system. You could walk or crawl through a cave with it, and it would make a detailed 3D map. I hadn't gotten into a cave for months, but maybe someday again...

I hired somebody to come and build an end on the barn. It was a kind of curtain that could be rolled up, but still cost enough to make me choke.

The school year wound up again and I got awful busy. Just getting some of the pieces took pulling all the strings I knew how to pull. I skinned knuckles and breathed glue and paint fumes. I fought to align curved pieces, make watertight seals and hard-wire microcircuits. I wasn't one of your boy geniuses from some comic strip. I didn't have super-skills. I had to use stuff people were already making. I just stuck it together in a way nobody had ever done before.

I stared at the half finished *EAGLE*. That's what I called it. It was the coolest thing spreading across the floor. But I had so much work and money in it now that it *had* to fly and dive. And I was scared it wouldn't.

Yeah, you heard right. Fly *and* dive. Dad could have told me all the reasons you can't build a flying submarine. But then I knew all the reasons he should have quit writing books and gotten a 'real' job. But his book had paid for all this, so I guess the impossible does happen.

I had dreamed of something that would do flips and loops and those kind of stunts. You know, the things that would have most people puking their guts out. Well, I knew enough about flying now to know if this thing got into the air at all it would be a wonder.

I had worked late and could barely hold my eyes open as I brushed my teeth. I peeled my clothes off and left them where they dropped, then sort of fell across the bed. I lay there for a minute till I started feeling cold, then rolled heavily to the side, rolled blankets back, and dragged myself under them.

I hardly ever cried anymore. But I was lonely as fury and mad at Dad again for dying. It was stupid being mad at him. It wasn't like he had planned it. So I was mad at myself for being stupid too.

It was getting too cold to work in the barn. I bought one of those pellet-stove things. It was probably against the law but I set it up myself. I didn't want anyone seeing what I had out there. I bought the biggest one I could find, but it barely kept my fingers from freezing. There had never been insulation in the place and I had too much stuff in there now to do it.

I was a slave to the work. I had never known what cold was until I lay on the cement floor working under the belly of the *EAGLE*. The scars on my face when I dropped things in the cold didn't seem to make much difference to the baby-face image. When I got too cold I'd go back to the house, mop up the blood, and work at the computer. I fought with the calculations. Math is stupid-easy for the most part but there was stuff I had to get right. Making the formulas work for an equation that looks impressive on the board is different from making them work where it actually matters. There were Acceleration tables, Induced Drag, Profile Drag, Thrust and Lift, and all that was for the flying part. There was also Buoyancy and Displacement, Water Pressure and the Variable Boiling Temperatures at different pressures. It wouldn't have been so tough, but this contraption was 10 times heavier than a small airplane. Nobody else was trying to make something heavy as a bloated whale fly. I couldn't ask for help either. How stupid would I have sounded if I told people, *I'm building a flying submarine. Can you answer some questions?*

There were internet sites where you could find all kinds of wild and wonderful formulas to figure out things nobody needs to know. But trying to find out how much pressure a reinforced glass bubble can stand before it caves in was a whole different ballgame.

I'd work for hours, then get mad. I'd stomp away from the computer and work in the barn till I was frozen stiff, then I'd go back.

The boiler was my first job. My uncle's disk gave the idea clear enough, but he'd never built one. It was a cool kind of furnace. Moving from the idea to the reality was anything but simple. I kept remembering his *accident* too.

I wasn't bad at welding, but the temperature and pressure that this had to work at stretched me. Forming the loops in the tubing saw quite a few kinks before I managed to do the bending consistently.

It was the other plumbing that drove me crazy. How could I make the furnace work at extreme temperatures and a thousand kilos of pressure, but have the drain under the sink leak?

I finally got a furnace built that actually worked. I made four more before I had one good enough to use in the *EAGLE*. I just about cooked myself when I hooked it up. But after a while I learned how to control the temperature enough that lying on a mat under the *EAGLE*, I could work in my underwear if I wanted to.

At the maximum depth the *EAGLE* could reach, the steam jet would condense almost instantly, but should still provide a bit of thrust. Propellors set onto the wing surfaces as well as the tail of the *EAGLE* would give a lot more maneuverability as well as a bit more thrust. Finding heavy-duty reversible electric motors totally oil-filled and sealed so water couldn't enter at the high pressure when deeply submerged took a lot of searching.

Christmas came and went. Somehow it made the loneliness worse. The rest of the winter dragged by. A pedal-bike is a lousy way to get around in a Canadian winter so I broke down and bought an old van. I pulled the extra seats out so I could use it like a truck. The insurance was pure robbery but I couldn't do anything about that.

The days got longer. The grass started to grow and I had to waste time cutting the lawn. The 'lake' was full and beautiful, though I didn't usually notice. I went fishing a couple of times, then made myself clean the fish and try to cook them. I have eaten fish I liked. These weren't some of them. Still, with what I had ahead, it looked like I'd better learn how to cook fish and like it. I just about lived in the barn working on the *EAGLE*. There were days I forgot to go to school, though the hassle of trying to answer all the questions wasn't worth it.

Summer holidays came and went. I'd work till I couldn't see straight, then try to sleep. My stupid brain wouldn't shut off when I went to bed.

School started up again with the time wasted in classrooms and on that stupid yellow bus. There were days I ached for a motorcycle, but the *EAGLE* kept me occupied enough that there didn't seem much point. I drove the van to school a few times, but it was a pig on gas so I usually took the bus.

Winter closed in again and things got awful slow. Somewhere along the line I realized there had been another birthday.

I hated going to school. I was getting so I hated going into the barn too. I guess I was scared that after all this time it wasn't going to work. The *EAGLE* was almost done but little jobs still took up hours and days and weeks.

Winter crawled by. My second Christmas alone approached. I had always thought killing yourself was stupid, especially for kids, but two days before Christmas I wanted to jump in the *EAGLE* and fly it into some cement wall. I got through it but started dreaming of dying. Do you know how bad Christmas stinks when you're alone?

I went to a counsellor after the holidays but she was no help. How do you tell someone, "I feel like killing myself?" They'll think you're crazy and lock you up. She told me I needed to let go of old-fashioned ideas of guilt. I guess I said something about reading the Bible and she got upset about that. I didn't tell her I had a piece of rope I kept tying in a noose and then untying. I thought about going to the preacher but it was like I was invisible at church. He'd shake my hand and mumble something but already be looking over my shoulder at the next person.

I read more in my Bible than I had since Dad and Tacye died. That helped sometimes, especially the Psalms. David, or sometimes that Asaph guy would rant and rave and then they always seemed to get over it. I tried to pray, but how do you tell God you think He blew it when He made you?

Much of the time I just worked on the *EAGLE*, forgetting everything else. I was getting almost no sleep. I don't know how I got through exams. I can't say I cared much.

I had to take time off school to meet with the lawyer. There were things I couldn't just leave. I wanted to sell the place but found out I couldn't till I turned 18. Even at 17 somebody seemed to be looking over my shoulder all the time.

The lawyer was a real pro. He never laughed out loud while I was there. He'd made good money handling the estate so he was smart enough to be careful what questions he asked. I told him nothing I was doing was illegal and that was mostly true. I had a driver's license now, but not a pilot's license. I didn't suppose they'd give one to a 17-year-old kid, or a license for a submarine, whatever kind that took.

As the days started getting longer I quit playing with the rope. It was a stupid thing to do anyway. The *EAGLE* was ready. I wasn't sure it would work but if I died trying, that didn't sound like such a bad thing. With winter behind I almost wanted to live again.

I bought two new computers. I'd managed to scare myself about viruses and worms and trojans. I didn't know much about them but knew being on the internet put me at risk. I got a notebook and one of those half-sized desk-top things. They wanted to fill it full of stupid software and a thousand mind-numbing games but I had them take most of that stuff out before I brought them home. I was mighty picky about what I transferred from the old computer to the new ones.

I rented a storage building in Owen Sound and had the spare power plants sent there. They looked like squat black bugs with a few strange pipes sticking out of them. With all the shielding around them they weighed a ton.

The *EAGLE* controls were like a stripped-down airplane. An artificial horizon, an altimeter, a depth indicator, and a gyroscopic guidance system dominated the panel. A computer monitor sat to the left of the pilot's controls. It was an extremely heavy craft for free flight. The design made it most at home just skimming the surface. It lacked the skirts of a hovercraft but the wings formed the underbelly.

Ready for its first flight, the *EAGLE* had a strange bird-like look from above. Below, it was almost snake-like, at least if you could ignore the wings. It spread over much of the floor of the barn. The hull of the 1.38-metre pilot's sphere was built to withstand the pressures of more than 900 metres of water. The other spheres, much larger, were designed for about 450 metres, but could be pressurized internally to give access to deeper water. Luxury? Not quite.[2]

Equipped with special tools, I hoped it could deal with anything underwater. It had a cutting laser and a couple of manipulator arms. It also had a tiny compressed-air motor that could draw a fishing lure a hundred metres from the *EAGLE*. I had put cameras, floodlights, and sensors on it too.

I started getting supplies. I hated some of the research I did. But if the only thing I could get fresh for the next several months was going to be fish, I needed to learn a bit about cooking it. Scurvy didn't sound like any fun either, so I got a bunch of vitamins and dehydrated fruits and vegetables. There wasn't much room, so I had to be awfully picky about supplies.

On May 18th church seemed a downer somehow. Broken glass littered the parking lot. Numbers were low and they sang like they were hurting or scared. The teens had mostly disappeared. The preacher warned of coming troubles. He seemed to expect someone to show up with guns, torch all the

---

2 *See Appendix A, Image 2*

Bibles, and kill the lucky ones. The rest of us would have to watch, lose our Bibles, our jobs, and pretty soon everything else. I went home depressed and didn't go to school Monday or Tuesday.

I went into town and bought some last minute things. If I'd been 19 I would have gotten a bottle of champagne and broken it over the *EAGLE,* but I could imagine the reaction if I walked into the liquor store. I figured they'd probably still be ID-ing me at 40. I didn't want anybody asking why I wasn't in school and I always thought it was kind of weird that people would build some big boat, then start things out by smashing a bottle on it.

Wednesday, May 21

Late afternoon storm clouds hung low and threatening. The radio posted a *Severe Weather Watch.* In a strange way it made it the perfect time.

For one last time, I showered, shaved, and slipped beneath the covers. I set my alarm for the middle of the night.

I was awake before the alarm went off. I dragged myself to my feet as rain rattled the windows. I boiled eggs and ate a bowl of cereal, then threw the empty box into the wood furnace.

I had mostly cleaned out the fridge but left it plugged in. I knew how fast it could get smelly. Flipping off the lights in the kitchen, I walked through the dark house to the porch. Standing for a moment as rain spattered against my back, I fought against tears that had snuck up from somewhere. Dragging in a breath, I ran to the barn.

CHAPTER THREE

FIRST FLIGHT

Friday, May 23

D im lights showed the *EAGLE* sitting sleek and low on the barn floor. The camouflage paint gave no reflective glare, but the glass of the pilot's sphere and the living sphere gleamed faintly. She was beautiful. I snorted, then fell silent again. I didn't know what made her female now.

I entered through the upper access panel and activated the nuclear furnace.[3] I went back out and rolled the curtain up. Wet wind blasted into the barn. I wished I had a catapult like they once used on some aircraft carriers. I'd done the math over and over and knew I could get just enough speed if everything worked perfect. If the lake had been a real lake it wouldn't have been a problem. It had more water in it now than any other time of year, but a couple of big maple trees at the far end meant I had to pull up steep when I was just getting up to speed. They were across the fence on the neighbour's property, so I didn't think I could get away with cutting them down.

I switched the barn lights off, then climbed onto the wing and up the traction plates to re-enter the *EAGLE*. I locked the hatch behind me.

---

[3] *See Appendix A, Image 3*

I stood silently in the biggest sphere. My world for the next several months would be the inside of three bubbles. "I guess it's time." I murmured. I wasn't sure if it was a prayer or if I was just talking to myself. "The *EAGLE'S* ready. I guess I'm ready. I've wanted a thousand times to die since the accident. But I don't want to die today." I bit my lip. "I don't want it to all be for nothing.

"Oh God! Make it fly."

Cold rain slanted out of the north-west, a tinny drumming on the barn roof punctuated by rolling thunder. The gauges showed storage water temperature increasing quickly. I regulated steam pressure. I had gone through this procedure over and over. But this was not a practice run.

Stripping to my underwear, I towelled off. I ran a strip of tape full of microscopic wires up each leg from above my ankles to below my armpits. Dressing in fresh dry clothes, I glanced at my watch. It showed 4:15 a.m. Dull light cast faint shadows toward the west. I sealed the hatches between each sphere, then belted myself into the pilot's seat. I clipped the wiring harness from the lateral-line sensors into the tape on each side of my body, then adjusted the power controls until I could feel the faintest hint of tingling. I brought the nuclear furnace up to full power, pouring heat back into the storage water as I waited for output to reach its maximum. Holding the disconnect to the tether cable, I fed steam to the jet. The craft trembled and strained.

I'd just been to the bathroom but felt like I had to go again. I wiped sweat from my forehead and rubbed wet hands on my pants. The roar of the jet was muted inside the sphere, yet amplified by the barn into dull thunder. I released the cable.

As the *EAGLE* cleared the end of the barn, we were rolling at 39 kilometres per hour. Two seconds later the ground dipped gently. At 52 kph, the craft was not generating sufficient lift to climb over obstacles. I'd checked repeatedly for potholes and bumps that might get the *EAGLE* rocking and dig the wings into the gravel. I don't suppose the run down to 'the lake' had been that smooth in 20 years.

The trail went downhill in a gentle slope that let us accelerate a bit faster. Lightning split the sky. Then suddenly the early morning seemed astonishingly dark. Driving rain soaked up the *EAGLE'S* lights. Heavy as the craft was, I could feel the buffeting of the wind.

I held a death-grip on the controls. As we raced out over the water of the small lake I heard somebody hollering. I retracted the wheels to reduce drag. I had tried to come up with some way to jettison them. It was doubtful I'd ever need them again because I'd always be taking off from water. But any idea I came up with increased the risk during that first critical flight—or, if I did it while still too low, bouncing back up and smashing the bottom of the *EAGLE*. So the timing couldn't work when it mattered most.

The wind and rain slammed against the craft. I leaned forward in my seat, seeking to coax a little more speed before we reached the end of the lake.

Those old maples were staring me in the face when I pulled back on the control. They passed less than two metres below at 230 kph. We followed an abandoned railroad right-of-way, cleared a power line by a perilously narrow margin, and then crossed a gravel road. The tops of several maples reached above her wing tips as the railroad line led us east of north toward a small town. As we came clear of the trees, I raised the nose several degrees. I swung westward to avoid passing over the town. A long gentle slope faced us with trees at the top.

I still had almost full fuel-water so the *EAGLE* was loaded to its maximum. We were losing speed as we climbed. As the trees approached, I gauged my timing with intense focus. I pulled back on the control. A warning alarm sounded. The nose rose sluggishly. I could feel the craft wallow and slow. Even before we passed the trees I had pushed back on the controls again, levelling the *EAGLE*. We had lost 37 kph, but gained 11 metres of height.

I'd have been in trouble if the hill kept climbing. The *EAGLE* was barely above stall speed. But as the ground dropped away below us, lowering our angle just a half degree saw us gaining air-speed again. A small branch clung to the right wing tip, leaves whipping in the wind.

"Yes!" I punched the air, my fist slamming into the ceiling of the pilot's sphere. I just about broke my hand. I could almost hear Dad's voice in one of those moldy clichés he liked to quote. "People who live in glass houses shouldn't throw stones." What it had to do with an aching wrist and stinging knuckles I couldn't say, but the longing to groan over one of Dad's sayings was suddenly intense.

Still at maximum power, the *EAGLE* slowly gained speed and altitude. A minute and a half later, we had 108 metres of air beneath us. I laughed, almost giddy with relief and joy. She was female and we were a team.

Because the craft was so heavy, and even more because of the nature of the power plant, I couldn't reduce power in free flight. The great simplicity and almost limitless output of the nuclear furnace had major shortcomings. It required three minutes to reach maximum output. The steam could be dissipated if necessary rather than fed through the jet. But to have full power on tap required the furnace to be kept at full output even if that power was being wasted. Full power wasn't any more than enough to keep her in the sky either, though she flew a bit easier as the water reservoir emptied.

Rain continued to curtain the world. Ragged wisps of clouds tore apart as we passed through them. I had caught a glimpse of blue sky through a break in the clouds when a flash of lightning blinded me. Even through the incredibly strong walls of the craft the shock-wave struck like a physical blow. It took several seconds before I could focus on the instruments again.

Black clouds piled up behind and on either side of us. Lightning flickered distantly. But our flight path showed open ahead.

I could pick out landmarks now. I changed direction slightly to pass between the Meaford Tank Range and Owen Sound, not too close to either. I knew there was a small airport east of Owen Sound and guessed the Tank Range had some kind of control tower for the helicopters that flew in and out, so I assumed I'd be showing up on somebody's radar. I hadn't filed a flight plan. I didn't have any call letters. I don't know how many regulations I was breaking, even if the *EAGLE* had been an Ultra-Light. At around 29,000 kilograms, 'Ultra-Light' somehow didn't fit.

My watch showed 4:33 a.m. We had been in the air 23 minutes when the rocky shore of Georgian Bay passed beneath us, west of Johnson Harbour. Fuel-water showed at five percent. That was cutting it too close.

Yes, that's right, fuel-water. The *EAGLE* ran on steam jets heated by the nuclear furnace.

I reduced power. As we descended, I searched the water for obstacles. I checked and rechecked the instruments. A fishing tug, one-and-a-half kilometres west of our path, pushed its blunt nose north past Pyette Point. Several kilometres east a freighter steamed ponderously southeast toward Collingwood. Otherwise, the water appeared empty. I descended quickly, watching my fuel-water gauge.

We flew on until the broad hump of dark shoreline turned west at Cape Commodore. Passing Deepwater Point on the southwest tip of Griffith Island, the storm was again closing in as I reduced power. I held the nose steady and descended to just above the surface.

A further settling to three metres and the *EAGLE* rode in a smooth glide. The long swells raced beneath us. Rain again fell heavily. A fog bank ahead hid Hay Island.

I reduced power more until the *EAGLE* lost most of its forward momentum. I reduced the sensitivity level of the lateral-line sensors as they reacted to the solid force of water.

The craft lay low in the water, rocking sluggishly. One-metre swells came from the right and broke over the front sphere. My head ached and my eyes burned. I wanted to scream and do back-flips and I wanted to stretch out and sleep.

A distinctly stronger wave-like sensation came from the right-hand lateral-line sensors. The left ones gave choppy, weak impressions. The craft had been largely completed when that idea stirred in my imagination. In the water where so much of my time would be spent, almost every creature had some form of lateral-line sensors. I figured if that many things had it there must be a reason, even if I didn't fully understand.

Rows of hair-like sensors, above the wings and below, fed information about anything moving through the water near me. Like learning a new language, I could only hope that over time my body and mind would learn to *read* the information the sensors brought me. In effect, I would be developing a whole new sense.

I carefully checked the gauges. I ran air pressure up in the anterior spheres searching for evidence of leakage. I had done this over and over before the craft ever felt water under it, but failure now meant a long time in a cold, wet place. This seemed like good day to stay alive.

My sonar showed the bottom of the lake 30 fathoms below me. I had tried to teach myself nautical terminology, but mentally translated that to about 55 metres. If Dad was still around he'd have changed it to yards, added a bit, and then changed it to feet. Old people had such a weird way of measuring.

Slowly, watching the instruments, seeking to pierce the secrets of the dark water, I opened the vents on the ballast tanks. I held neutral buoyancy about six metres below the surface for quite a while. It's a scary thing the first time the water closes over your head. Left and right-hand sensations from the lateral-line sensors were almost identical now. I *felt* the rippling of waves overhead, undisturbed by the craft itself. Only the stimulators at the back of the strips of tape were active. It was more than cool that I could tell the sensors above the wings were detecting the surface waves and I could feel the difference.

The muscles in the back of my neck felt as tight as guitar strings but weren't making any music. We began a long slow descent, swinging in a wide loop around the base of the island. The propellors were more effective than the steam jet underwater. At full power they sounded like I was inside a laundromat with too many machines running. The noise started to drop off at about 60 percent power and they ran almost silent at 15 percent power—at least with my present ability to know what I was hearing.

We finally came to rest about 10 kilometres from our landing place. North of Hay Island, my chart showed me three kilometres east-south-east of a First Nations village with an unpronounceable name: Makataewaukawauk. I was pretty sure if anybody's radar had seen the *EAGLE* go down, or if someone from the shore had seen it submerge, we were far enough away that they would never find the wreckage if they went looking.

When the *EAGLE'S* lights first reached it, the lakebed appeared nearly featureless, a nondescript grey. As we approached closer we stirred up enough current to disturb a dusting of silt over milky white, glacial scoured granite.

I released a little more air from the ballast tanks, adding weight, then settled onto the lake floor. A cloud of silt swirled around and for a few moments seemed to swallow the craft. A slight current carried it away.

Exhausted, and with my body making urgent demands, I went carefully over a checklist before leaving the pilot's seat. Then I opened the bulkhead separating the spheres. My hands reached up, gripping the handholds provided. I pulled my body through the 33-centimetre hole into the much roomier second sphere.

The demands of space had placed the toilet in a tiny room with less than a square metre of floor space. It wouldn't win any prizes but it met the needs of the moment. I found it funny that the completion of the first flight and dive after all the intense effort should end in this mad rush to the toilet.

There were some strange features. The toilet used water jets and warm air rather than tissue. A threshold you had to step over and a small motorized disk set into the floor of the bathroom created a clothes washer using parts from a dismantled compact apartment washer. The theory was better than the reality. After trying it a couple of times I wouldn't be applying for a patent.

In the tiny kitchen a previously prepared meal went into the combined microwave-convection oven. While it heated, I scrubbed my face. I ate standing, then washed my dishes and left them in the sink. There was nobody to write reports now if I didn't do the dishes, but with so little room and nobody else to do them for me, there wasn't much choice.

Tired, but too keyed up to sleep, I made a journal entry on my computer.

```
Friday, May 23

It has finally happened. I can hardly believe
it. I'm under water. The EAGLE flies and it
dives. The controls work. I can actually
figure out some details from the Lateral-Line
Sensors. I thought that would take months.

It's hard to leave the old place behind. There
are so many memories. It seems like I've been
alone forever.

The chart shows 50 fathoms. That works out to
87 metres. Water temperature is 6.4°C. The
water's clear with quite a bit of light down
this far. Colours are starting to be a bit
strange.

The pilot's sphere got cool and air quality
wasn't great with the hatch sealed between
spheres. Air quality may need some work. I'll
try to get some sleep if I can turn my brain
off.
```

"Stupid dictionary," I muttered, staring at the spellcheck flagging *Colours*. "This is Canada. Is it a crime to use Canadian spelling?" I saved the file, then turned off the computer. Kneeling on the floor in front of the sink, I leaned across to grasp two small straps against the opposite wall. A quick sharp tug and a narrow section of floor lifted, turned over, and settled into the same space, covered with a thin mattress.

I tried to pray. It seemed like the right thing to do but my mind drifted. My only words in an almost inaudible whisper were: "Father, teach me..."

It was strange. I'd heard sermons a couple times about Jesus calling God, Abba, "Daddy." The preacher would have been shocked that I'd listened to even that much. I liked the idea of that, but "Daddy" seemed a bit too much. "Father" felt a whole lot more comfortable. I sighed, then undressed and slid between the blankets. I leaned over and turned down the lights.

The loneliness came then. Guys my age aren't supposed to cry, especially guys who can build flying submarines. But tears welled in my eyes, then overflowed. Once again, a prayer reached into the darkness. "Oh God, teach me..."

My meal had been skimpy. Hunger woke me after a couple hours sleep.

For the next several weeks I explored my underwater world. I moved along the Niagara Escarpment ridge where it separated Georgian Bay from the rest of Lake Huron. My skill with the lateral-line sensors improved. With sight not mattering much, my hearing became fine-tuned. I learned to block out the murmuring sounds of the *EAGLE* itself. But the breaking of waves against a rocky shoreline, the soft slap against a wooden boat, the sharper slap against aluminum became clear, sharply focused images. I learned to distinguish the churning of the screw of a freighter, the whine of a speedboat propeller, or the hiss of a jet-ski.

Saturday, May 24

Georgian Bay had its share of shipwrecks. Many of them were in shallow water divers could easily reach, or even be seen from those expensive glass-bottom cruise-boats. In the deeper, cold waters, below the reach of all but a handful of divers with sophisticated high tech support equipment, the wrecks that lay at the base of the escarpment were virtually undisturbed. Many of them were protected as National Historic Sights, with "Salvage" defined as the ultimate curse.

A new generation of submersibles had been developed, but the richer pickings in southern waters, legal or otherwise, lured them away from the Great Lakes.

Surprisingly well preserved in the cold waters at the floor of the lake, I examined anchors, wooden and steel hulls, and broken masts. Some boats had burned. Some had been driven onto rocks or smashed by giant waves. Some showed little damage. It looked as though they had simply buried their bow under a wave and never come back up. I never approached too closely, assuming there might be listening stations or cameras set up, although I found an occasional shipwreck that didn't show on any charts.

Each wreck was somehow magical, and at the same time desolate and lonely. Dad would have wanted to write about them, spin some fanciful story for each one. I just wished I could raise the ones still worth money. It probably meant something was wrong with me. I mean, how many kids do you know who own a flying submarine and have a couple million sitting in a bank account, but still want more?

The hermit's life seemed to suit me although at times I craved company. I had no pressing need to stay in hiding. I had proved well enough what the *EAGLE* could do. I didn't know much about patents, but was pretty sure the design for the power plant was worth millions. That or the energy companies would kill me to kill it. I mean, what would it do to oil prices? Electric cars had become much more common, but the hybrids were the ones gaining the most ground, so oil prices still impacted almost everyone. I hadn't forgotten my uncle and his "accident." It somehow suited my fancy to think I had to hide from them.

I read a lot. I worked out on the treadmill I had built into the *EAGLE*. I kept records the Captain Nemo guy from the Jules Vern book, *Twenty Thousand Leagues Under the Sea,* would have been proud of. I took pictures of wrecks and I even wrote a few stories. I don't suppose they were very good and I didn't know any publishers except Dad's. I didn't think they would care much. I also got pretty good at fishing, though it was a strange and awkward business from inside the *EAGLE*. I would charge the little motor with compressed air, then send out the lure. Using one of the manipulator arms, I would reel it back in. Down deep like that there were some pretty big fish, but there wasn't any fun in landing them. Once they grabbed the hook I just hauled them in like they were on an anchor chain.

Getting them inside the *EAGLE* presented the biggest challenge. I had a collection basket I'd put them in. It would easily hold a five-kilo salmon. Sometimes they were too big and I had no choice but to let them go.

The basket would get moved under the *EAGLE*. A sealed pressure chamber in the bottom of the *EAGLE* would open up. The basket would lift into position. The opening would close again. The pressure would be reduced to the same as inside the *EAGLE* and then I could lift up my bed and go under it to open the inner door of the pressure chamber.

Those big fish weren't shy about slapping me around when I tried to get them up out of that hole. And cleaning them without filling the whole inside of the *EAGLE* with fish-guts and scales proved a challenge.

The winter dragged long and cold. I explored the depths of Lake Huron and Georgian Bay. I poured over maps, added details to underwater charts that nobody but me would ever see, and I read for hours. I even explored a few underwater caves. I didn't go in far. Usually the *EAGLE* was too big so I couldn't.

I did get outside a couple of times. I knew a few places near Tobermory where some crazy people practiced winter diving. Setting the *EAGLE* down on the lake floor and putting on an insulated diving suit, I could let myself out through the pressure chamber and fit right in with other crazies. I'd then go into what was almost a ghost town in the winter and eat the biggest salads they would feed me, along with anything but fish. I'd indulge in steak or roast beef, pie and ice cream, or anything with chocolate on those times. Then I'd usually feel half sick by the time I returned to the *EAGLE*.

When winter finally released its grip on the harbours and docks, it was a relief to sneak into some of the little inlets and bays, surface the *EAGLE* and get outside on dry ground for a bit. It felt strange and almost wrong though, and I always feared someone would find the *EAGLE* when I was away from it.

I got to listening on the radio when I was at the surface, trying to understand a bit of what was happening in the outside world. I didn't like most of what I heard. It kept reminding me of that last sermon the preacher had given, with all the warnings.

Chapter Four

The Hiding Place

Wednesday, May 28

eeling that I had learned the capabilities of the craft, with an uneasy urgency driving me, I began to search for a hiding place for the *EAGLE*. I guessed I couldn't stay underwater forever, though the idea of being with people again scared me somehow.

My world had turned upside down the day a drunk snuffed Dad and Tacye. When I listened to the radio it sounded like the world outside had been stood on its head too. Doctors were almost forced to give lethal injections on request. Pastors, priests, and chaplains were being called "public parasites." Churches had lost their charitable status and had government cameras installed.

Searching for a suitable place to hide the *EAGLE* consumed weeks. The French River[4] maze of shallow channels that drained Lake Nipissing into Georgian Bay had always intrigued me so I searched there. I'd done

---

4 *See Appendix A, Image 4*

enough reading about caves to know there wasn't much chance of the big karst formation (dissolved limestone) caves there. It would be a fault line I needed, with a subduction zone where one tectonic plate left a gap as it nosed under another one. My geology teacher from high school would have been shocked that I even knew the words.

Maps didn't give much promise anywhere in Ontario, but there were fault lines and even earthquakes, though they weren't the kind to bring down buildings. Most people never felt them.

I wasn't particularly hopeful when I took the *EAGLE* into a long backwater on a foggy evening. Fishing season had already opened and I still had this thing about anyone seeing me, so I relied mostly on the lateral-line sensors. I could feel my way in the dark with them now, though I'd practiced where there was lots of room in the open lake.

Local fishing guides bragged about the trophy fish caught in the area so I figured there had to be deep water somewhere close. There's a different feel when there's no bottom under you, so I knew when the *EAGLE* went over some kind of trench.

I'd already checked to be sure there were no other boats close. I didn't have much wiggle room, but the trench dropped 80 metres from the surface. A couple shifting shadows might have been trophy fish, but they knew all the hiding places and I didn't. My lights kind of messed with them though, and a few of them poked around the *EAGLE*.

The edges of the trench looked like some giant had got his fingers into a crack and pulled the rock apart. Jagged pieces stuck out and deep cracks reached way back. The temperature kept rising and a slight current became more noticeable. The current had to be coming from some underground source, so probably stayed the same year round.

I inched my way under the south-west lip of the trench. The *EAGLE* cut off almost all natural light and took up so much of the channel that the current felt stronger, stirring up sediment and sweeping it past the glass.

Twenty metres back the bottom began to drop again, but a dome reached above me. Turning off all lights I could still see a faint glow coming from the entry tunnel. I couldn't be sure, but there seemed to be light coming from above as well. With more maneuvering room I turned lights back on and slowly raised the *EAGLE*. The sandstone gave way to a layer of granite and then sandstone again. The *EAGLE* broke surface under a low, dull ceiling of reddish-grey rock. A sliver of light probed down into the water somewhere below the craft, promising access to the outside.

I spent an hour examining the walls for the best anchorage possibilities, then pulled on a diving suit and exited through the upper hatch. I had just enough headroom to sit on the upper curve of the living sphere. I slipped into the water, cold even with the insulated suit. Sucking in a lung full of air I swam three metres down to where I could see the light entering. It was a narrow tunnel. I called myself a fool as I gripped the rock lip for a moment while my head-lamp revealed details before I risked moving into it. It narrowed more but I broke surface with enough room to crawl up a passage. A candy-wrapper and a rusted beer can told me this part of the cave had been entered, probably more than once. I dared to believe they would have stopped at the water and not tried to go deeper.

It was a tight squirm to turn, but I swam back to the *EAGLE* where I checked all supplies and prepared a pack for the next part of my journey. I knew roughly where a resort lay relative to my position but this was wild country. It was liable to be a half-day's tramp.

After the best meal I could manage with the supplies that wouldn't keep, a sleep and a shower, I shut down the *EAGLE* and entered the water the next morning.

Once out into open air I fixed a homing beacon into a crevice. A coded message from within 20 kilometres would activate it.

I crossed the hump of rock that separated the backwater from the main French River channel. Swimming across the current took me farther downstream than I had anticipated.

Cool rain fell as a rusty hump of rock swelled out of the muskeg. Near the base of the rock, a cedar had gone down in a storm. The root-bowl provided the closest thing to shelter I expected to find. I peeled off the diving suit, shivering in the damp air. I quickly dressed in jeans and a plaid shirt.

This was wild and beautiful country. Much of it was bald rock. Much of it was muskeg and swamp. The rest seemed to be open water. My leg muscles, attuned to the unchanging treadmill, soon began to ache. It felt strange and surprisingly difficult walking. I'd done it rarely since launching the *EAGLE*. Five hours of slapping mosquitoes and black-flies finally brought me to a rutted trail. As the day wore itself out, the sun won a long argument with rain. Only the flies forced me to keep moving. I carried a clipboard as well as my pack, and I wrote down things I saw along the way. I didn't much care what I was writing but wanted some excuse for being out in this backcountry that I could pull off without lying. Since I had no tan I couldn't pass myself off as a dedicated fisherman or hunter, although I did carry a camera.

As I stumbled up the trail, I could hear voices and laughter. The smell of wood-smoke, roast beef, and outboard oil hung in the air, mingled with tobacco. When I stood below the deck of a small resort quizzical grins greeted me.

"Better come on up for a cold one," a man's overly loud voice shouted as he held up a beer. "Looks like you could use one. Where in God's name have you been?"

I hadn't talked to real people for months. I never thought that would be something to scare me. "Don't even ask." I didn't try to keep the tiredness out of my voice. "I'm doing a wildlife survey. Forty-seven million mosquitoes. Half again as many black-flies. If there is anything else alive out there it's still oozing out of the mud.

"I want a shower, a meal, and a bed. In that order. I smell like swamp water, so you don't want me up there, but thanks for the offer."

"Room's $105.00. Roast beef dinner's $26.00. I'd throw in a cold beer, but you look on the young side."

I fought against a gasp and a protest. "I knew I should have held out for all expenses paid. I'll pass on the beer. I never could develop a taste for it. But I'll go for that dinner. That's what, $131.00 before tax? Will $150.00 do it?"

I peeled three $50s from a small roll and passed them to the hands of the proprietor, even though he had a debit machine there for me to use.

The size of the room seemed almost overwhelming. I could have lain cross-wise in the bed. And the bathroom... I had almost forgotten what a big tub looked like. After the *EAGLE* it felt like someone had blown my world apart, knocked out all the walls. It felt too big to undress.

I scrubbed myself. Soiled clothes lay on the floor of the tub, a brown stain swirling down the drain. Bone-aching weariness seemed to swirl with the dirt.

I shouted, "Just leave it on the table," when a knock sounded on the door. Stepping out of the shower, I towelled myself and ran a brush through my hair. I wrapped a towel around myself, opened the bathroom door, and stopped. I almost dropped the towel.

She was probably a few years older than me, maybe early-twenties. I don't know if she was really a looker or not. I hadn't seen a girl in months, but her smile sure turned up the heat. She had a wide, sensual mouth and big eyes. There was something about them though. Almost predatory, like a cat.

"Gordon asked me to bring you your supper." Her voice was soft, inviting. She stood in profile to the window, the evening sun glowing through her light summer blouse. I had forgotten how much you can see when the light hits at just the right angle.

"Thank you." My voice came in little more than a whisper, high pitched. "It looks good." I fought to control the tremor in my words, wondering if I was talking about the food or the girl.

She grinned, somehow knowing and triumphant as she turned back to the door.

I dumped my pack out on the bed. After dressing I sat down to the meal the girl had brought. I think it was good, but my mind was going places it didn't belong.

Back in the bathroom, I half-filled the tub. I knelt and scrubbed my clothes, then wrung them out and hung them to dry. An hour later, freshly shaved, I clicked on the TV while I skimmed the movie directory from an acrylic holder.

"Too young for beer..." I muttered as my gaze took in the XXX ratings. These were pay-per-view movies, probably a good thing because I wasn't going into the office to let anybody know I hungered for that kind of stuff. What if it was the girl I had to pay?

I clicked through different channels on the TV, but finally turned it off. It was too much too fast after my time alone in the *EAGLE*.

I slept fitfully and finally gave up in the small hours. At three in the morning I pulled on the damp clothes, put the other things back in my pack and walked out the door. Sunrise saw me slapping black-flies five kilometres northeast of the resort, feeling my leg muscles complaining again. The rutted trail had quickly led into a narrow paved road. It was 29 kilometres as the crow flies to Alban. The road, including a section of the Trans-Canada Highway, made it 42.

Nine hours later I thanked a trucker as I stepped down from the cab in Sudbury. Another four days saw me armed with a map, my camera, and booking a charter flight out of Sudbury.

CHAPTER FIVE

SMOKY RIDGE

Tuesday. June 14

After my long isolation, I dreaded crowds. I wanted seclusion with access to deep water. The shore-line of Lake Superior seemed a good place to search. Several charter flights narrowed my focus to three specific locations. Calls and visits to real estate agents were followed by the tedium of tracking down absentee owners of two locations. The calls worked better. They didn't know how young I was on the phone.

The real estate agent made it a bit too clear that he thought I was wasting his time so I went to the bank. Two collapsing log cabins, piles of rotting garbage, and rocks could be purchased for back taxes not too far from White River.

Sunburn and fly bites made me look like a pimple-faced kid so I made a great impression when I sat down with the bank manager. "We don't give mortgages to school kids. And we won't be pouring good money into that place." He stared at me from behind his desk. "It can only be reached by helicopter or boat." He leaned back in his chair and looked me up and down. "The Indians tell wild stories." His use of the *forbidden word* startled me. "There was a gold claim staked there years ago. I don't know that they ever brought any out. But that's probably what those hunters were looking for more than moose.

"And what about you?" A sneer crept across his face, though he seemed to fight it. "What is your interest in this property?"

In my 18 years I've wanted to tell off smart-mouth adults more then once but this was one of the first times I had the means to do it. Too bad I actually wanted the place.

"I don't like crowds much," I said in a deliberately quiet voice, trying to suppress the desire to spit in his eye. "I'm an orphan Mr..." I searched for the nameplate at the front of his desk. "Mr. Thompson." I paused. "My dad and sister were killed by a drunk." I fought the tears that suddenly threatened. I think it was the first time I had said the words out loud.

I had printed an update at the ATM just before my appointment. As I spoke, his eyes glanced disdainfully at the paper, then the pupils dilated and he sat forward. He reached across to grasp the paper, but I pulled it back. "Dad had pretty good insurance and he was a writer. His last book has sold more than a million copies." The tears were still dangerously close, angering and embarrassing me. "I wasn't lookin' for a mortgage." I found myself slurring words as I fought for control.

I stood up. "I guess my money's not good enough. G'bye, Mr. Thompson."

As I walked out of his office he almost tipped his chair rushing after me. "Wait. Wait," he called. "Don't be in such a rush."

I turned, standing just outside his office door. Blinking back the tears that still threatened I pulled out a pair of business cards, cheap home-made things. I glanced at them quickly, then flipped them toward his desk. "Call my lawyer. He hasn't heard from me in months. Maybe he'll confirm all your suspicions." I glanced around the lobby where people stared with bored curiosity. "I'll be back in a day or two."

I wanted to say more, way too much more, but didn't trust my voice and was losing my battle against tears. I hadn't cried for months!

I heard the bank manager sputtering after me. People stepped aside as I headed to the door, looking me up and down and whispering to each other.

I stumbled down an alley beside the bank, then sat on the curb in the parking lot behind the building. I desperately wanted privacy but couldn't see any place better at the moment.

An hour later I went searching for a phone booth. I finally found one at the public library and called my lawyer. I reached his receptionist and learned he was in a meeting. I expected that, true or not. I gave instructions to be cooperative with the banker *if* he bothered to call. I also asked that the lawyer confirm with my local bank that I was probably buying some property.

I didn't know if they would let me in to Charlie's Pub and Café but they did without even ID-ing me. That would probably change if I ordered beer. I'd eaten in better looking places but I ordered a meal. When I paid I asked about the possibility of renting a helicopter. The boss turned and bawled to someone in a dingy corner. "Hey Sam, kid wants a chopper ride. He's even paid for his supper. Maybe could you put down your bottle long enough to talk at him?"

"You make it a habit of shaming your regular customers?" I asked.

The man snorted and backed away from the counter, holding both hands up. "Okay, kid. Okay." In an almost inaudible whisper, he muttered. "SOB Indian lover. Oughta make 'em wear a sign." Out loud he continued. "No offence, kid. But I ain't running a charity here."

I glanced over at Sam, then leaned over the counter, my hands spread on the scuffed surface. "It was good food but I can't say I'm impressed by the company." I clenched my hands into fists, then spread them again. They're big hands. I'd lost most of the baby fat that had labelled me for so long, and by now I could almost pass for somebody the football coach at high school should have been trying to get into a uniform. The man's jaw worked as he backed farther from the counter. I turned away.

Sam wasn't a promising prospect. Piercing black eyes glared from under wild salt and pepper eyebrows. A dirty hat clung to a mat of heavy hair. His wide, heavy lipped mouth wore a scowl. He nursed a beer bottle. His hands were meaty and red. A scar ran across the back of the right one. I guessed he was late forties or early fifties but anyone over 30 looked old to me.

His beer had sat on the table long enough to sweat in the humid air. He had been watching me, the way people always watch when somebody new shows up. He stared at me, sizing me up, and like everybody else, guessing my age and probably writing me off.

"You want a chopper ride?" His right fist clenched the beer bottle.

"I want to get into a pretty tight place, then back out again." I fumbled a bit for words. "If I could meet you some place tomorrow morning, ah, could we talk about it then?" I almost said "sober" but caught myself. It seemed he could hear me thinking it though.

"You think I'm drunk! Just a dirty, drunk Indian. That what you think?"

I drew a long slow breath, searching desperately for words. "I see one bottle. If that'll do it then all that locker-room stuff about a six-pack in ten minutes was an even bigger lie than I thought." I paused a moment, then continued. "Can I meet you here in the morning, say 8:30?"

"I'll be here. And I'll be stone sober." He slammed the bottle onto the table. A glass tipped and rolled slowly in a half-circle. "You might like me better drunk."

He turned to stare at the café owner. "You'll get your money, Charlie." He seemed to chew on some other words before he continued. "Even if I have to sell the chopper. But I'll fly this kid to hell and back first if that's where he wants to go." He stomped toward the door. "He doesn't like the looks of this dirty old Indian. Maybe I'll come with war paint and feathers and see how he likes that. Maybe bury a tomahawk in a certain big mouth's skull."

I wasn't too impressed with myself for picking Charlie's Pub and Café for a meeting place, but by the time I finished my breakfast I saw Sam waiting outside.

"Can you take me to the old Smoky Ridge[5] Hunting Camp? And would it be possible to take a canoe in with us?"

"You should stay out of there." Sam spoke almost too quickly, bitterness in his voice. "It's mud slides and the garbage and graves of treasure hunters.

____

[5] *See Appendix A, Image 5*

"Never was any treasure but white-men will never believe that. Don't suppose the bank told you about the people who died. I used to fly people in all the time." Sam stopped abruptly, then continued slowly. "My people have a legend. They believe there is a curse."

"Is it a Native burial site?"

"No." He shifted. He seemed uncomfortable yet almost eager to talk. "It involves a people more ancient than the Chippewa. Whoever they were they hunted here before the Chippewa came this far north."

"Does the curse cover the entire valley, or just part of it?" I asked.

"You aren't suggesting you believe an Indian legend?" Sam couldn't keep the hint of a sneer from his voice.

I searched for words. This guy wasn't making things easy. "I'm not the kind of history nut my dad was, but I doubt if the old legends have changed much. Dad was sure most legends had some basis in truth. He was weird, Dad I mean, but he wasn't stupid. Can you tell me more about this one?"

It got to be a long silence. "I think you're saying you can't take me into the valley," I finally blurted out. "Can you bring me close enough to hike or canoe in?"

"There is a rock shelf on the west side of the inlet," Sam responded. "There is just enough room to set the helicopter down if it isn't windy. On a stormy day, the waves break right over that part of the rock and there isn't enough maneuvering room. I can take you if the weather cooperates. Know how to handle a canoe?"

"Looks easy enough. I've never tried."

"Only looks easy 'cause you've watched people who know what they're doing." Sam stared at the ground. "Curse won't matter. If you listen to the old stories the serpent likes his meat with some colour. But he'll pull a white man's canoe under just for practice. If you ignore the old stories, the waves will swamp you without any help from the serpent. And you could shave with some of those rocks. Dying takes about as long one way as another.

"There is one other way." Sam chewed on his lip and scuffed his boot on the ground. "I wouldn't normally consider it but..." He paused and then interjected. "You know how much a charter costs? Your old man got too much money?"

He sighed and then continued. "The legend surrounds a mud slide. The Indigenous name for the valley, in English," he added disdainfully, "is *The Snake Pit*. At least five people have died in the last 40 years. East of the slide, around a hump of rock, I can set down in shallow water. That part is solid rock."

"How much will it cost me?" I bit the words off, fighting the anger that seethed in me. "If it's not too much bother, anything else I should know before I go in? Any specific taboos related to the legend?"

Sam stared at the ground.

"The fellow in the restaurant didn't impress me much, but he mentioned your name was Sam. My name is Roland." I forced myself to reach out my hand. He grabbed it with a crushing squeeze but I gave back as good as I got. It was fun watching the look on his face and I felt the anger drain away.

"If you've been in a slump you probably need an advance for fuel. How much do you need?" I asked.

An hour and a half later the helicopter, with a canoe firmly lashed to its support struts, lifted from the clearing. An 18 minute flight put us over the valley. Sam pointed out the snake-like streak of the mudslide. "First Nations people call this valley the Snake Pit. The last bodies were never found." He shouted over the roar of the motor and pulsing thump of the prop. "It's as if the mud slide, or the serpent, swallows them whole. Every time it rains the mud comes down like a mad bull moose." He paused for a moment to consider. "It never fills the valley. It's been doing that for longer than the memory of my people, but the mud never advances farther than that line." He pointed out a rock lip, visible beneath the clear water.

"Some swear it's where the Great Serpent lives." Sam swung eastward and brought the helicopter to rest in shallow water, spray billowing up around us, then reached across and switched off the ignition. The roaring of the engine immediately stilled. The thumping of the prop continued, gradually slowing and finally coming to a stop.

"First Nation's people talk of *Making Medicine.* White men have pictures of African Witch Doctors with a whole crowd in a trance. But Indigenous people's visions almost always come after fasting alone for three or four days."

Sam opened his right hand. It was only as he flexed it that I realized he had gripped the controls tightly. Something seemed to be worrying him. He began to speak again.

"The legend says two warriors loved one girl." His eyes restlessly searched the valley. "Even among First Nations that means trouble." He laughed, a harsh, mirthless sound.

"These guys didn't try to kill each other. It wasn't a time of war, so they couldn't earn honour that way. They tested their skill hunting the bear and the moose. They cut the ice and dived and brought back amethyst from the depths. They called it *the rock with purple fire.* They asked the spirit of the Turtle and the Hawk to guide them. They prayed to *Michabo*, the Great Hare, and to *Edáyíné Nezqi,* the Great Manito. They sang their spirit song in this valley.

"They sought the strongest shamans from all the tribes. Many spirits were called upon. The smoke of their fire drifted over the Snake's Pit.

"Thunder shouted from a clear sky.

"A maiden's voice mingled with the spirit song. She sang so beautiful the smoke forgot to rise. She ran to the rock. She stood in the fire, unburned, caught the hand of each of the men who loved her and lifted her voice to *Edáyíné Nezqi.*

"She sang of the joy and pain that she should be so loved. She asked the Spirit to take the three of them to the place beyond coupling and beyond parting.

"Thunder shouted again. The rocks shook and broke. The bay boiled. The fire flared up and surrounded the three. The rock they stood on sank.

The maiden and her lovers sang, until they were seen no more."

Sam sighed deeply. "The legend tells of a cave, old even then. A painting on the wall shows a man. Beside the man a creature comes out of the water. Many people shelter under the wings from a wild storm.

"The reasons have been forgotten for unnumbered years but the shamans teach that when the man is purified in the whirlpool, the lovers will show him a world so new that *Michabo* has not yet painted the sky blue or let an eagle's feather fall to the ground. They teach that the serpent still lurks in the dark waters and hates all sons of *Edáyíné Nezqi*."

"Who's Adyne Nezqui? I asked.

After another long silence Sam sighed again. "*Edáyíné Nezqi?*" He drew a long slow breath. "Guess you might call him the white man's God, when they're not chasing money or sex. Except they've got their god shrunk down so he's not god anymore. *Edáyíné Nezqi* is bigger than most whites will ever understand."

I felt like I had stuck a screwdriver into a wall plug while Sam related the legend. The story caught me somehow, sucked me in till I was part of it. Sam had brought an uneasy blending of First Nations tradition and educated white man into the telling, with skepticism and belief somehow warring against each other. But the First Nations part seemed to be the stronger.

"I can keep the clock running if you want to sit here and listen to Indian stories," he told me.

I had to force myself to step down from the helicopter. My mind whirled as I splashed through the shallow water, unlashing the canoe. I gave the valley a thorough exploration, but part of my mind clung to the legend, turning it over and over. I didn't know what Sam believed, but something had him spooked.

Limestone that glaciers had chewed on formed the floor of the eastern section of the bay. Towards the south shore a ridge of granite stuck up. It formed the rugged shoreline and boundary between the bay and the lake. Lichens coloured the rocks with patches of green, white and orange. Patches of wet sand showed through a scum of algae.

The advertising had mentioned two cabins. It took some creative writing to say that without flat-out lying. One, backing against a cliff face, barely showed its shape any longer. The roof had long since fallen in. Porcupines had chewed through old barrels and boxes. A pot bellied stove could be seen between two fallen timbers that had rotted away to almost nothing.

The other cabin looked better. Log rafters were still sound, although the roof had collapsed where two rafters were spaced farther apart. A stone fireplace formed one end. A cast iron stove could be seen beneath the rubble from the roof. Shelves lined half the north wall. A crude bed took up the rest of the wall space. The only window opening formed a gaping hole. A black spruce, thick as my wrist, grew through the remains of the door, lying to the right of the opening. Two wooden crosses leaned at crazy angles. Thin wild grass tried to hide a rubbish pile.

It was the kind of picture some artists can make look cool. To me it just looked like something had died but never been buried. I could hear the burble of running water but couldn't tell where it came from. It was a dreary place but could be made livable. Weird as it sounds, though, I felt like I had come home.

The mudslide dominated the valley, splitting it. Back in the canoe, I gazed at the mud bottom, then glanced up the slide itself. *Snake Pit* seemed like a good description. It felt strange and creepy to be paddling the canoe over a lip of rock that somehow channeled mud into an underground passage and had done so for about forever. I looked at the cloudless sky because it seemed like I could hear distant thunder.

Looking up the rusty streaked grey of the mudslide it was easy to believe in the legend, easy to believe in the curse. I back-paddled the canoe, then maneuvered it clumsily across the rock lip that formed the underwater boundary of the Snake Pit.

A small stream meandered across a meadow, then tumbled and gurgled into the bay. Deer and raccoon tracks showed in the sand along the edge.

The west side of the bay had a tranquil beauty that had been missing somehow on the east side, but there was something more. It seemed like some mighty, watching presence filled the valley. There was no numbing, hypnotic spell with it, so I didn't think it was something awful like a ghost or a demon. I guess I half believed in demons since the Bible talked about them like they were real. It's probably crazy thoughts for an 18-year-old but I was pretty sure if I bought the valley and had all the right papers, it would never really belong to me.

It seemed strange that I *could* buy it, with the legend and all, but maybe because of the curse the First Nations people didn't want it.

I wondered about the Great Spirit the lovers from the legend prayed to. Was he the same God I believed in, just called by another name?

Thursday, June 16

The price I offered for the hunting camp was almost shamefully low. The bank manager acted insulted but I used his own words against him; *"We don't give mortgages to school kids. And we won't be pouring good money into that place.'* If my memory is right, that's a quote. I'm not a school kid anymore, just in case that was too hard for you to figure out. You made yourself pretty clear before you knew I had money, so I'm talking a one time deal."

His face got red, then almost purple. It sort of started at his neck and worked up.

"If you have the papers ready we can finish this, then I'll get out of your sight and you can go back to thinking how awful teenagers are."

He controlled himself, his jaws clamped like he was trying desperately to bite off something that was trying desperately to escape. He shoved a bunch of papers across the desk at me.

I made myself take the time to read through all the mindless legal trash. I grabbed a highlighter off his desk and marked two paragraphs. After I had waded through all that mess, written so nobody can understand it and not written that way by accident, I went back to those two paragraphs. I read them again, then a third time before finally stroking them out.

"Mr. Handson…" His voice came through strained, high-pitched. "Those documents have been drawn up by lawyers. They've spent many hours…"

"They've spent hours writing it so it needs another lawyer to read it." I cut him off, then fell silent as I signed my name at all the places marked with an X. "I'll sign with those paragraphs removed. Your assistant is witness to that. If you can't accept that, I'll go somewhere else and you'll still have your hunting camp that you're not willing to pour good money into.

"I'm an orphan, Mr. Thompson. I'm alone. But I'm also old enough to do this legally now, so you don't have to bend the law to make this work."

I pushed the completed papers across to him. The purple on his face had gotten even deeper. His assistant was also red, though I think from a different reason. If she wasn't trying to choke back a belly-laugh, I'm one poor judge. Half an hour later it was all done.

CHAPTER SIX

CLOUDS WITHOUT RAIN

Tuesday, June 28

A property deed for 104 hectares of inhospitable rock now had my name on it. The timber rights had been sold 14 years earlier, but except for a couple of places where a logging trail slashed its way between boulders, the property was largely untouched. Having taken out the logs they could get easily, without doing any reforestation or clean up, the company sold the timber rights back. They made more than enough profit, but at least that cleared the place of any other claims.

Mineral rights had stayed with the property for some strange reason. I could keep any gold nuggets I found. *Fat chance.*

Four helicopter trips brought in enough supplies to restore one cabin and set up housekeeping. Sam's edginess seemed to lessen with each trip in.

I had bought a cell-phone. I couldn't quite figure why. There was almost nobody I wanted to talk to and I wasn't giving the number out to anyone but Sam either. The craziest part was it didn't work in the valley. I had poor radio reception for either regular broadcasting or a cheap Ham-Set I had bought. The mass of rock on all sides cut me off from short-wave towers. I didn't much like anything I could get on the radio, but not being able to listen bugged me. One of my early projects was a climb to the highest point on the property. A wind-blasted jack-pine thrust its way another 12 metres into the air.

I struggled to get about seven metres high. I wound a thin strand of insulated wire around a limb, then made several wraps around the trunk of the tree. As I descended, I continued to circle the trunk with the wire. I didn't know much about aerials but thought I should be able to make something work this way.

A south-facing slope of granite became the anchoring place for a small photovoltaic collector. I mounted the collector in an irregularly shaped backing, coloured to blend with the rocks. A small battery pack nestled into a recess between two boulders, where I camouflaged it too. I made connections, then sealed and waterproofed them. Then I began the slow descent, feeding wire off a spool, burying it where possible. Dusk was settling with a chill in the air as I stumbled into the cabin door.

The next day I completed the electrical hook-up at the cabin. I could use the connection as an aerial for the cell-phone as well as Ham or regular radio. It also let me charge the batteries on my computer. I listened sometimes on the ham radio but couldn't seem to transmit from my new antenna. It had to have the right number of wraps to transmit properly and I hadn't researched that enough. It wasn't important anyway, especially since I didn't have a license or call numbers.

With the cabin in livable condition, an old chair sitting beside the fireplace, and a lamp hanging from the ceiling, I got to thinking books would be cool. I had a bunch in the computer, but it's not the same as sitting down with something you can smell the ink on. Most of the people my age that I knew did almost all their reading on their smart-phones, so I guess that love for real books was another thing I got from Dad without even knowing it.

I was getting stronger fast with the very different exercise from the treadmill alone, but some days I felt like an old man by the time I crawled into my bunk.

Sam was doing a stint of steady flights for a surveying company so it took three weeks before I could coordinate a trip to Owen Sound where I had supplies in storage. After several phone calls, I found a trucker running empty from Owen Sound to Thunder Bay. The driver was happy for even a small payload for some of those *dead miles.*

A forklift that had seen better days rattled and groaned as it lifted surprisingly heavy packing cases onto a flatbed trailer. As the truck rumbled away 20 minutes later, I stuck three boxes of books into the helicopter. I had to leave the rest for now. They were mostly Dad's and I wasn't feeling old and grey enough for some of them yet. Back at the hunting camp I carried the books up to the cabin and set them on my bunk.

"Like a mother duck with a new brood," Sam grumbled good-naturedly. "Put 'em on the shelves. I'll scare up some grub if there's any to be had." He grinned. "I suppose supper's still out there swimming in the bay."

Sam insisted I have a rifle and a shotgun out here in the sticks, and wouldn't take no for an answer. I didn't have a Fire-Arms Acquisition Certificate, but that didn't stop him. He brought two cartons of shells with him, shoved a gun in my hands, pointed out a target against the stone wall of this narrow valley, and made me start blasting away. The rifle wasn't too bad for kick, but the shotgun proved pretty nasty. But he didn't let up till I had gone through those boxes of shells. I was hitting the target as good as him by the end, although my shoulder felt like somebody had been beating it with a baseball bat.

He tried to pound a couple things into my head with more stubbornness than Dad had ever shown. "Most accidents happen with guns people think are empty, so ALWAYS, ALWAYS, ALWAYS treat a gun like it's loaded, and NEVER point a gun at anything unless you're willing to pull the trigger."

Twenty-four hours later I paid a modest fee to Don Jensen at the Trading Post in White River to offload the packing cases. I wanted them away from curious eyes, although inside the cases, like squat black bugs with antenna slapped on by a drunken creator, there was little to excite the imagination.

I had gotten used to the weird looks a teenager gets when he tries to do any kind of business. I had also learned that most people would shut up and take your money. Jensen fit the type. With a heavy timber set across the struts of the helicopter, lashed in place so it couldn't shift in flight, we attached one case beneath the hovering helicopter. Giving slack to the short loops of thick rope, Sam lowered the helicopter as much as possible. I clambered onto the packing case, swung myself up onto the struts, then crawled through the open door. With the blades slashing the air we laboured heavily upward, straining the helicopter to its limits.

Slowly, carefully, the packing case was maneuvered over the chosen depression in the valley floor and lowered. I crawled out the door and dropped onto the packing case. As Sam gave slack to the ropes, I slipped the loops over the spikes and slid them off the plank. I then slid the timber away and waved Sam clear. As he moved out over the water and set the helicopter down I shoved the canoe out and headed to pick him up. We hadn't found a better place than the rock in shallow water where he had landed that first time.

"Come on, Sam. You can see if I've learned anything about cooking since you were here last," I hollered as the blades slowed.

"Is that a threat?" he shouted.

"Ah well," I shot back. "If you don't survive I can come up with some place to bury you. I've heard rumours that if I just put you in the right spot and hold a rain dance, it will all be taken care of. But you better teach me to fly that egg-beater first."

Sam's voice became pensive. "Don't mock what you don't understand." Then he grinned. "You're too stubborn to teach new tricks. Best use I can make of you is a scalp to hang on my belt and the rest of your carcass for bear-bait. Besides, you need real red-man's blood to fly one of these in this country."

"I thought scalping was out of style." With good-natured laughter we paddled around the limits of the mudslide, then pulled the canoe up onto the shore and headed to the cabin.

"What'd you do with that treasure trove?" Sam pointed to where the garbage had been scattered. "That was a national treasure. There's a lady in town works for the Heritage Society. She was raising money to preserve it and restore it."

I put the coffee pot on.

"I see you've got the grave markers nice and straight. New paint too," Sam said. "That ought to make the dead feel better. I'd get awful grumpy if I was buried in a messy grave. Probably come back and haunt somebody if it wasn't too much trouble." He stared around at the books lining the shelves. "Looks like a preacher's house," he commented.

"The bank manager doesn't like you much. Says you robbed him blind." He grinned with delighted amusement. "But he says it's his own fault. Says he opened his mouth when he should've kept it closed. Said you latched onto his words like a blood-sucking leech and wouldn't let go." Sam looked with undisguised interest around the cabin. "He's sat on this property for years waiting for some sucker to buy it. I flew some guys in a few years back. They sniffed the bait but didn't swallow the hook. The bunch before that laughed at fool Indian stories. They had more whiskey than blood in their veins. The ones I brought out were blithering idiots. They'd seen their friends go down in the mudslide. Nothing left of them but one soggy hat." Sam paused for a moment. "What's different about you? Why do you believe?"

I took awhile to think about that one before I replied. "It would be handy to write off legends as the superstitions of ignorant people. I can feel better, more intelligent. I can even make it a religious thing." I searched for words.

"I believe in the God of the Bible, Sam. I guess you know that. I think the missionaries who came to your people included some of the best men this country has ever seen. Probably a few of the worst too. I know whiskey came in under stacks of Bibles. But most of them, even the good ones, didn't know your people. Some of them never bothered to learn. You were the *Noble Savage*. Your stories of serpents and lightning, turtles, wolves and beavers were good entertainment, and *proof* that you were backward and *heathen*. Your religion was rejected. But you were expected to jump at the chance to adopt ours." I snorted.

"You didn't talk about land ownership. When some white man was crazy enough to pay you for what belonged to everyone and no one, you laughed at the stupid white man and took the money. Then we started to shoot you when you came onto *our* land." I paused, reflecting.

"In religion we talked two different languages too. We used the word *Manito*, thinking that was an accurate translation of God. But it meant something different to you than it did to us. We never figured that out. A lot of us still haven't.

"You've been around white-men long enough to know that most of them couldn't give a rip about God, even some who go to church all the time. Why should you believe anything I say?" I paused.

"Your people have been screwed, Sam. I can't change it. I don't know what I can do." I fell silent.

"Steak's burning." Sam commented dryly.

A shaky laugh escaped me. "Sorry. Didn't mean to get all preachy."

"Hey! I haven't met a lot of whites I respect." Sam stopped for a bit. "How 'bout you rescue that steak. I don't like it still kicking, but I don't like to break my teeth on it either."

I quickly opened a tin of mushrooms, then drained and dumped them into the fry-pan. A few moments later, the steak and mushrooms were slapped onto plates while a slab of bannock dough went into the hot juice on the pan.

"We had to do essays on the residential schools—all those bodies found. It was enough to make a guy sick. We couldn't ever use the word, 'Indian.' You were 'First Nations' or 'Aboriginal,' or 'Indig… Indigenous.' But it was all stuff from so long ago that nobody could fix it—and the stuff that could be fixed—well, we had to put our pipelines through there, so you still didn't have any say." I shut up and poured coffee, then opened a tin of evaporated milk. Sugar in a coffee-tin sat in front of Sam. I pulled up a stool and sat down. Sam waited, knowing the routine. I bowed my head.

My prayer was brief, with one added request: "Help me not to be a pain in the rear when Sam is crazy enough to ask some question about You."

Sam burst out laughing. "This God you talk to," he sputtered. "He's big enough to carve out this valley with his little finger, but he'll let you talk to him like that? He doesn't sound like your typical white man. Someday I gotta meet the guy."

The summer wore away, hot and dry. As July passed into August the sun scorched the valley. On the shoreline of one of the biggest bodies of fresh water on the globe, you wouldn't think drought could be possible. But the grass on the little meadow grew dry and yellow. The deep green of black spruce had sickened to a lifeless grey. The leaves hung limp and dull on a scattering of birch along the south-facing slope. The stream that meandered across the meadow flowed sluggishly. Cracks opened in drying mud. A milky broth trickled into the bay.

The sun glared off the water. It reflected from the sloping rock on three sides of the valley. Only the north-facing slope gave some relief, casting narrow, sharp-edged shadows.

It was too hot for a cooking fire in the cabin. The risk of sparks from a campfire in the tinder-dry conditions prohibited that too. Even the fish were listless, though I caught enough to survive. Gutted and split, I cut them into thin strips and hung them on wooden slats to dry. I shot a deer, although it was out of season. I dried some of the meat, but made most of it up into sausage, using a recipe Sam gave me. He dropped in often enough to show me what I had to know and I muddled through other things on my own. I ached for the *EAGLE* and the cool comfort of deep water.

Using a barrel and an old two-drawer filing cabinet, with a skeleton of branches and clay dug out of the bank near the mudslide, I made an outside stove and oven. Raised off the ground, I wove a bed of soaked willow bows into a snug cradle. I added a coating of mud, then pressed the barrel into it. In the stifling heat, the mud dried fast, cracks opening in it. I removed the barrel and added a second layer of mud, filling the cracks as I went, adding to the thickness. By repeating the process three times, I had a thick coating of clay forming a bed for the firebox.

I removed the drawers from the file-cabinet, cut the fronts off them, then rigged crude hinges and reattached them. I put a screen into the chimney before lighting a fire.

My first attempt at baking bread was pretty sad but I could cook on the hot surface without making the cabin even hotter. Cracks opened and had to be refilled. The oven seemed ridiculously huge for one guy alone. But the file-cabinet had been there, the drawer runners too badly rusted to be useful. And I had other purposes in mind for a large cooking capacity in the future. I spent three more days building a simple shelter from the sun.

A breeze sighed along the cracked slope of the parched mudslide. Wearing a wide-brimmed hat and a shirt glued with sweat against my body, I took advantage of the relative safety to explore the mudslide itself. I wanted answers but I felt strangely tight and tense.

Channelled along a rent in the rock face, the slide spread in places as wide as 30 metres and in others to as little as seven. Fine grit rolled under my feet. Dust with a strange sooty odour rose with each footfall, then settled quickly, as if even the tired air could not carry it. The granules, small and spherical, made walking tiresome.

The winding slope reached back almost three kilometres, way past the boundaries of what I owned. It then opened into a wide grey wasteland. Fingers of mud reached back into muskeg, now a steaming gumbo in the heat, reeking of decay. Just below the dusty surface, the grit felt damp and cold.

Largely featureless until it reached into the muskeg itself, several upwellings had the appearance of huge frost boils. I didn't know what else they could be but thought this was too far south for that. Whatever the cause, some upthrust continued to feed the granular mass. A moderate rain was enough to sweep waves down the channel. I guessed freeze-thaw cycles might do the same.

The upwellings of mud intrigued me but I'm no geologist. I had no theories except permafrost and that seemed illogical. Some weird tectonic activity might also be a possibility. I sure didn't know. I trudged slowly back to where a shelf of rock let me leave the slide itself and work my way through the intermittent shadow of black spruce, cedar, and tamarack, all drooping in the hot still air.

When a light spattering of rain broke the heat wave for a couple of days, dimpling the dust, I turned my attention to the large packing case Sam had set into the hollow. I built a frame and draped a tarp over it. It gave just enough room to work, while sheltering me from the sun, though it still felt like I was working in an oven set on high. With the crate dismantled, the nuclear furnace itself looked ridiculously small and uninspiring.

Deeply pocked limestone formed much of the floor of the valley. The thin dusting of soil filled some of the depressions. Many caught rainwater and seepage. Minute fissures channeled some of that away. Others slowly evaporated, or spilled over into lower pools. Where a smooth sided bowl held a stagnant pool two metres wide and one deep, I widened a crack. I bent a piece of copper tubing, hammering and coaxing it into shape to follow the crack, feeding from another nearby depression that drained from fissures in the bottom. I tamped moss in place and pressed the tubing into it. Adding additional moss, I covered it all with stones and rubble.

Hours of work set several lines into moss insulation, connecting the nuclear furnace to a depression I called my 'hot tub' and also to the cabin.

I installed a sink in the cabin. A drain fed through the wall into a fissure in the rock. Enlarging the pipe formed a funnel. The faucet arm of the cold water line discharged continually into the drain, or could be swung over the sink.

Having hot water available but concealed demanded much thought and effort. I couldn't explain my reasons for keeping it secret, even to myself.

A flexible tube with a ball valve at the end tapped into the closed loop of copper pipe where it entered through a concealed recess in the wall. I worked a loose knot in the windowsill free. A hand drill bored a hole down to a gap in one of the lower logs. With just enough length of tubing to pull up from the window and reach the sink, and the recess enlarged enough to allow the excess to lay smoothly when it was set back, hot water was readily available but invisible. A hundred other wood knots lay above or below the surface of the rough logs. Nothing made this one appear more significant than any other.

I checked the *hot tub*. Stagnant water had been flushed clear. A steady, clean stream flowed from beneath a limestone recess. The pool stirred in a slow, gentle swirl.

I built a fire on the bare rock, already shimmering with heat waves in the July sun. I grunted as I hauled four-litre paint tins full of the solidified amalgam[6] to the fire, pried the lids loose and set them into the coals. It's hard to believe such a small tin could be so heavy.

The furnace I had hauled out of storage was one of the first ones built with the coil fixed in place. The amalgam had to be added. It took an hour before the first of three tins was fully liquefied.

I poured the amalgam into the reservoir of the nuclear furnace. Within seconds the discharge pipe began to warm, even as the amalgam itself solidified in the bottom of the sphere. A thermometer on the discharge line showed the temperature creep up from 16°C to 29°C. As the temperature continued to rise, I opened the valve feeding cold water to the cabin. On the hot-water line I opened both valves allowing the loop to the house to fill, then closed the bypass valve, forcing hot water to take the loop.

Back in the cabin, I watched as the cold water line spit and sputtered for several moments. With gentle pressure, it forced bubbles down the pipe. Another three-metre drop along an 18-metre length brought the water pressure up to 76 kilopascal (11 psi).

---

[6] *See Appendix B*

Over the next hour, I added amalgam until the temperature at the furnace held steady at 52.2°C. The water flowed into the pool at 41.7°C. The amalgam had solidified again, the water cooling it below its melting point. But the furnace functioned in the temperature range I wanted.

Sweaty and dirty, I stopped for a supper of venison jerky. I made a salad of watercress and plantain, with a dribble of oil and vinegar over it. A cup of scalding coffee brewed on my outside stove completed the meal. Washing dishes was almost a pleasure with hot running water, although the entire valley, cabin included, felt like the inside of a blast furnace.

The light was fading when I rechecked the pool. The inlet temperature had risen to 42°C. The mixing was inconsistent. The overall temperature showed 34°C.

A little fine-tuning of the direction of the inlet would improve the situation. The overflow had filled two lower pools, each with a cooler temperature. A cluster of small fissures swallowed the outflow from the second of those pools.

The sun blazed through the late summer. The drought hung on for three more weeks. Fearing a fire, I cut grass and hauled water, widening a strip of bare ground close to the cabin.

Heavy clouds rolled in from the southwest. A cool wind gusted and eddied through the valley, picking up dust and swirling it. The clouds promised but swept on. I stood at the cabin door and watched them longingly. Two days later I woke to a drumming on the roof. Standing at the door as mud spattered my feet, I laughed out loud, then walked outside in my underwear. I stood with my face raised, letting the cool torrent beat on me.

CHAPTER SEVEN

BLOOD MONEY

Sunday, October 23

skin of ice on the bay greeted me in the morning. I tried to tune in a Christian radio program, but if any were broadcasting I couldn't find them. I recognized the tunes on a couple stations in some strange language but couldn't find anything I wanted to listen to in English.

It was close to noon when I headed out to the *hot tub*. The overall temperature held steady at 41°C. The skin of ice on the bay had melted. Steam swirled in grey eddies above the pool. I stripped in the cold air, then stepped into the water.

What a feeling. I lay back against the curving side and basked in the soothing warmth.

Within another two weeks I had the nuclear furnace covered with slabs of stone and a tent over the hot tub. The privacy in this valley would be hard to increase, yet it felt weird to be naked in the open air.

After the first light snowfall in early October, I had begun stripping the other cabin, looking for anything useful. It backed against a towering slab of limestone. The rotting walls were cut into a rubble of coarse sediment. Animals had tunnelled into the back. As I shovelled away the mess, I found a cave. The entrance was low, forcing me to stoop. Broken slabs of rock covered the floor. The ceiling made a rough inverted bowl, with a bent handle pointing toward the entrance. Reaching up nearly four metres, it dropped slowly toward the back where the floor rose to meet it. At right-angles to the 'handle,' a 'spout' thrust a finger farther back into the rock. A trickle of water flowed from that spout. The tiny stream disappeared under the rubble of the floor, to reemerge in a small clear pool near the centre.

The cave measured six metres across. Along the southeast side, rotted wooden boxes had been torn open by animals. Tins and bottles littered the floor, some still intact. A case of whiskey had been scorned by the animals while tins of beans and soup had rusted through and been pawed over. Moldy scraps of grey-green cloth resolved themselves into an army uniform when a couple of medals glittered. The animals had ignored a box of books, moldy and damp. A mildewed newspaper showed headlines from the Canadian Declaration of War, September 11, 1939. It seemed likely that was the last time anyone had entered the cave. A mud slide had covered the entrance. The man who had hastily stored supplies had apparently never returned. Latecomers, unaware it even existed, had not found the entrance.

The cave was too damp to be an ideal storage space, but with a proper door to keep out animals it offered great potential. I wished I had found it before going to the work of rebuilding the other cabin. Through the heat wave it would have been a delight.

It took two days to clear the doorway. I then built a door to fit the opening. Bands of flat iron covered the face of the door, with one inch spacing between them. I ordered a battery powered electric fencer to be brought in on Sam's next trip. Hooked into the power supplied from the solar collector for the antenna, few animals would ever sniff at the door more than once. With a switch to shut the power off any time I wanted to enter, I had a bear-proof storage area with lots of capacity.

There was a lot to do before winter closed in. I fished daily, taking the canoe out through the narrow wave-choked inlet when the weather was dead calm, staying inside when it was too rough. A deep hollow under a rock shelf intrigued me. The few seconds of calm between waves gave just a hint. I longed for the *EAGLE*. Each time I took the canoe out, I gained a bit more skill, but I never took foolish chances.

I built a wooden rack for drying fish and learned to quickly split and gut my catch, wasting almost nothing. I didn't learn to like dried fish. My tastebuds compared it to shoe-leather that had seen years of dirty feet.

Friday, November 4

I cut firewood, splitting and stacking it, waiting for enough snow to drag it back on a sled. I figured eight cord was a minimum. That much I understood, although heating the cabin, tiny as it was, differed greatly from heating the insulated house I had left so many months before.

Twice I had been lucky enough to shoot a deer. Most days I was able to snare a rabbit. Dad might not have liked it, but I was getting to be an okay hunter. Maybe it was Sam's influence, but some part of me ached for every animal I killed. I got so I thanked them for feeding me.

The shorter days cut into my working time. I often fished by moonlight. Wolves frequently howled along the top northeast rim of the valley. I never got fully over my nervousness about them. They featured in too many of the stories I'd read as a little kid. Sam told me those stories had been written by people who had also read too many wild stories when they were kids but didn't actually know a thing about wolves. Still, I liked to have the rifle with me if I was far from the cabin when the howling started.

A bear ruined my fish drying rack and stole much of the meat I was preparing. Two rifle shots, close but deliberately missing, drove it away. For some strange reason, I didn't want to kill it.

Two days later I woke to a loud snuffling at the door. As I slipped out of bed, I could see the bear heading towards the drying rack. I reached for the rifle, paused and lifted the shotgun off its pegs instead. I rammed four shells into the gun. Swinging the door open, I raised the gun to my shoulder and fired.

The bear, a large black male, was reaching up to the fish when the door opened. From 40 metres, the pellets slammed into his back. With his heavy coat of fur, they could do little damage unless they hit his eyes. But the painful blow must have stung like a swarm of hornets. A screaming snarl burst from him. He swung around, his huge paw whistling as the claws sought whatever enemy had attacked him. A corner post snapped. The whole structure collapsed over the frightened bear. Again, he bawled out a panicked snarl, twisting, slashing with his forepaws, searching for a way out.

As soon as his head turned so the eyes were not at risk, I fired another shot. The bear leaped straight up, then flung himself out of the wreckage and galloped away, spurred by a third peppering of buckshot.

As the grey half-light faded into full darkness, a rumble filled the valley. Startled, I looked up from where I was reading by lamplight. The booming of heavy waves against the rocks of the shore was distinct. It had to be the mudslide. I thought again of Sam's description of *a charging bull moose*. It seemed to fit.

Winter settled into a predictable routine. I spent several hours reading every day. I even did a bit of writing. I fished through the ice and I hunted, trying to never let my supply of meat get too low. I got pretty good on snowshoes, and I almost always carried the rifle if I went any distance. My sister had laughed herself silly over Farley Mowat's book, *Never Cry Wolf*, but I'd been in one of those crazy little brother stages where anything my sister liked had to be bad, so I'd never read it. Now when I heard the wolves howling, I kind of wished I had.

The chain-saw was another tool I used, but reluctantly. It seemed obscene to disturb the peace of the valley with the roaring of the motor and the oily smoke. But the stockpile of firewood close to the cabin slowly grew through the winter. Hauling wood on a homemade sled was hard work, but on a trail of hard-packed snow I saw visible results for a day's sweat.

There wasn't much reason to stand in front of a mirror but I hardened up. The toughs at school would have had more to face than just bad timing if they tangled with me now.

I made two trips to Toronto during the winter. I also got together with Sam a number of times. Sam fiercely defended the Indigenous People's Treaty Status. I called it *Blood Money*, *Conscience Money*, and *Prostitute's Pay*. I didn't really know that much about it, but had great arguments with Sam.

"You want to be recognized as a full citizen? Getting what everybody else in the country sees as a handout? It'll never happen."

"The whites owe us. Big time. Why shouldn't we take it?" Sam's voice would become harsh. "God knows, we've earned that much."

"Money so you will hide away on reservations and drink your beer out of sight of the rest of us. That's what the money's really for. It's to get you out of sight." I snorted. "I sound more like Dad every day. He'd have been impressed with all I just said. Only problem. I haven't a clue if it's right or not." I stared at Sam. "What do I know? I'm a real expert on the Indigenous Peoples problem, aren't I?"

"A guy's liable to starve to death while you solve all the Red Man's headaches." Sam's gruff voice had a hint of a chuckle in it. "I thought I might at least get a rabbit's leg to chew on after I set the chopper down on your high-tech helipad. But it looks like I'd better head back to White River."

Four hours later I stood on the ice beside the helicopter. As Sam buckled his safety belt, I leaned through the open door and placed a small package on his lap. With a frown, Sam unwrapped it. A broad grin split his face as he held up a fried leg of rabbit. He lifted it in a salute, leaned forward, and twisted the ignition key, then swung the door shut as I stepped back.

I was cutting firewood on the east side of the valley when the helicopter returned. It had only been a couple of days since Sam had left so I was surprised to see him coming back. I stuck with my work though and watched him head across to the cabin. It was a sure thing it was no emergency or he would have come to where the chainsaw was tearing up the silence.

Sam hadn't said much about his change in status but I knew it galled him. He was everybody's friend now if he showed up at the pub. Don Jensen at the Trading Post would slap him on the shoulder, asking how much fuel he needed. It was only a few months since they had all treated him like dirt. No wonder he wanted to deck the lot of them.

When I finally dragged a loaded sleigh up two hours later, Sam greeted me at the door with a self-satisfied smirk. "Come on in. Make yourself at home. Supper's cooking and the coffee pot is on. You're just in time."

"You taking over, Sam?"

"I figured if I want to get fed around here I'd better do something about it myself. I tried to get some new teeth to handle your steak too, but White River's all sold out of false teeth."

"It's been a long time since I walked into this cabin to find food already cooking, Sam. If it's safe to eat I might invite you back." I stripped off my parka and mitts. "I must be paying you too much. Or is it just my wonderful company? What brings you out today?"

"Why, it's your cooking. Don't you know? Where else can you find a steak worth sinking your teeth into? I've probably left two or three in your steaks. They must be ornery critters you shoot to be so tough."

"I don't shoot them, Sam. I found a woolly mammoth frozen in a glacier. He's only been in the deepfreeze a few thousand years. That's almost as good as fresh. I hack a slab off with the chain-saw every now and then. The chain oil adds a different flavour but I feed that to crazy characters who fly in. There's one who tells me he's man enough for anything."

"Ha! I should have guessed," Sam chortled. "Set yourself down there.

This kitchen wasn't made for two bodies, even if one of 'em's only half a man and that half is crazier'n a treed coon."

I pulled two coffee cups from the shelf, poured the steaming liquid from the pot, then sat down. "You know, one of the few things I miss out here in the sticks?" I exaggerated the longing in my voice. "Cream for my coffee. It's never the same without it. I lassoed a cow moose the other day. Thought she'd be glad to trade a bit of milk for me coming that close without a rifle, but she dragged me across three counties, then wrapped me around a tree. No consideration at all."

"You've read too many Cowboy an' Indian stories. But you'd never make a cowboy. Don't have the right hat for it."

"Ah, it's the hat that makes the difference. I've always wondered."

The food, prepared and served by a different male hand, was remarkably similar to the meals I routinely ate, although Sam boasted of it being *real* food. We spoke little as knives and forks scraped against plates. Finally, Sam pushed back his chair. "Now that was a man's meal," he said with a sigh.

Afterwards we played a game of chess. I led with my right-hand pawn, then quickly brought my rook out. Sam countered with his queen and a bishop. A dozen moves on each side had traded three pawns. I had lost a bishop and Sam had lost a knight.

Neither of us were highly skilled. We settled down to a slugging match, waiting for a mistake. Sam lost his queen as he laboured to get past my defences. My fist came down solidly on the table as my knight jagged across the board for the kill. My triumphant grin faded as Sam followed up the sacrifice with a rook and a bishop lined up on my king, after a lowly pawn moved forward. "Checkmate," Sam said gruffly.

I stared reluctantly at the board, then shook my head. "I was going to stick you for cooking Christmas dinner after I won. I was planning on turkey with all the trimmings, and mashed potatoes, yams with that gooey marshmallow topping, and hot mince pie for dessert." I sighed. "I haven't sat down to a meal like that since..." I paused for a long moment. "I think I've only read about those meals. Bannock and fried onions work pretty good at keeping a bit of something between a guy's backbone and belly-button, but they just aren't quite the same."

"You need a woman in the kitchen for that." Sam chuckled. "Me, I figure one woman in the kitchen is too many. Trouble! That's what they are. They get a man thinking with parts of him that aren't too bright. His brain turns off and all the rest of him turns on." He snorted. "Was it your God that designed us that way?"

"He's the guilty one, Sam." I looked up with a broad grin. "He told Adam and Eve to fill the earth. I wonder how thrilled Eve was with those instructions? Then He wired Adam to some high-voltage charger. He never did tell him exactly where all the switches were." I stopped for a moment. "Does it get easier, Sam, when you get older? Living without girls?"

Sam grunted, but did not answer.

"I was sure I had you whipped. With your Queen down, you were out of the running. Must have been a bit like the old devil felt like when ..." I stopped, grinning. "A pot of coffee, a friend, even if you did whip me, and a lonely kid who must be infected with preacher blood... It's a dangerous place to visit."

"Guess I'll have to up my prices," Sam grunted back. "Eighty dollars an hour to fly you places. Double that to listen to your sermons."

"You've got it all wrong, Sam. It's the preacher who gets paid. Of course, if the sermon is too bad you can knock him out of the pulpit. Twenty-dollar bills made into a tight roll are the proper thing to throw, though fifties or hundreds work even better."

A log dropped in the fireplace with a loud pop. A burst of sparks streamed upward. The fire flared brighter for just a moment. I pushed back my chair. I asked a silent question as I held the coffee pot over Sam's cup. Sam nodded. I poured, then topped my own cup as well.

"I can't figure you," Sam finally broke the silence. "You're barely out of kindergarten, but you think like a man. You don't just give lip service to this Jesus guy, though most of the time you manage to keep your preacher blood down. I'm just a crazy Indian guy who has tried to find something better than a treaty cheque and a bottle. But there's something different about you."

I stared at Sam for a long moment. "I'm nobody special, Sam. There are thoughts in my head that would make a sailor blush. I was awful disappointed in the church I went to. They said all the right things and I learned to say them too, but after Dad and Tacye got killed, I didn't seem important. I hurt like crazy but nobody was there, except the police and Child Protection Services."

I struggled for a moment before I continued. "It's funny that Child Protection Services was more interested in a 14-year-old orphan than the church I had gone to most of my life. Real, belly-laugh haw-haw kind of funny, you know."

I couldn't stop the shudder that went through me. "Why wasn't the church there for me, Sam? How could they say all the right things but not be there?" I paused, raising my gaze to meet his. "Don't let me get like that. Scalp me if I do. If I ever get talking 'religion' and it's not something I'm trying to live, even if I'm messing it up most of the time, use me for bear-bait."

I hadn't realized till after Sam left that I had turned 19 a few months back. It seemed strange, but I felt older than that. I had got through Christmas this year without that morbid rope and the noose I had tied and untied a thousand times. I actually loved the winter out here where the snow stayed white and clean and there weren't a million stores telling you life was one big party and all you had to do was spend more money to be happy.

During a couple of trips south through the winter I found an old, run-down building with a set of massive doors opening directly into five metres of water. It would allow a 60-metre boat to dock inside. The landlord owned several waterfront warehouses. I reached an agreement with him and began to accumulate supplies. They were weird supplies, but I was making weird plans. I guess I didn't look quite so babyish any more. I got treated almost like an adult most of the time.

I found a beat-up old barge that I managed to buy. The diesel motor belched oily fumes from a stack that had lost an argument with a low bridge. One of the blades of the propeller was bent, causing it to vibrate badly at anything over a slow idle. As elegant as a sow in mud, it could still carry a huge load while drawing only two metres of water. I had the propeller taken off and straightened. I also got the diesel engine overhauled, and cleaned fuel lines and tanks.

Before going back to the hunting camp I made an extra stop and talked to my lawyer for a few minutes. He seemed to have everything under control. He gave me a strange warning though. Said the government and the banks were doing weird things. He didn't know what would come of it but thought I'd be smart to put some of the money from Dad's book into things that couldn't just disappear by pushing a button on a computer. He seemed scared to say more, like his office might be bugged or something. It didn't make much sense but got me thinking. I mean, the only proof I had of money in the bank was a piece of plastic with some coded numbers on it. If somebody messed with that plastic, what could I do?

Chapter Eight

Bear Bait

Thursday. February 5

*I*f White River bothered me with the crowds and noise, Toronto was a madhouse. I was glad to get back north. It took everything in me not to have Sam fly me to check on the *EAGLE*, still hidden along the French River. He didn't even know it existed, though he was the only real friend I had.

A growing restlessness stirred in me. The wilderness valley and the physical demands for survival had been healing and emotionally restful after the aching loneliness mixed with those awful, endless days of school.

Hiding the *EAGLE* while I searched for a proper location had seemed right, though I couldn't tell you why. It seemed like the *EAGLE* fit the legend of the valley. It seemed like I had some reason to be here, though it also seemed stupid and arrogant to dare to think that.

Spring came slowly to the north shore of Lake Superior. Within the enclosed bay, ice reached a metre thick. Along the inlet where the waves churned up a froth, cakes and mush ice ground and sloshed against each other. Close to either shore where the spray reached high, a layer of slick white armour covered every surface. A canoe could be crushed or swamped at any second, and a man on foot could be swept off the narrow band of ice clinging to each rock face. I had hoped the ice would allow me to explore the small rocky island that protected the inlet, something I always intended but never got to during warmer weather. But the only cold spell that succeeded in choking the inlet closed was followed by a rapid rise in temperature. The mid-afternoon sun, striking on the east rock face, caused slabs of ice to peel off and crash onto the floor. I got some cool pictures, but stayed on the landward side.

Monday, March 9

It was late afternoon. The sun's meagre warmth was long gone behind the western rim. Four small fish lay gutted and cleaned on the ice. A damp, chill wind blew. I gathered my gear to head back to the cabin.

A snuffling, then a woof alerted me. A hunched figure, black against the greying shoreline, swayed on its feet, sniffing. The smell of freshly cleaned fish was strong. Just out of hibernation, a bear would be surly and unpredictable. The bear shuffled toward me, continuing to snuff loudly, then broke into a lumbering gallop.

I don't know why I hadn't brought the rifle with me that day. The cabin suddenly seemed impossibly distant. I peeled my mittens off, cupped my hands and brought them together in a single loud clap. At the same time I shouted. The bear braced all four feet and came to a sudden stop, claws scrabbling against the snow. I clapped and shouted again. The bear turned, uncertain. I hurled a slab of ice that hit by its front paws, spraying tiny shards into its face. An instant before it hit another clap resounded. An angry woof burst from the animal. It leaped backwards, startled, then turned and galloped away. I pulled my mitts back on, gathered up the fish and tackle, then headed across the ice back to the cabin.

The smell of fish drew the bear back. I could see a black shape moving against the shadows. I fought the urge to drop the fish and run. From what I had read running might trigger an attack.

The bear charged just before I reached the cabin door. I didn't know if this was for real or not but wasn't waiting to find out. I wrenched the door open, leaped inside, and slammed it. The fish hit the floor as both hands came up to my mouth. My teeth grasped my mitts. I jerked my hands out of them and reached for the shotgun, aware of the fishy taste as I did so. The bear's claws hit the door. I could hear its angry snarl and loud grunting breath. I rammed a shell into the chamber, then shoved three more into the breech. The glass of the window shattered as a huge paw reached through. The gun came up to my shoulder and I squeezed the trigger.

Nothing happened.

Fumbling like mad in the semi-darkness, I found the safety. *Why'd you set it on an empty gun?* I took a strip off myself.

The blast inside the cabin sounded incredibly loud. An explosion of splinters burst from the log just inches to the side of the bear's muzzle, thrust through the window opening. A snarling scream escaped the jaws. Teeth gleamed in the semi-darkness. The bear flung itself backwards as the second blast tore through the opening. I rushed to the window and fired a third time.

I could see the black smudge against the snow falter, then gather itself for a swift, panic-stricken escape. The gun roared a fourth time. A guttural wail tore from the beast's throat. A hollow click came from the next squeeze of the trigger.

I backed away from the window and sat heavily on the bed. I shuddered, then bolted up from the bed, struck a match, and lit the lamp. My hands trembled and I wasn't too impressed. I shoved four shells into the gun, then levered one into the chamber. I left the safety off.

I stirred up the fire, set two of the fish on to fry, then dug out a piece of canvas and nailed it over the window opening. I turned the fish and seasoned them. While they completed cooking, I cleaned up the broken glass and wood splinters.

After cleaning up the dishes I wrote in my journal:

Monday, March 9

Caught unprepared by a bear today. Somebody set the alarm too early and hadn't bothered to put the coffee on. It was in an ugly mood.

The brute broke a window. It apparently had a fish-fry in mind, but claimed it had ordered them rare and complained about the service. It didn't leave a tip for the waiter. I'm guessing by its table manners it might not have turned down a leg roast for dessert.

I'll probably have to kill it. There was a little blood around the window. I may have taken out an eye. If it can't hunt properly it will be even more dangerous than before.

If it was a grizzly, I could make some sense of its behaviour. But it's a black. I guess I just don't know that much about bears.

Dad always told us never to have a loaded gun in the house. Heck, he wouldn't even have an empty one. Now I know why. A shotgun inside a log cabin makes a heck of a lot of noise.

A close-up with the camera next morning caught huge paw-prints, plus the claw marks on the door. Droplets of blood testified to the bear feeling at least some of the sting of the shotgun blast.

The canvas over the window left the room dark and gloomy. I didn't have replacement glass.

Carrying the rifle loaded and ready, I walked out on the ice. The bear had returned and clawed at the bloodstained snow. I could see fox tracks as well. I followed the bear's tracks. They meandered from an east-north-east direction. Each place they crossed one of the game trails they showed evidence of stopping and sniffing before proceeding. From reaching the ice-fishing hole, they turned toward the cabin. Where the morning trail intersected its path from the night before, the tracks changed.

I could almost visualize the shaggy hulk rocking on its front paws, head swaying, lips curled back, low guttural snarl coming from white fangs with yellow roots. The vision was a bit too rich in detail. I shivered slightly, checked the gun, then made a slow full circle. I could not shake the feeling I was being stalked.

I followed the bear's back trail. Where the track crossed one of the main game trails, the bear had milled in indecision, then sat on its haunches. A slight pink stain in the snow suggested blood, but in the early morning light I couldn't be sure.

As I approached the trees along the east shore, my gaze was drawn to the left. A shadow seemed to keep pace with me. I couldn't pick it out and stopped often to scan the area through binoculars.

I checked and re-checked the rifle. I worked the bolt, making sure the action was smooth and sure. I circled twice and searched the ice behind me.

A bear looks pretty clumsy, but even a skilled hunter with a heavy rifle is no match in skill and stealth. Against snow and ice, the challenge for a large black bear to remain invisible would seem impossible. But with broken boulders, trees, and shadows this surly creature was successful.

For long moments I scanned the broken ridge and shoreline through binoculars. A raven croaked its harsh cry. A snowshoe hare watched from a hollow below a boulder. Tree branches whispered in their squeaky voices as they rubbed against each other. The breeze sighed and teased a few parched, dry leaves hanging from a birch.

The sun melted through the mid-morning mist that had shrouded the top of the ridge. It lay warm and gentle on my shoulders. Shadows suddenly stood out bold and sharp. Large tracks, invisible seconds before, led from boulder to boulder, tree to tree. Only brief glimpses of the trail appeared. The creature had made excellent use of sparse cover.

A jumbled mass of boulders with a clump of stunted black spruce drew my attention. Deep shadows almost materialized into the black muzzle and short ears of a bear. I could not be sure. The track led in that direction, but repeatedly disappeared. Clouds drifted across the sun. Bold shadows faded into grey.

I knelt in the damp snow and raised the rifle. I sighted on a patch of white rock just above the deepest shadow, then squeezed the trigger.

A tiny explosion of white dust burst from the rock. With a loud startled "WOOF," the shadow exploded into motion. Straight up the bald face of the ridge the bear heaved himself in ungainly flight. I held him in the cross-hairs of the rifle scope, my finger tight on the trigger. When the bear stopped at a crest in the ridge and half turned, a steel-jacketed shell hit the granite beside its head.

The bear leaped sideways, scrambled and slid several metres on the steeply sloping ridge. It claws tore deep furrows in the softening snow, caught in a rocky crevice and arrested its slide. Then it heaved itself upwards once again, crossed the narrow crest, turned and disappeared among the spruce trees.

For several moments more, I could see a black shadow appear, than melt back into the deep blue-grey of the spruce forest.

My heart pounded and I was breathing heavily as I lowered the rifle. I loaded two shells, then picked up the spent cartridges. Setting the safety on the rifle, I looked again at the tracks I had been following. I started to turn away, then shrugged and turned back. The area was riddled with small caves. A bear was as likely as any creature to lead me to one of any size.

It was a tough climb up the snow-covered rocky slope with patches the early spring sun had managed to melt bare. Black spruce clung tenaciously to cracks in the rock. In little pockets of leaf mold and moss, tamarack had taken root.

The bear had walked this trail several times. Claw marks nearly three metres up a tree gave the first clear indication of size. Fresh, dark dung made a pile beside the base of the tree. Close by, a rotting stump had been torn apart.

The bear had clambered over a boulder where a shelf of rock appeared to taper off into empty air behind a cluster of tamarack. A strong, earthy smell greeted me. The shelf, scarcely wide enough to carry a man, overlooked a dangerous drop. Gaunt branches of the tamarack reached like bony fingers to stop my passage. Wisps of black hair clung to lower branches.

Crouching low, with the gun at the ready, I pushed against the branches. Sweat stung my eyes. My collar rubbed against my neck. My clothes rustled against the rock face on one side, and the branches on the other.

A narrow slash in the rock face, hidden from only a metre away, gave back an earthy, barnyard smell. I shoved the muzzle of the rifle through the opening. As it tapped against the rock, a hollow sounding echo came back. Bits of hair clung to the sharp edges of the rock face.

At its widest, the opening spread about a metre. Standing outside in full sunshine I could see nothing looking into the blackness. I wanted to charge right in, but it seemed to make sense to live a little longer. I guessed I'd get a light.

A pair of ravens quarrelled near the inlet to the bay. Binoculars showed a large fish, half frozen in the slush ice. A whiskey-jack screamed and chickadees chattered with cheerful carelessness. I found myself basking in the sun's warmth, strolling lazily back toward the cabin. I flushed a deer just at the shoreline. Instinctively, the hunter in me responded and the rifle came to my shoulder. As the cross-hairs lined up behind the animal's shoulders, a voice in my brain whispered, "Now!" But no crack resounded and echoed across the valley. I lowered the gun with a slight smile. "You're probably ready to drop a fawn. Go on. Get away." She flashed her tail and was gone.

Where the sun had cleared a boulder of snow I leaned back. I gazed around me. My glance fell on the rifle in my hands. I levered the bolt, drawing it back, taking the gun out of ready-to-kill mode. I leaned the gun against the rock beside me, setting it down with the practiced care of long habit.

Before the day was over, I made one trip back to the cave, carrying supplies.

Only fools, usually skinny as a snake, enter caves alone. I had read enough to know that much about caving. I had weighed 84 kg (185 lbs) when the high school coach was still trying to get me onto the football field. I had still had the baby look I hated so much, though I was stronger than I looked. I was leaner now, and with a lot more muscle, so I guess that made me a BIG fool. Still I explored the first small chamber, about three by five metres. It opened off a three-metre tunnel. Slabs of broken rock formed the floor. The walls and ceiling of white and blue-grey granite reached up two metres, shot through with seams of limestone. Two protruding flat-topped plates of rock formed giant steps against the northwest extremity. A thin mat of black hair showed where the bear had bedded down in a hollow around the bend of those stone bulges. The absence of refuse indicated the bear had used this place for hibernation only, never a place where kills were hauled to eat. A short tunnel, almost too small for me to squirm into, came to a dead-end off the east wall two metres back. A second tunnel, dropping toward the south-south-east, channeled a slight air movement deeper into the cave. I spent a half hour or so toying with the mobile LiDAR mapping system. I had fooled around with it in the storage cave, just to see if I could understand how to work it. But this would be the first place it actually made any sense to try to use it. I think this was a second or third generation system. The earlier ones were hand-held, but this mounted on my helmet and connected to a tiny computer worn on my belt. It was supposed to be water-proof, dust-proof, and shock-resistant and kept a detailed three dimensional record of the cave, supposedly adjusting for every time I nodded or turned my head. I finally stashed the equipment in the tunnel leading deeper. I hoped it would prove too small for the bear if it returned. Then I reluctantly headed back to the cabin.

I took more pains with supper than usual, cooking biscuits, vegetables, and a venison steak. The washing up seemed tedious, standing before a stained square of canvas rather than an idyllic scene.

I opened the door for a few moments and looked out over the late twilight lake. A pair of snow-shoe hares played on the white expanse. A snowy owl, strangely dark against the purpling sky, swooped soundlessly over the hares. One thumped a warning, then leaped to one side. The other responded instantly. Two great leaps to the right, then one straight ahead and another to the right. The owl swept away looking for easier prey. It was a ballet. The warning thumps reached me faintly as the drama played itself out, a soundtrack out of sync with the movie.

The night was cool and I stood at the door as the sun descended over the west ridge. I saw a deer running across the ice-covered lake. Two wolves flanked it only a metre or so back. Four more followed. They were the first wolves I had seen in the valley itself. The deer ran heavily, feet cutting into the softening surface. The distance was too great to see clearly in the growing shadows. The leading wolf leaped for a shoulder. The deer flung itself sideways. The second wolf tore at its throat as one of the following ones leaped for the thigh muscle. A youngster I think, inexperienced, took the full force of both hind feet across his muzzle as he tore into the fray. Leaping straight up, the deer had kicked back in a last desperate effort to defend itself. For one endless, agonizing second, the deer's head and shoulders held a proud, beautiful profile as fangs tore at its body. Then it fell. The shadows were too deep to see it kicking or struggling for one final breath.

My eyes filled with tears, surprising me. The leader of the wolf pack raised its nose to the sky and howled. The others joined him in a triumphant, wailing cry.

Such a proud, beautiful animal. Such a gruesome death. Yet there was something far more wholesome than the crack of a rifle. There was the grace and beauty of an eternal dance.

A deep ache stirred in me as I stepped inside again and closed the door. With the ache came a sense of completeness. There was pain in the hunt, in the kill, but no willful cruelty. There was death, but no malice. I ached, but it was somehow similar to the ache of listening to the call of geese or the song of a loon.

First light saw me at the kill. The deer had not been large. Little remained. I wondered about the pup that had been kicked, hoping it had not been badly injured, yet paradoxically cheering the deer at the same time.

Before I reached the east shoreline I looked back to see a fox nosing the remains, searching for some small scrap. I stepped into the trees and began the climb to the cave.

With the rifle ready, I approached the cave entrance again. I talked loudly, listened, then talked again. I shouted into the opening. I held the rifle at my hip, finger on the trigger.

I wore a miner's helmet and switched on the light. No eyes caught the gleam and reflected it back. With the business end of the rifle ahead, I entered the cave.

The supplies left the day before were undisturbed. A barely perceptible movement of air seemed to drift down into the cave. I struck a match. The smoke trailed lazily deeper. The stone walls and floor revealed no evidence of human touch but I was struck by a sense of a watching presence, brooding with infinite patience. *Waiting for what?* I wondered.

I activated the mobile LiDAR mapping system. With the small backpack, I could just squirm through the tunnel leading from the entrance. I had some tense moments when the pack snagged on the ceiling. I expected to see bats sooner or later, but now, as my body formed a plug in the passageway, I hoped it would be later.

I moved with deliberate slowness, frequently checking a compass. It was a smart-watch on my wrist, one of those cool contraptions with time, pressure, temperature, altimeter & barometer, stop-watch and compass all behind one small digital face. It also allowed a wireless connection to the LiDAR computer, so added more detail to the 3D map being produced.

Popsicle sticks with florescent paint were the markers of choice in some of the cave exploration reading I had done. With one end aiming back to the surface, they caused no defacing of the natural wonders of a cave. The bright paint was hard to miss even when you were returning to the surface exhausted. I didn't have florescent paint, but the clean creamy-white of the sticks showed with startling brilliance against grey stone. Even with high-tech things like LiDAR, everything I'd read stressed physically marking your way back out. And since I still distrusted computers on some level, I took those warnings seriously.

My headlamp could switch from white to ultraviolet. In this particular rock, ultraviolet added nothing.

The passage dipped at an easy slope. It became high enough to stand erect, but frequent loose stones demanded caution.

I know you're never supposed to go into a cave alone. There's a lot of things you're not supposed to do alone. But what's a guy do when some drunk wipes out his dad? I had lived through building and flying the *EAGLE* and done that alone. I had lived through enough days worse than dying that the risks of dying didn't seem all that great.

After 40 metres, twisting and turning, levelling, or falling gently, a vertical chimney opened before my light. A noticeable draft of cool, damp air settled soundlessly. I could hear the murmur of water, muted through stone walls.

A thin stream fell from somewhere above. Breaking on a rock, it settled as a fine mist. I studied details carefully before proceeding. Little trickles of water broke into the shaft in numerous places.

The shaft averaged three metres in diameter for the first eight metres, then expanded out to five. Recesses offered precarious hand and foot holds on an undercut bank. Rappelling offered greater safety than climbing. With an anchor set into a crevice, I tied a rope. I tested and retested the knot, a simple bowline, then fed the loose end down the shaft.

Clipping the rappelling harness onto the rope, then testing my weight against it, I backed over the rim of the shaft. Perpetually wet and slippery, the hand and footholds were widely spaced. I had special gloves, thin and rubberized, giving protection and grip. The rope still seemed slick and treacherous. A painful throbbing radiated from my right knee after banging it against the rock face just as I started my descent. The falling mist mingled with sweat in a clammy coldness.

My light, close to the rock face, blinded me. When I shut it off, the darkness closed in with a sense of physical crushing. I changed to ultraviolet. Little glimmers of yellow and purple, plus a subdued muddy grey were easier on my eyes. But it was far from the stuff legends are made of.

Twenty metres down a hump of rock thrust into the shaft, narrowing it to a tight squeeze. I stood in a puddle, my feet in a tangle of rope. I leaned over trying to get a glimpse below. With water flowing it was hard to be sure, but there seemed to be a large chamber under me. I shoved the end of the rope on down and listened, but the little stream, tiny as it was, created too much noise to hear the rope hitting bottom.

I had to slip the pack off to fit, so tied it on a three-metre length of thin rope and hung it from my waist. I then got a firm grip on the rappelling rope and stepped into the hole, lowering myself quickly, writhing a bit to let my hips and then my shoulders slide through the squeeze. What looked like so little water from above felt like a flood as my shoulders plugged the opening. Then I was through and descending into a large chamber. But the rope held me directly under the falling stream.

Rising to a seven-metre ceiling and smooth sand floor, it provided an excellent resting place. As my light pierced the darkness, a chorus of high-pitched squeaks accompanied the rustle of small wings as bats dropped from their roost. With a quick whir of wings, they swept past me and up the shaft. But it looked like they found a way beside the water.

I came down in a shallow pool, fed from above but also by a stream flowing from the northwest. The cave widened to four metres and reached back 25. The stream flowed through several pools across the lower side, spilling into the shaft with a soft, tinkling burble. I pulled my gloves off and stuffed them into a pocket.

Human touch showed on a sandy ledge that stretched back from the water. Drawings on limestone walls showed a deer-like creature surrounded by four hunters. Three of the hunters carried spears. The fourth had hurled his. A cracked earthenware bowl held a handful of wild rice. The charred leg bones of a deer lay beside a small mound of ashes and charcoal.

Paintings could be identified as bison, fox, and bear on the other wall. A red clay-like substance had been used as well as charcoal. At least that was my guess. Closer to the shaft, where a narrow ledge offered a tenuous foothold, a drawing seemed to depict a battle.

I washed my hands in the stream, then drank deeply from my canteen. Locating a sloped area free from bat droppings, I slipped my pack off and stretched out.

Several handfuls of trail mix formed an unexciting lunch. After resting an hour, I took a number of pictures. Using my tiny portable filter, I refilled my canteen.

With the camera handy I thoroughly explored the chamber. I took pictures of more paintings. Like so much ancient art the skill was incredible.

My nose and eyes confirmed the ammonia in the air. No surprise with all the bat droppings. The temperature showed at 9.8° C. My elevation showed 288 metres above sea level. That placed me 83 metres above the surface of Lake Superior. I had descended 20 metres from the cave entrance.

I secured the camera, munched on another handful of trail-mix, then left the chamber. Clipping my safety harness onto the rope once again, I continued to descend. Still almost vertical, the shaft tended slightly to the northwest. Another squeeze, not so tight this time, left me descending under a more forceful stream until I reached the bottom of the shaft. I could stand fully upright in ankle deep water for a number of metres. Then two tunnels led away, nearly horizontal. One rose slightly towards the east. Marking the way out with a popsicle stick, I followed it. It varied between a hands-and-knees crawl and a 'bear-walk,' a killer on the back but faster than crawling. Crossing a low hump I had to go belly-down in water through a short squeeze with another pool beyond it. I could stand up in that pool, giving a brief rest to my back. An upward crawl took me into a slightly higher section of tunnel that allowed me to crouch, but not stand. Another puddle and another climb took me over a hump of rock and reduced me to a hands-and-knees crawl once again.

A murky pool smelling strangely foul hid a drop in the floor. I got a face-full and spit and gagged. The stink became even worse after I'd stirred up the water. I'd read of hydrogen-sulphide, a swift killer, but this wasn't a rotten-egg smell. More like something dead.

Another squeeze and belly-crawl took me to one more pool. The water was clean and sweet here, at least compared with what I had just crawled out of. I flushed my mouth, though avoided swallowing, trying to clear the taste. I also washed my face and so far as possible my clothes, although the mud already caked into them had prevented too much of the last pool's muck from sticking.

A quick climb, a crouching passage, several more pools and finally a larger chamber that allowed me to stand fully upright led to a final crawl and a large lake. I could stand in shallow water at the edge of the lake but could see no possibility of going farther.

The ceiling of this chamber sloped gently back to touch the water at the limit of my light. The murmuring of a distant waterfall seemed more imagined than real. Water lapped around my feet. The silence seemed amplified by the slow plink of dripping water.

The walls and ceiling showed a deep blue-green. Purple and white glittered from a handful of spots. Under ultraviolet, bits of amethyst gleamed out of a muddy-grey background. The light brought a reaction in the water as well. A number of drab grey fish, 15 centimetres long, rose to the surface and hung there swaying. At a slight stirring of the water, like the bow wave from a boat, they flitted away. I had the camera in hand as a spiny fish, two metres long, broke the surface.

In my startled leap backwards, I hit my head on the rock. I went down hard. My pack broke my fall as my back struck a ridge of rock, but my head snapped back, then slammed against the floor. My hands slapped hard against sharp gravel in shallow water. The helmet protected me, but my light glowed red for a second, then went out.

In the blackness I could hear the writhing slap of a tail against water. The scrabbling sound of sliding wet gravel died away in a quick swirling burble. Then silence reigned again. My breathing seemed unnaturally loud.

Wincing as I sat up, and with my head spinning, I lifted the camera off my belly, aimed it vaguely, and pressed the button. The flash seemed like an explosion in the blackness. The startled fish whipped the water into a boiling froth as it fought to reach deep water again. I took two more pictures before the water surface calmed.

I shrugged the pack off and fumbled in it for a flashlight. I leaned forward and washed blood and grit off my hands. They would ache for days, but the injury was minor. I watched for the return of the fish. I had received a close-up look at those jaws. My pant leg was torn and a strip of flesh burned. The fish had won the argument and I had to leave it at that.

I worked my way painfully back to the most recent chamber where I had adequate room. The cuts and bruises on my hands, as well as the abrasions on my leg turned crawling into agony. Where the gallery widened out I slipped my pack off again and leaned against the sloping wall. I replaced the bulb in the miner's lamp. I only had the one replacement. After the feeble glow of the flashlight, it seemed like full sunlight. I only had one replacement.

I pulled my jeans off to get a better look at my leg. Rows of scratches formed a crude pattern against the flesh and oozed blood. It had to be the hard, bony dorsal fin. Those teeth would have taken a hunk right out. I wouldn't bet on them not taking the whole leg off.

Medicated ointment burned, then soothed. I wrapped the leg as well as I could. I had to get through that one hole again, though it was as inviting as a cesspool. I'd already got a mouthful of it. I didn't need infection in my leg too. A couple of bats flitted around above me as I dressed again.

It must have taken two hours to reach the bottom of the vertical shaft. I muddied up the first clean water after the sewer one, but at least I got through with my mouth closed this time. Again I washed as thoroughly as possible, although it was almost criminal to treat those other pools that way.

Shrill squeaks and the flutter of bat-wings suddenly filled the air. Some of them swooped and swirled around me before fleeing up the shaft. Moments later more bats came out of the channel I had just emerged from.

They too fluttered up the shaft. My watch showed 5:15 p.m. I realized the bats would clock the cycles of the sun even if I had no watch.

In my journal I wrote:

Wednesday, March 11

Caving – spelunking – has its moments. But I'm not sure it's my thing. If the pictures turn out, I can probably sell tickets as a fishing guide. But they'd probably want me to carry the monster back to the surface.

I feel old and tired. I can't quite figure what I'm doing down here. But you've got to admit it's a new experience. I've bruised both hands and punctured them on sharp gravel. I've got battle scars from some fishes first ever glimpse of light. I've crawled through something that would make a sewer smell sweet and I'm sitting in bat-poop as I write this. Surely I can sell tickets.

If I come down with Rabies, (I've heard bats are carriers) I hope I can get these pictures to Sam first. He'd like to see them so long as I don't bite him.

Don't know how I'm going to explain the pictures without having 400 heritage protection buffs tearing this place apart to "protect" it.

I've never seen large flights of bats. They would have been a give-away to a big cave. I suppose coming out behind the tamaracks, they would spread out and fly along the face of the slope. They would be scattered before a guy would ever see them. But I have noticed the black flies aren't as bad as I had expected. I wonder if these handsome fellows deserve a thank-you for that.

My neck is starting to tighten up. If I tell the doctor a four-metre fish attacked me (I only exaggerate a little) he'll probably lock me in the psych ward. Stupid enough to be down here alone, I probably should be there anyway.

It's been quite a day and I'm tired.

The temperature is steady at 9.8°C. I'm 278 metres above sea level. That puts me 73 metres above Lake Superior. I have 56 metres of climbing ahead if my math is right, most of it vertical climbs. The way I'm feeling, it sounds like a tough job.

The air quality is better here than in the higher chamber. Not so much bat poop. I still feel like something or somebody is watching. (Better reserve that bed in the psych ward.) It feels like some awesome power – nothing to be tampered with, but nothing awful either.

I scraped a level place in the coarse sand mostly free of bat droppings. I rolled out the small self-inflating mat, then spread my sleeping bag on top. Undressing, I beat as much of the ground-in dust out of my pants as possible, then crawled in. Shutting off my light brought instant, crushing darkness. I resisted the urge to turn it back on. I needed to save the batteries. For long moments I lay silently, images playing through my mind.

A deep aching void gaped before me. I was falling down an endless black well. Hands reaching out slashed against the rock face. Differing coloured streaks of rock flashed brilliantly before sightless eyes. The roar of a million wings whipped the air into a swirling vortex. I could see blues and purples in the swirl. The blackness was impenetrable. My mind could not reconcile the two exclusive realities, but my mind was left far behind as I plunged endlessly downward.

CHAPTER NINE

A BIT OF SNOT

The whir of wings and the high-pitched call of bats roused me. I lay for long moments in absolute darkness. My breathing sounded harsh and laboured. Cold sweat shrouded my body. The dream seemed more real than reality.

Pain exploded in my brain when I switched on the miner's lamp. Even through closed eyes, the light seared like a laser. Knife-thrusts of stabbing pain greeted the first movement of my head. The muscles in the right side of my neck screamed protest. I forced myself to turn it, my breath catching in shallow gasps. Taking a light sweater from my pack, I rolled it into a loose, twisted cord. Wrapping it around my neck, I fastened it with a pair of safety pins. It gave some relief.

The weight of rock above me seemed crushing. My leg burned. The palms of both hands stung. My neck screamed protest at every movement. I felt physically and emotionally drained. Broken nails and torn fingertips added stabs of fiery pain to all the other sensations assaulting me. Added to that was a nagging pressure in my bladder and bowel.

The weary climb back up the shaft seemed to take hours. Almost totally dependent on the rope with water pouring over me, muscles in fingers, arms, and shoulders protested by the time I reached the squeeze and ledge.

The first climb wasn't long, only about 17 metres. There was just no place to rest. Besides, water poured over me the whole time.

I spent a long hour in the *Indian-Paint Gallery* as I had dubbed it, though I'd go with a clumsier, politically correct name if I tried to describe it to anyone else. I ate most of my remaining provisions and rubbed salve into my hands.

I forced myself to my feet and tackled the longest stretch, the vertical shaft in the falling mist. The slick rope and meagre hand and footholds taxed my strength to the limit. With pig-headed persistence I forced myself to keep going, one tortuous pull above another.

I finally crawled over the lip of rock where the tunnel entered the chimney. I lay there, chest heaving, arms aching, hands strangely weak. After ten minutes I pushed myself to the bear-walk and hands-and-knees crawl back to the entrance chamber. The rifle waited there in case the bear had returned.

A half hour later I dropped the pack on the cabin floor and sank into the chair beside the cold stove. After a few moments rest the door closed behind me again. My stiff limbs took me the few metres to the out-house. The stop there seemed somehow more appropriate than a hole in the sand down in the cave.

Opening the flap of the bath-tent, I stepped into the warm enclosure. I stripped, then lowered myself into the gently stirring water. My hands and leg stung for a long time, but aching muscles slowly relaxed.

I made myself pull the dirty clothes in. Rubbing a bit of detergent into the wet cloth, I worked it with my hands, still strangely weak. The overflow carried away the suds. I squeezed the excess water out and lay the clothing on a rock, then scrubbed myself. Stepping out into the cool afternoon air, I seemed to feel exhaustion in every muscle. The walk back to the cabin seemed long.

Sleep does wonders, but the muscles that could swing an axe or handle a chain-saw all day still complained about climbing ropes. My hands and neck also needed time to heal. I had a strange conviction that I needed to return to the cave, but it could wait a few days.

After puttering around the cabin and yard for several hours, I phoned a travel agent and arranged a flight to Toronto. Calling Sam, I contracted a trip to the Sault Ste. Marie airport.

In the couple hours before Sam would arrive, I ran an insulated wire from the electric fence installation protecting the door to my storage cave. Using the steel bands from the packing crate the nuclear furnace had arrived in, I formed a grid covering the window and the door of the cabin. Flipping a switch could shut both off. I hoped the bear would not return, but guessed this valley had been part of his territory for longer than it had been mine. I finally gathered the few things I wished to take, then sat down with a good book.

I asked Sam to fly me along the shoreline of White Fish Bay. With the village of Gros Cap behind and the city of Sault Ste. Marie ahead, a series of docks and warehouses squatted low and dark against the shore. Old rotted pilings and racks of rusted steel peeked from tangles of second growth tamarack, young maples, sumac, and cedar. With the rusted, abandoned look softened by snow cover and evergreens, there was something almost quaint about it, like the ruins of old castles.

Before I went through security at the airport, I phoned the Essar Steel Algoma Company and made tentative arrangements to rent one of their properties. I hoped eventually to bring the barge and dock it inside.

Tuesday, March 17

Security at the Sault Ste. Marie airport had been stepped up. The news reports on the radio and an occasional paper Sam brought on his infrequent flights into the valley had only partially prepared me.

Travel documents were not yet needed within Canada. But my identification, fed through the computer, triggered some kind of alarm. A government agency, seeking to identify and screen *subversive* types, had pictures of me in church. I hadn't known that had become a crime.

I'm afraid I'm not a very convincing Christian. I didn't answer their questions very well. They put me through a strip-search. I don't know what they expected, that I was smuggling Bibles in my underwear? The guard was a bit of a snot, but maybe that goes with the job. Strip-searches are awful things. They mocked me but didn't touch me. I think I'd have decked them if they had.

I had arrived at the airport three hours before departure time, but the final call for my flight had just been given. "Security" had wasted all that time. I rushed to the departure gate where the stewardess smiled professionally and said, "Welcome, sir. We hope you enjoy your flight," as she glanced at my boarding pass and then waved me onto the plane. We had an uneventful flight, with lots of empty space.

There was a prominent police presence at Toronto Pearson International. I half expected to be stopped there too but received only a casual nod by those who acknowledged me at all.

I took a bus from the airport to the subway station. Passing through a turnstile, I got on the southbound Spadina line. At Yonge and Bloor I left the train and entered the shopping centre. At the bookstore that once claimed to be the largest in the world, I spent two hours browsing the shelves. I found Dad's book. Blazed across the front it said: *More than 3,000,000 sold*. I should have been thrilled. That was 2,000,000 more than I had known. But it was a thumbed-over copy on a discount rack. It seemed to have fallen from favour. I had been less than three hours in the city. The noise and smells already wore on me.

I took the subway to the bottom of the loop at Union Station. Before leaving the station I picked up a few over-priced groceries. I walked the last couple of blocks to the water, then strolled east for a half hour. In a rundown section of derelict boats, I reached my barge. A key let me into the cabin. The stale smell of rust and tar greeted me. I started up the big diesel. It wheezed and complained before settling down to a muffled roar. With electricity now, I turned on fans and ran the bilge pumps, clearing out stale water from below decks.

I brushed cobwebs from the cooking surface of the stove, then wiped off the table. The entire water system had been winterized so I didn't use it. I looked with distaste at the bunk. The musty smell did not invite.

Early morning saw me walking four kilometres to the waterfront warehouse I had leased. Ice caked the inside of the massive doors. A couple of windows were broken, but the small stockpile of supplies appeared untouched. I unlatched the heavy steel beam that spanned the sea-door opening. The electric winch groaned and screeched as it raised the beam a few centimetres, then stopped. I'm pretty sure the old fuse box violated every safety code in the book. There was a rat's nest of wires disconnected within the box, bent out of the way. Half the sockets had no fuses in them at all, and several others were burned out.

I locked the warehouse behind me, then searched the area until I found a hardware store. I purchased the four 30 amp screw-in fuses they still had in stock, a pail of grease, a bag of cotton rags, and a pair of leather welding gloves, then lugged them slowly back. My hands and arms complained about even that weight before I got back.

At the warehouse again, I thrust a stick into the grease and smeared it generously on the cable that lifted the beam spanning the door. On a rickety wooden ladder any safety inspector would have instantly condemned, I climbed up to the winch at each side of the building. I thoroughly lubricated each one. I screwed a new fuse into the correct socket.

Loud grumbling accompanied the winch now, but the high-pitched squealing of dry metal was no longer part of it. The hydraulic cylinders that worked the doors moved part way, shattering ice, then they too stopped. The reservoir no longer held sufficient oil. I returned to the shop where I purchased a pail of oil. With that added, I could fully open the doors.

I secured the building again and walked to the harbour master's office. After paying the docking fee for the old barge, I found a greasy waterfront café where I ate an unidentifiable meal. I caught a city bus back close to the barge, then fired up the engine again.

A "pilot" arrived a little later. I could not legally guide the barge within the harbour area. I didn't ask, but probably couldn't legally run it anywhere else either. Other than the *EAGLE*, I had never been at the controls of a vessel larger than a pleasure boat. I grilled the pilot for as much information as possible. In spite of regulations I held the wheel as he basked in the role of instructor and master-mariner.

The barge was a squat mass of scrap metal. Once underway, it steered with slow but predictable response. It took an hour and a half to reach the warehouse. Maneuvering close enough so I could leap to the dock, enter the building, and open the doors took an additional 15 minutes.

The building and boat seemed suited to each other. I played the role of a foolish kid dreaming of a gleaming yacht, waking up on a garbage scow after smoking something. The pilot shook his head in pretend sympathy, pocketed his fee, and I'm sure wrote me off and promptly forgot about me.

I spent three more days in Toronto making contacts and securing provisions. Scanning newspapers, I found two jewelry stores in receivership and three others for sale. A couple of phone calls eliminated three of the five. Toronto Transit carried me to the first of the other two.

After an hour examining inventory lists, I questioned the manager closely. The wholesale value listed at $367,742. I offered $340,000 with all stock removed that day. My gut feeling was the manager was honest. I wasn't so sure of the agent handling the receivership. My questioning revealed the manager would come out broke whatever the figure. The price I offered would at least leave him debt free.

The agent was a professional. I think he figured I was young and stupid. But I had learned a few skills too. I made my proposal. When the agent pretended to be dismayed and wounded, I simply thanked him and walked out the door. I hadn't gone ten steps when he caught up, saying maybe he had been a little too hasty.

Fifteen minutes later we had drawn up an agreement. I delayed signing until I had a rental van at the loading dock of the store.

Two hours later I closed and locked the van door. The diesel motor rumbled and the vehicle pulled out into traffic. I made repeated turns and twists, watching my mirrors. I saw no evidence of anyone following but clocked 26 kilometres before I reached the warehouse. A garage door let the van inside. I secured the small treasure. Two truckloads of clothing from thrift stores had already been brought onto the barge. I had taken care that they were seen entering the warehouse. It was a simple thing to cover the surprisingly small storage space required for the jewelry with bags and boxes of clothes.

Over the next two days I used the van to bring several more loads to the barge. I purchased another jewelry store's stock without mishap. I also bought caseloads of discounted fluorescent lights, plastic pipe and copper tubing as well as reels of wire. I bought a bunch of LED lights. They had come done in price but were still pretty costly. Unskilled in lying, I gave non-committal answers to the questions people asked. I'd had to go into the bank three times and sit down with someone to prove I was who I claimed to be and get permission to spend so much money. It seemed like 40 kinds of ID they wanted, as well as a death certificate for Dad and a thousand other things.

I ran my bank-balance dangerously low. I had spent a million give or take. With the added sales of Dad's book there should have been lots left, but there wasn't. I thought again about the lawyer's hint that the money wasn't safe.

I returned the van to the rental agency, then walked back toward the waterfront. On a whim, I purchased a ticket to a movie but found it mindless and boring. Somehow the city made my loneliness worse.

I spent a long, restless night on the barge. In the early morning, I took the subway toward the airport, transferring to a bus to complete the trip.

Tuesday, March 31

Security was tight and thorough before boarding the return flight. I was astonished when the guard apologized for the indignity of the strip search. Nothing was said about my church background.

At the Sault airport, I scanned the crowd as I waited for my luggage. It was just after picking it off the belt that I recognized the snotty security guard. I don't know why but he seemed to have it in for me. I should have done some checking to see what kind of crime church attendance had become but had pretty much forgotten about it during my time in Toronto. In the instant we made eye contact, the man's pupils dilated. He stood away from the wall he was leaning against. His hand went down to the gun he carried. Then he shook his head, pasted a smile on, and leaned back against the wall again. He turned away from me, but just enough that he could keep watching.

I couldn't be sure, but it seemed to me a car followed the taxi.

I paid for a motel room with cash, giving an assumed name and a false address. It was probably just my crazy imagination, but something didn't feel right. I slipped back downstairs after dropping my luggage on the bed. I couldn't see the face, but someone from airport security was there, questioning the man behind the counter.

I went back to my room and searched through my luggage, checking all my pockets as well. I'd read about drug dealers stashing stuff in other people's luggage but I couldn't find anything that didn't belong. I didn't even have a Bible with me this time. I had assumed, wrongly, that there would be one in any hotel I booked.

I double-checked the lock on the door, then had a quick shower. I called the Essar Steel Algoma Company and finalized rental of a waterfront warehouse. Two hours later, with the key in my pocket and the rusty smell still in my lungs, I returned to my motel room.

I couldn't be sure but I thought a couple things had been moved. I did a quick check of the room but found nothing wrong. I checked all the drawers. I've seen a few movies where they have those listening bugs. They're usually so tiny that you can't tell, and I didn't even know what to look for. Besides, I was nothing to anybody. If somebody was crazy enough to listen in on me, they were in for a boring time.

I checked my luggage again and did find something that looked like a hearing-aid battery. It was stuck inside a pocket where the seam half hid it. I doubted it was anything but threw it in the garbage

I kicked my shoes off and stretched out on the bed. It had already been a long day. An argument in the room next door dragged me out of a deep sleep. I sat on the bed and pulled my shoes back on. I had fallen asleep still dressed.

I must have been getting really paranoid. I pulled the battery-thing out of the garbage, wrapped it in toilet paper and flushed it down the toilet. I grabbed a towel and rubbed everything I could think of that might have fingerprints on it. My jacket was reversible but I left it the way it was for the moment. Pulling it on and grabbing my cap, I reached for my bag.

CHAPTER TEN

ON THE RUN

Wednesday, April 1

I was a half block from the motel walking north when a police cruiser turned toward me at a major intersection. There was no shelter anywhere close, but a transport rolled up beside me, slowing as it approached the lights at the intersection. I turned to watch and saw the police car pull into the parking lot of the hotel I had just left. I stepped a bit faster to stay beside the transport.

Another glance back showed a second police car in the hotel parking lot. I didn't know what they were looking for and was sure I had committed no crimes, but at 3:00 a.m. walking the Second Line East, I felt exposed and wanted to hide. I crossed the street to where the exit from a soft-touch car-wash stood open. Somebody would likely be in trouble for that but I breathed a prayer of thanks. The doors closed and the lights dimmed moments after I entered. The air was hot and steamy, so maybe the doors hadn't been forgotten.

There was no dry place to sit but I slid down in one corner beside a barrel. I must have dozed because the rumble of doors rolling up, creaking and thumping, roused me. Lights came on and a vehicle entered from the far end.

I fought the urge to jump and run, waiting until the car had moved onto the track and the huge spray bars began to cover it with foam. When the spray reached the windshield I slipped out the door, the cold air striking me forcefully.

Traffic was heavier than an hour earlier. A few people walked the streets as well, tramping doggedly toward some fixed destination.

The dampness had penetrated my clothing and the frigid temperature demanded that I move. I slipped my jacket off and turned it inside out, changing the colour but making me even colder. Then I jogged north.

A truck-stop and service station on Highway 17 was busy enough that I could slip into the all-night restaurant without being too obvious. I didn't try to pass for a trucker. I didn't think I looked old enough or knew the jargon well enough for that. But there were a couple of other teens there looking like they had partied all night.

They still had a payphone so I called Sam. When the machine answered, I left a message: "Hope this doesn't wake you up so early. It was a long shot that I might catch you before you head out for another job. I'm back at the Sault. Hopefully I'll see you in a few days." I'd have said more, but someone walked close behind me, so I hung up.

I bought a meal, slowly warming as I sat at a booth. I fought against the urge to duck and hide when a police officer came in and took a searching look around the room. His gaze lingered on the other two teens for a while, then he turned and left.

After a washroom break I checked out the parked transports. A police cruiser was still sitting in the parking lot, the man inside sipping from a mug. I intentionally ignored him and made myself walk purposefully, as if heading to a specific rig. Two other men came out just behind me.

The temperature had dropped through the night to well below freezing. My light jacket was almost dry now, but not adequate for what I had in mind.

A swift glance eliminated nine of the rigs that faced the right direction. If I could get out of sight on most of the others, exposed to the full force of the wind, I would freeze to death. Only two had tarped loads. One of those was close to the gas pumps. No shadows would allow a guy to slip in along the side. Lights from the highway repeatedly swept one and the other received the full benefit of the floodlights bathing the parking area.

Moving into the alternating light and shadow, I checked the tarp until I could feel a gap between sections of the load. I unclasped two bungee cords, astonished but thankful that any trucker would use them rather than the more secure canvas tie-down straps. I waited until a break in the traffic promised several seconds of darkness. Reaching up under the tarp, I worked my fingers into spaces between layers of lumber, then drew myself up. My buckle caught against the steel edge of the trailer. Lowering myself slightly, bracing my elbows and forcing my body out against the straining tarp, I managed to wriggle up into a narrow gap between two lifts of lumber.

It took a lot of fighting and feeling blindly against cold steel before I managed to re-attach the metal S-brackets of the bungee cords. The tarry smell of creosote combined with the turpentine odour of green pine. Some unidentifiable chemical smell was mixed in.

By the time I heard the dull thumping as each tire was checked, I was beginning to feel light-headed. The rumble of a rig pulling up along the side sounded. Air hissed as the brakes were released on the trailer I was riding. The crunch of tires and swaying of the trailer brought a quick draft of welcome fresh air.

If "Air-Ride" was one of the boasts on the side of this trailer, the paint should have been faded. Wedged between lifts of lumber that shifted with each bump, I feared being squashed like a bug. I fought against sleep.

I mulled my money losses as I tried to distract myself from the freezing wind that cut through my clothing. When the crunch of tires on gravel penetrated my consciousness, I was almost comatose as the truck rolled to a stop. From inside the tarp, my clumsy fingers could not unfasten the bungee cords.

I could hear occasional traffic roll by on the highway. It was impossible to check for spectators. I timed my move to just after the whine of tires went past. Straining against the tight cords, I slid down between the tarp and the side of the trailer. The steel edge scraped across my belly, chest, and arms. My legs collapsed under me as I hit the ground. The tarp flattened back against the load. I rolled under the rig as the sound of another vehicle approached. Crawling across under the trailer, stinging life came to aching limbs.

I staggered to my feet. By the time I had covered the length of the trailer I could walk almost normally. Gas pumps showed to my right, with a wild looking store beyond it. The moose on the step, "Henrietta," I realized with a chuckle, located me at Wawa, close enough that I'd probably just passed the famous goose.

I wanted a sit-down restaurant where I could thaw out with a cup of coffee in my hands. But Young's General Store was known far and wide and I had never expected to get here.

I turned back and checked that the bungee cords tying the tarp down were properly fastened. Straightening my clothes then, I turned toward the door, glancing at my watch. The eastern sky showed pinks and purples, but I was too cold to appreciate the beauty.

"You just come in on that rig? You caught a ride with John? Didn't think he ever carried riders. You must be family." A man had just unlocked the store and stood there staring at me.

"Well," I responded, even my lips slow and stiff. "I caught – a ride – but – he doesn't know it. I've come a bit – too close to – freezing – to death."

"None of my business. But get on in here and get the frost out of your blood. You gonna steal from me too? Do I need to call the cops?"

"I hadn't thought of it – as stealing," I replied slowly. "I guess that's one way – of looking at it, though I don't think – it cost anybody – a thing." My whole body shuddered with the cold. "You can check – my pockets – before I leave – if you want. I'll park – my bag – at the door."

"Ah, let it go. The ones who steal make a big song and dance about how honest they are. My grandpa rode the rails way back in the 30s. Now get on in here. Wadd'ya take in your coffee?"

"Black, usually. A bit of cream – when I'm lucky. I spend most of my time – out in the sticks." I stepped into the delightful warmth of the store, the smells of fudge and leather surrounding me.

"You from 'round these parts? Don't think I've seen you before." The man grilled me in a polite, but persistent way as he poured a huge mug full of coffee, then dumped in a generous amount of cream. "For sure no sugar? It'll help get your blood pumping."

"Thanks. No." I ignored his earlier question. My hands gripped the cup, trying to pull the warmth from it. I raised it to my lips, savouring the hot steam. "I've read about your store." I took a scalding sip. "Coffee's great. Thanks. What do I owe you?"

He looked at me for a long moment then chuckled. "Guess it's okay if you have reasons not to spill everything. Coffee's on the house. John'l be coming in a couple minutes from now. He usually rolls in a half hour before we unlock. Guess there's no harm done. He'll buy a coffee, maybe a bit of beef jerky, and be rolling again in ten. I think you need more thawing before you look at hitching another ride."

"Thanks," I said with genuine appreciation. "I'd like to put together – an outfit. I'm just back from the city – where I don't fit. But these clothes sure don't suit out here."

The door opened and he glanced up and called, "Hey, John. The usual?" He turned back to me, shrugged, and then filled another huge coffee mug.

Ten minutes put together a modest outfit. A sturdy hunting knife, a pair of hiking boots, a pair of jeans, four changes of underwear and socks, and two pairs of heavy rubberized fishing gloves sat on the counter. Added to that was a kilogram of beef jerky, two kilograms of trail-mix, 100 metres of thin nylon rope and a coil of snare wire. Along with a tin cooking pan and canteen, I added chlorine tablets for treating water and a tin of bee balm lotion. I also added a lighter and a disposable flashlight. A sturdy backpack to carry it in, and an over-coat, with durable grey-green duck shell rather than the lighter nylon, plus a hatchet, joined the pile.

"Mind if I change?" I asked after paying for the first lot.

After a few moments in a bathroom the casual street-wear geared to

Toronto was gone. My weathered face set off crisp new jeans, unscuffed boots, and a coat that would disappear among the trees. With the knife sheathed at my belt and the hatchet attached to my backpack, I didn't look so much like a greenhorn in spite of the obvious newness of my outfit.

When I came back out I added a pair of sunglasses, then lifted a pair of snowshoes down from the wall. I started to return them, then thought better of it. The snow still lay deep in places in the bush. I purchased them as well, clipping them to my backpack.

The best local topographical map available was none too good, but I bought it. Major features like ridges and gullies were crudely sketched.

At 8:42 the lights blinked, then went out. The hum of the computer died and the whisper of fans stilled. The man behind the counter shrugged as the receipt printer stopped. Questioning voices sounded from other places in the store, suddenly dull and shadowed.

"Need a receipt?" he asked.

I shook my head.

He grabbed a flash-light and counted out change. "Quite a pack you've got there. But I don't think there's a wasted thing in it. So ya knows something 'bout this country." In the shadows he scrutinized me. "You got me curious, I gotta admit." He grinned as he listened to customers groping in the shadows.

"Thanks, for everything." I nodded toward the change on the counter. "For the coffee," I said. "Besides, it's weight I don't need in my pocket. I hope your power comes back on soon."

CHAPTER ELEVEN

FREEZING FIRE

*T*he transport had rolled out just before I left the store. I sat on the step for a few moments, studying the chart I had purchased. It looked like about 60 kilometres in a straight line to reach home. With the climbs, descents, and detours around cliffs and rivers I'd probably have to triple that distance. There seemed to be a road that might shorten it a bit.

"Anybody in town sell used cars and trucks?" I questioned when a couple came out of the store.

"Sorry, we're not from around here," the lady answered.

"I did see a truck with a for-sale sign just up the road a bit. All dented and rusted up," the man with her responded. "A Dodge Ram I think."

Up the road *a bit* turned out to be a kilometre in the wrong direction. It had been a Dodge Ram—once. Now, the license plate looked like the only thing holding the rest of it together. I couldn't see anybody around and thought the $500 asking price sounded $450 too high, so I started the long tramp back.

A weary trudge later I took a secondary road and left Henrietta the moose behind as I angled south-west toward the Trans-Canada highway. I wanted to avoid it as much as possible. I was a little too visible there if the security guard from the airport was pushing his search further. But the bridge that crossed Magpie River cut off a lot of hard hiking.

Five minutes down the road a rusted pick-up pulled up beside me. "Long trail ahead looks like." An unshaven face with cigarette hanging from the mouth spoke to me. "Where'ya headin'?"

"Tremblay Flats Road would be ideal," I answered. "But anywhere across the bridge would be a help."

"Want good shoe-leather for that one. Bear country too." He chewed on his cigarette. "Tell you what. I was heading for a little berg at the end of Red Point road later today, but can just as well do it now. That work for ya?"

"Red Point?" I dug my map out and scanned it. "It turns off just before you hit Cemetery Road?"

"That's the one." He chewed on his cigarette. "Don't know I'd choose that name if'n I was going tramping."

"That's better than I could have hoped for. Can I give you something for gas?"

"Oh, heck, I'm going there anyways. Climb in. Don't mind the junk."

I tossed my pack into the back. The door squealed as I opened it. Empty Tim Hortons cups, beer cans, and cigarette packages littered the floor. An open 24 pack and a carton of Players sat on the passenger seat. A can of Budweiser nested between the man's legs. I shifted things till I could slide in and pull the seat-belt across.

"Sure ya wanna be tied to this old wreck?" the man questioned with a smirk. He nodded at the case I was half cradling. "Thirsty, or need a smoke? Help yerself."

The pickup lurched forward, engine coughing and sputtering, worn shocks wallowing. He took a swallow from his beer can, somehow shifting his cigarette to the side of his mouth. "No bad habits?" he questioned.

"I wish that was true." I had to speak loudly over the creaks and rattles of the old truck. "A drunk driver killed my dad and sister. Beer has had a bad taste for me since."

He lifted his can and looked at it for a moment, then rolled his window down and tossed it. "That's a tough one," he said. "That's my first for the day, so don't think I'll be killing no one, so long as the wheels don't fall off this ol' rattle-trap." He watched the road for a moment. "Don't smoke neither, looks like. Smarter'n me."

He pulled over before turning onto Highway 17. "Cops seem to hang out on this stretch. Best have my friend Bud ride in the back. Give you more room too." His door squealed even louder than my side had. He grabbed the case of beer and dragged it across his seat before grunting as he lifted it over the side of the box. The back was even more cluttered than the cab. He rummaged by my feet to grab a couple of empties and threw them behind as well.

The door banged as he slid behind the wheel again. He cursed as he pulled the seat-belt over his shoulders and fumbled to latch it. "Hate these things. Don't believe in them neither. But can't afford 'nother ticket."

The truck lurched forward again, then turned right on the highway. New paving on this stretch quieted the rattles. We crossed the bridge, my first objective, then passed an RV park as a long motorhome pulled out of the driveway. "More money than brains, people who drive those things," my driver observed, talking around his cigarette. It had gone out but he continued to chew on it. "Wisht I could try one once though. A whole house on wheels. Then I'd let you fill the gas-tank."

It seemed like we had gone too far and I was starting to get nervous when he slowed and turned left onto Tremblay Flats Road. I let out a long breath, realizing I had begun to tense up. He fumbled with the seat-belt and it wound back clear of his shoulder. "That's better," he muttered.

"Beautiful country up here," I commented.

He looked at me strangely. "Guess so," he admitted. "If you likes boulders and swamp. We raise a great crop of black-flies and mosquitoes too. Need a shot-gun for some of those mosquitoes, they're so big. You oughta have a gun you know. Not just mosquitoes out here."

"I know," I responded. "I've run into a couple of bears. Only one nasty one so far." A pot-hole caused the truck to buck and wallow. A cigarette pack fell off the dash.

"Wouldn't want 'em to waste money patching these roads up now, would we?" he grumbled good-naturedly. "Run into a nasty one ya say? Lived to tell the tale, looks like. Maybe yer not so green as some who come out here. Though they're usually packing 'nough guns for a army."

We stayed on surprisingly level ground for a while, crossed a railroad line and a few minutes later began to descend on a steep curving road, heading almost straight south. "Magpie Falls over there." He shrugged to his left. "Never been to it, though I've lived most of my life here."

We followed the ridge overlooking the river until the road kinked to the right and hit Michpipcoten Harbour Road. Turning right we headed north-west, getting rare glimpses of Lake Superior off to the left. The rugged beauty fascinated me, but more than once when the worn shocks of the truck bottomed I heard the driver mutter curses about this "God-forsaken land."

We made another left turn onto Red Point Road and followed it west until it dead-ended at a T intersection. The truck ground to a halt. "End of the line I guess, 'less ya wanna go down ta the water," the driver informed me.

"Thanks so much." I put my shoulder to the door when it resisted opening. "You've probably saved me a couple day's walking. You sure I can't give you something for gas. It's worth it to me."

"Hell no! Just don't let no bears trim yer toenails for ya."

I grabbed my pack out of the back and raised my hand as the truck groaned and rattled, turned left, and rolled away.

Pulling out my chart I saw that the road might still give me one-and-a -half kilometres before I was committed to the wild. Dirty snow filled ditches on both sides and still showed in folds of the land, especially where trees gave shelter from the spring sun. The pack was heavy enough, but I walked at a good clip north, then west. This seemed like the back end of nowhere but I passed an outdoor skating rink, then began to see houses in the distance and smell wood smoke. It was a tiny community and was probably reached more easily from the lake than by the road. I'd stick out here even more than on the Trans-Canada highway.

I left the road a hundred metres past the rink and pushed into the bush, giving the closest houses a wide passage.

A dog barked, then a couple more took it up so I hurried my pace, getting farther north of the little hamlet. The breeze was coming from the north-east, so they would be getting my scent. Hopefully their owners would assume it was a bear or a moose the dogs were smelling and wouldn't bother to investigate.

I began to work my way west then, already aware of stiff new boots. The barking grew more distant and intermittent before stopping completely. I stopped for a short rest before taking a new compass reading and heading as close to due west as the terrain would allow. Where the trees thinned out enough I wore the snow-shoes. Where they grew too close I had to slog through knee-deep banks, though the sun had found its way in and melted some spots bare.

An hour later I stumbled onto some kind of old road or fire cut running almost directly north-south. That should have put me straight north of Seagull Island but I got only brief glimpses of the lake. I could see open water farther out but ice wherever the shoreline showed. I hadn't made much more than a kilometre since leaving the road. The ground did not slope steeply to the shore here but rippled and folded so I was almost constantly climbing or descending. Snow lay in the bottom of every fold. The chart offered little promise of improvement farther inland so I kept to my present course.

A ridge and gully showed along an unnamed inlet at the north shore of Doré Bay. The gully seemed to go way inland with a string of tiny lakes heading upstream to the larger Doré Lake. My cave research flagged the area as a perfect place for caves. The chart didn't tell me if it was karst formation or not. But this seemed different than most of the Canadian Shield. Undoubtedly the glaciers had covered this, since they'd reached so much farther south. My untrained eyes thought they had just glided over the top here, rather than ripping the whole top off.

This country seemed different, older somehow, so big caves were a real possibility. I wanted to spend days exploring and call the author of that

Rockwatching book and see what he knew of the area. But I had to get back home.

Cave country means potholes and deep cracks. It means the snow can betray you at any moment. If you're crazy enough to mix a broken leg with the hope of not being found, you might just get your wish and leave your bones bleaching out here for a hundred years. I slowed even more as my chosen trail descended the gulley.

I had hoped for spots where ice still bridged the stream. It looked narrow on the map but at the moment, swelled with snow-melt, it ran swift and turbulent. Heavy bush kept the snow deep where the current hadn't flushed it away.

After twice breaking through snow into water up to my knees, I ploughed my way across a wider area of shallow water. Mounds of snow painted a blend of spring promise and winter wonderland. Cold, wet feet made the beauty hard to take delight in.

I climbed carefully over small crevices and pits in the stone, with the fantastic contortions of tree roots where they showed through the snow. I crossed another smaller stream twice as I climbed, then the trees thinned as the rock face heaved itself upward. Fifteen minutes of scrabbling brought me to a gentler slope. Tree roots found purchase in crevices of bald rock. From a distance it appeared solid forest but the spacing made walking relatively easy. Catching the sun, the slope was mostly cleared of snow as well.

I stopped and gathered enough dry wood to build a small fire. Pulling my boots off I rung water out of my socks, then propped the boots on branches where they would at least start to dry. I rubbed bee balm lotion over the blisters on my feet and rested as I checked the map again.

The ground still rose beyond me. I could see a rounded ridge curving south-west. Doré Bay spread below me, shore ice reaching well out into the lake. I could not pick out the small islands my map showed.

Pulling wet boots back on defeated new, dry socks even before I had taken a dozen steps. I had done my best to tape over the blisters to gain a bit of extra protection, but the lotion prevented the tape from adhering. I could feel the sting of rubbing as I started out again. I reached the highest point for quite some distance, then began a gentle descent, snowshoes sinking into soggy snow much of the time once again.

Little streams seemed to be everywhere. I resigned myself to wet feet. Two hours later I crossed another larger stream, wading up to my knees in icy water. Then I found myself following a twisting creek flowing from the west. Narrow ridges separated streams of water often flowing in opposite directions as they meandered blindly before finally spilling into the lake.

Where the stream came more from the north I left it once again and struck out westward. The ground became more rugged as I pushed on, with fewer trees and more rock. The pack seemed to grow heavier and the angle of climbs or descents steeper, but I had several hours of daylight left and wanted to make the most of it. The sun shone strong, more into my eyes as the day grew older. Yet raw, cold gusts kept coming from the east. *A lazy wind.* Wasn't that the cliché Dad used to rattle off? *Goes right through you 'cause it can't be bothered to go around.* Strange how many of those moldy old sayings he had used, though he was always on high alert for any in print, at least in essays I wrote for school.

I pushed on a bit longer but I knew my limits; had tested them repeatedly in the months spent in the wilderness. Two hours later a half circle of huge boulders promised as good a camp site as could be found out here.

I gathered wood and lit a fire, positioning it where the boulders would stop the wind and reflect the heat. I gnawed on a piece of beef jerky as I set a snare into a tunnel of juniper boughs. Bending a limb down from a spruce that shadowed the juniper, I formed a trigger, ready to snap the snare upward at a slight movement. With that done and enough wood gathered to last the night, I unlaced my boots and pulled them off. New boots and wet feet are a bad mix. The cold had prevented me from realizing how much damage I was doing. One blister had broken.

I hated the taste chlorine tablets gave to water that looked pure, but this wilderness was "pristine" only in tourist brochures. Untreated water was host to any number of parasites.

After placing a couple large blocks of wood that would sustain the fire for some time, I prepared a crude bed by stripping boughs from black spruce. Giving some cushioning, and more importantly, holding me up off the ground, I lay with my back to a crevice between two boulders.

An almost human cry that died into a strangled whisper roused me. Disoriented for a few seconds, I looked at my watch. It said 3:42 p.m. Rolling to my feet, I pulled wet boots onto sore feet. Four strides brought me to the snare. A snow-shoe hare was kicking violently as it hung suspended. Its strained breath, not fully cut off by the snare, came in gasping grunts. Grabbing the loose skin at the back of the neck, I brought the handle of my knife down with a solid crack on the rabbit-like creature's head.

I had never mastered the polished ease with which Sam butchered. What skill I boasted was clumsy as I severed the head, then gutted the animal. I placed the liver, heart, and kidneys back inside the abdominal cavity, then punched holes through the flesh on each side of the opening. Using whittled skewers of green wood, I fastened the cavity closed. Without skinning it, I dug a hollow in the hot embers of the fire and placed the hare inside. It doesn't sound too appetizing but Sam had taught me quite a bit. He would have added the lungs and had told me that a couple of generations earlier the stomach contents might have also been eaten, although usually only when other food was scarce.

It would take a couple hours to fully cook the meat. I built up the fire and wished I had purchased coffee.

I explored the little clearing, again aware of a raw wind knifing through the trees. The land fell away slightly to the south. A tiny stream murmured gently, a faint promise of spring that the wind with its hint of snow seemed to laugh at. The smell of crushed cedar drifted on the air.

I gathered more firewood, breaking or cutting pieces to usable lengths. Chickadees flitted around the clearing, undisturbed by my presence. A whiskey-jack screamed insults from the edge. Farther north, a raven croaked. Branches rasped against each other as gusts swept through them.

I gathered more boughs, firming up my bed. A pungent piney smell wafted from them as the sky turned a soft pink to the west, deepening into rose, then purple. To the east it was more of a slate grey.

The cooked hare, when I peeled the blackened skin away, was tough but juicy. There was a strong gamy taste with a woody overtone. No doubt bark and twigs made up a large part of the animal's winter forage. It dressed out to about two kilograms.

Wrapping the remains in lengths of bark stripped from a nearby yellow birch, I placed them in my backpack. Earlier I had tied a piece of wood to the end of my rope and flung it over a limb eight metres high. Attaching my pack to the rope, I raised it up to the limb, then tied it off. The tree stood 15 metres from my bed. The stars shone brightly and the night promised to be clear and cold. Northern lights gave a pale, flickering glow.

Banking the fire with several large blocks, I snuggled down into my nest. A wolf howled in the distance. Several answered it. All those crazy stories I'd heard started rattling around in my brain again. The stirring of small woodland creatures brought slight scampers and rustles. Two bats flitted through the air. Just before sleep claimed me, I found myself wondering what they fed on in the winter.

I woke once, chilled, and put more wood on the fire. The heat reflected from the rock had kept me surprisingly comfortable. I woke a second time just before dawn to see a wolf standing at the edge of the clearing. I lay still and silent, drinking in the beauty, trying my best to convince myself I wasn't scared. The moonlight gave a silver glow to the stiff guard-hairs along the animal's back. Then it seemed to melt into the shadows and was gone.

Thursday, April 2

At breakfast, I sat beside my fire and watched as the grey, cold light increased in intensity, but gave no warmth. The cloud cover was heavy enough that I couldn't see the sun.

Seven-thirty saw me on the move again. Salve and a bandage over the blisters almost stopped the rubbing against sensitive spots on my feet and ankles. I scattered the embers from the fire, smothering them with snow. An hour later I began to work my way across a deep, narrow gully.

A steep, treacherous jumble confronted me. I half walked, half rappelled down another 30 metres, my rope draped around a tree but not tied. I had to hold both sides of it at once. With the ends of my rope seven metres below me, I found a secure spot. I simply drew one end of the rope to me as the other trailed up the cliff, around the tree, then fell at my feet again. Carefully coiling the rope, I returned it to my pack, then picked my way to the bottom of the gully.

It took two hours to gain the top of the other side. A raw east wind continued to threaten when I stopped for an hour. I ate the remains of the snow-shoe hare, drank deeply, then lay back against a smooth sloping rock and rested.

Well before nightfall I had chosen another campsite, set a snare, built a fire, and prepared a bed. Just at dusk my snare yielded meat for another day. I cleaned and cooked this one the same as before. With supper behind me and the remaining meat safely hung above harm's way, removed a good distance from my bed, I curled into my nest between the fire and a boulder and slept.

I added wood twice during the night and slept poorly, the wind snatching away the heat from my fire. Morning dawned dull, grey, and cold.

I broke through a crust of deep snow at the edge of the clearing and rubbed my face and hands briskly with the more granular stuff from beneath the crust. I ate a hurried breakfast as a ground-drift of ice pellets rattled around my feet.

With breakfast behind me and the campsite tidied, I set out. I pushed hard. There was a menace in the wind. I stopped for a hasty lunch on the western lip of rock overlooking home. I didn't build a fire. Flurries of dusty snow swirled across the valley. The wind sounded a sad moaning. Haze shrouded the far side. Where I could see the lake, huge grey swells rolled in. Even from this distance I could hear the boom of waves breaking on the rocks. Snow blanked out the horizon into grey nothingness.

Hard, dry ice pellets stung my face as I pushed on again. Gusts drew smoky streaks across the rock face.

Using my rope, I rappelled down the cliff-face. Where massive slabs of shattered rock slowed my progress, I pressed on with urgent steps, yet forced myself to care. The wailing of the wind deepened. Snow fell thicker.

One hundred metres of cracks and crevices, treacherous in the false-twilight, still lay ahead as the full fury of the storm broke. Huge wet flakes of snow fell, cutting visibility, painting the unforgiving rocks with deceptive softness. The temperature dropped and the wind increased. The snow changed again to hard pellets, stinging my face. I tested every footfall.

A weary hour later I stood on the sloping mound 200 metres from the cabin. A full-blown blizzard screamed its fury. The wind, enraged by the obstructing rocks, whipped and eddied, changing directions, howling, wailing, sobbing and moaning. One second I could see two metres. The next second ten. To walk two metres was to risk getting lost.

Reluctantly I turned back into the rocks. I found a sheltered hollow and scraped snow away until I reached a dusting of leaf-mold and moss. Stripping my pack off and using it as a pillow, I lay down and waited. I dozed fitfully as the storm howled above me. As the afternoon half-light deepened, I ate beef jerky, making another boring meal.

The cold bit through my pants with icy fingers. My heavy coat kept my upper body almost comfortable. But lying still, without a fire, a numbing lethargy crept up my legs.

Saturday, April 4

I drifted on a sun-washed raft, my hands trailing in emerald green water. Gentle waves rocked it. Childish laughter rang, close enough to bring visions of wide-eyed delight, far enough away to have lost the piercing quality of young voices. A wave, bigger than the rest, dropped its curling crest over my face. I sat up, gasping and sputtering.

My brain clung to the vision, fought against the encroaching knives of cold. I spit snow from my mouth. Where my elbows had bent, piercing pains shot up my arms. I could not feel my hands. I drew my knees up against my chest, gasping at the electrical stabbings. The skin of my backside felt like it was splitting. With a groan, echoed by the storm that my brain registered again, I forced myself to my feet.

I slapped my arms against my thighs. A million needles stabbed into each finger. An explosion of fiery pain shot out from my legs. I raised one foot after the other and stamped, driving needles of freezing fire to the very bone.

As circulation brought aching life to my extremities, it brought deepening cold to my guts. I began to shiver violently. I forced myself to eat the remains of the snow-shoe hare, half frozen in my pack. I shaved off thin slices, chewed them slowly, and swallowed. I forced my arms and legs to continue to move. Storm or not, I dare not lay down again.

IT'S SOMEBODY'S JOKE

Ten minutes later, I thought I could walk without collapsing. Moving out of the jumbled rocks, I caught fleeting glimpses of the far side of the valley. The storm, still wild, was no longer the shrieking blizzard it had been the night before. The cabin appeared and disappeared. No welcoming smoke rose from the chimney.

Knowing a fall might prove fatal in my weakened state, I tramped slowly and deliberately in my snowshoes. Leaving a trail of snow across the floor, I shuffled to the stove. My stiff fingers would not cooperate. I broke three matches before the newspaper ignited. Kindling and blocks soon brought a cheerful crackle. I opened a tin of soup, frost rimming the outside, and set a pot of water to boil. A lump of half frozen sourdough sizzled in the heating fry-pan. Burned on the outside and doughy on the inside, it flattened into a sad looking slab of bannock.

It was far from a gourmet meal, but my shivering became less severe. With the fire crackling cheerfully and the chill of the cabin reluctantly giving way to warmth, I stepped out the door again. The cold hit like a physical blow.

Clearing the snow away from the entrance, then opening and quickly closing the flap of the tent that covered the hot tub, I stepped into delightful damp warmth. As badly chilled as I was, the water was too hot to enter quickly. I sat on a cool rock, my feet trailing in the water. That first touch of cold feet against 41°C water felt like liquid fire, then like a magnet, drew me deeper.

Three quarters of an hour after leaving the cabin I shut the door behind myself again. Freshly bathed, with a sense of tired well-being, I curled up near the stove with a book. Two hours later, I put the book down, turned on my computer, and spent some time journaling. My fingers slow and stiff on the keyboard.

The stepped-up security at the airport and the suspicion of all things "Christian" disturbed me. There had been "End of the World" books among Dad's collection. I hadn't read any of them, though I had watched a few movies. It seemed people had been predicting the end of the world for 2000 years. Dad had talked about it being a big thing when he was a kid.

The storm fought a losing battle for another 24 hours, finally dying into sullen grey coldness. I spent many of those hours with my Bible. Somehow, if going to church had become a crime, it seemed like I needed to know what the book actually said. It's all well and good to be a 'believer' when it's the expected thing, but if things got rough, a guy needs to know if it's worth the cost.

I tried to tune in the Thunder Bay and Sault Ste. Marie radio stations but got nothing. I could pick up several ham operators. My aerial was so poor that I couldn't get much. Listening for a while I realized something big had happened. As near as I could figure, a virus had wiped out a bunch of computers. It appeared to have been between the time I left Sault Ste. Marie and the time I arrived home. The storm had come after, adding to the chaos. That focused the *ACTIVATION TIME* between March 31st afternoon, and April 4th. The power had gone out in the store on April Fool's Day.

Dad used to talk about how vulnerable everybody was if computers went down. I always thought it was just old-man talk and didn't pay much attention. It sounded like he had been right. He'd been right about quite a few things actually.

The chaos seemed to have included traffic signals, trains, and air traffic control, though I suspected the stories had grown like stories do. A lot of people had died.

I did some journaling on my own computer. I don't know why it still worked, unless it was that I had never been on the Internet with it while I was building the *EAGLE*. I was too busy after I finished the *EAGLE* and it's kind of hard to get a hookup out in the sticks where you have to fly in with a helicopter.

```
April Fools! What a joke! Are the dead all
laughing?…
```

I tried to find stuff in the Bible that might make sense of everything but I didn't know where to look. I stared at the computer monitor for a long time, then began to pound the keys again.

```
Sounds like a computer virus somebody has planted.
It had to be simple enough to escape virus checks.
It had to be in the system for years, doing
nothing but reproducing itself. Somehow, it had to
do that without anybody cluing in. It seems
impossible that it could have been an accident and
it was April Fools Day. Funny joke! Ha ha ha! Are
there really as many dead as it sounds like from
the reports?
```

Did air traffic control computers and the on-board computers of jumbo-jets crash at the same time? *Sorry, that's an awful pun.*

There's supposed to be three men and one woman out in space. Are

they running circles waiting for their oxygen to give out, or did life support
fail right away, killing them quickly?

> "We have to be the stupidest species on the
> planet." That was one of Dad's lines that I never
> used to believe. How can I *not* believe it now? The
> virus is somebody's joke. Oh, we're smart. We're
> smart enough to find a million ways to be stupider
> than any other animal that ever lived. Our
> "Intelligence" makes me want to jump off a bridge.
> There seems to have been some weird, self-destruct
> reaction after the electricity went down. Short-
> wave and hydroelectric towers have been destroyed.
> Power and telephone poles have been cut down. What
> do people do with electrical cables when there is
> no juice flowing? How many years will it take to
> rebuild, even if they could turn the power back on
> tomorrow? HAPPY APRIL FOOLS!
>
> Is it the end of the world?
>
> Would God play an April Fools Joke?
>
> If what I'm hearing is right, the whole thing
> repeated an hour west, and then again an hour
> later, though by that time they had clued in
> enough to have almost all planes on the ground and
> trains stopped.

I saved the file and shut off the computer. From what I could determine,
rioting and looting had tapered off. Most things worth stealing were
already gone. Fires burned in alleys in every city and town. As garbage

burned, meat cooked, scrounged from freezers no longer working.

Rainstorms and freezing nights added to the misery of some, brought others to the end of their pain. *End? Eternity is a long time for people who have pushed God out of their thinking and their lives.* I snorted. Realizing I really did believe didn't give much joy at the moment. Unfortunately, or perhaps fortunately, God wasn't exactly the Santa Claus in the sky I wanted to believe in.

Tuesday, April 7

Early morning found me in the hot tub, washing clothes. When I heard the thump of helicopter blades I jumped from the water, stood at the flap of the bath-tent, and waved a towel. As the helicopter settled towards the landing spot I dressed and trotted down to the lake's edge. Before the engine was cut, I was half way across the slushy ice.

Sam looked weary and old as he stepped from the cockpit. A worn smile creased his lined face. He wordlessly gripped my hand. I felt like my own face was cracking.

"I'm glad you're all right," I said, and I've never meant anything more.

Sam cut in. "I figured you'd have killed yourself with your cooking by now."

"For such a miserable guy, you're a welcome sight, Sam. I'm thinking if what I hear on the radio is right, you've been putting in overtime, and not getting paid."

"Oh, I could bring you bales of money if you fancy coloured toilet paper." Sam's voice took on a bitter edge. "Now with a case of whiskey, you could buy a house with a grand piano and a wife to keep your bed warm. From what I see of wives though, you'd need to keep the whiskey just so you could put up with one."

"You're real sour on the women today." I laughed at him. "One just about beat you out of the chopper in a poker game I bet."

"Be nice if life could be that normal again." Worn sadness tinged Sam's voice.

"You know, for an ornery old guy, you sure care a lot, hard as you try to hide it." I choked a bit. "I'm proud to call you my friend. Just want you to know that."

The day wore away. Sam slowly relaxed.

"You've seen what's happening in the real world." I stared at Sam. "I've been picking up bits and pieces on the radio. Toronto seems to be hard hit. I have the ugliest boat that ever floated there, sitting in an old warehouse on the waterfront. I have been collecting clothing and other things I thought I was going to need." I paused, not wishing to reveal more details. "There is enough fuel on the barge, if your helicopter will run on heavy diesel. What do you say?"

Sam sighed heavily. "I was afraid you'd ask. What stinks is I'd have been disappointed if you hadn't. Your diesel would let us run just long enough to get us killed. I guess that would let us off the hook." He stared at me and shook his head. "I've got a bit of fuel left in the chopper. If you can scare up a cot so this old red-skin doesn't have to sleep on the floor, we can be on the way at first light."

It was not a promising sight that met us when the helicopter arrived over Toronto. Flying parallel with Highway 427, we crossed the northeast corner of Pearson International Airport. The wreckage of a jumbo jet and at least four small planes littered the tarmac.

A mile southeast, a trail was razed through the heart of Etobicoke. A piece of tail section from a 747 proclaimed SWISS AIR. One half of a school lay untouched beside that trail. The other half was spread for 400 metres.

The burned out shell of a transport and four cars marked the intersection of Eglinton and St. Clair Avenues. A bloated tank with a long ragged split had sprayed flaming death over a wedge half a block wide and a block deep. A fire-truck, caught in a traffic jam, formed a strange part of the burned mess. Snarls of twisted wreckage jammed many intersections.

Three crows rose from the blackened shell of a high-rise apartment building. I fought nausea as I stared at a half consumed body lying across the threshold of a patio door.

A small crater at Yonge and Dundas must have been from a subway collision. The Bond Place Hotel had burned and partially collapsed. Rubble choked Dundas St. and a parking lot beside it. A beat-up old building with a faded sign saying MISSION PRESS still stood beside the hotel. Gaping holes had been torn in the roof by rubble falling from the taller building.

St. Michael's Boys' School had lost several buildings. A few metres away from blackened walls, trees were pushing out spring greenery.

Putrefying contents of freezers without power spilled their added assault on the air. The cumulating stench of sewage, garbage, disease and death hung like a shroud over the city. I groaned. It just sort of slipped out. I drew the stench deep into my nostrils and lungs. I felt the hunger, the disease, the hopelessness. I felt the fear.

My fists came up and I screamed, "WHY, GOD?" I bit hard on my lip. I pulled clenched fists tight to my body, feeling mad and sick.

The building beside my warehouse had burned. Some kind of heavy boat had plowed a trail of destruction when its computer controls died while the screw was still turning. But it looked like it had managed to back away from the wreckage it had created.

When the thumping of the propeller finally stilled, Sam turned to me. He asked: "How, in God's name, could one stinking computer virus do all that?" His voice rose in anger. "And how... could your God allow it?"

I stared back at him. "I don't know, Sam. I can figure out the virus, sort of. But I'm asking myself the same questions about God. And damn it! I don't have any answers." I couldn't stop the sob that shook my shoulders.

"Whoever planted that virus had a lot of patience. They made it simple enough no virus check on any of the main computers caught it. They made it so it would copy itself onto every computer it could reach, and onto every back-up file anybody made once it was in their system. And they made it so it would just sit and wait with the dumb patience of a piece of plastic.

"When it took out air-traffic control and the computers on a 747 at the same second, there was not a thing those poor suckers could do. The computer does more of the flying than the pilots these days."

"I was up in the clouds in a jet when the computers went down," Sam interrupted.

I stared at him, hearing, but not taking in what he said. "When the subway signals stopped at the same time as the driver's controls stopped," I drew a harsh breath. "What were the guys supposed to do? The only good thing about it was that if they didn't have brakes, they didn't have power to keep pushing them either. How many people are still buried alive under there? What's it been, six days, with a blizzard thrown in?

"When the traffic lights mucked up, nobody paid attention. How many people died? How many people roasted alive in their cars after somebody with a trailer load of gasoline ran them down. And the guy driving the rig was a professional. He knew the timing of the lights. He knew he'd roast alive if he piled up. He was just doing his job. But somebody messed with the lights.

"How many train wrecks have there been? How many fires? Where is there a hospital that can still function? They use computers for everything."

My fist came down on the panel at the front of the helicopter. "You think I'll make excuses for God?" I shook my head slowly. "You know what Sam? I'm mad at God! I'm mad as blazes!" My voice became quiet again. "He's still God. He's got the right. He's got the power. But I don't have to like it."

I flung back the door and lurched forward. The seat-belt held me. With a frustrated groan that was half sob, I drove my thumb into the button. My fist struck my own groin. Heaving myself from the cabin as the pain exploded and spread, my feet struck the ground and folded under me. I burst into sobbing laughter, kneeling on the cracked pavement. The laughter sickened into body-wrenching shudders.

When I could finally stand almost straight, I looked sheepishly at Sam. He was struggling desperately to maintain a sober face but failing. As a chortle slipped past Sam's fight for control, I gasped in my own effort to suppress a laugh, then gave up.

When I could speak again, I stared at Sam. "What did you say back there? A jet at how high? You were in the air, but not in the chopper?"

Sam responded. "That's what I said. But you were so busy spitting nails you weren't listening." He stared at me, pain in his eyes. "A man can't avoid getting close to death once in a while. Others died and I lived. I don't know why. I'm not sure I'm glad."

We weren't sure who to connect with or how best to start helping. I unlocked the warehouse and we poked around inside a bit. Sam started to share his story, and for a while I forgot all about trying to rescue anyone else.

Chapter Thirteen

Sam's Story

It's better if I let Sam tell this part of the story. It starts back on April 1st, April Fool's Day, although I didn't hear it until the 7th.

Sam Deerfoot
Wednesday, April 1

I was returning from Windsor. A layover in Toronto had wasted most of the night. I hate flying with someone else at the controls, but a little part needed for the helicopter had grounded me. I had to take a cracked bushing to a machinist who could make a new one. Not many people can do that anymore. The part was small. It fit my jacket pocket. I only needed an hour's work to get the chopper in the air again, but it took a 48 hour trip to get it.

You know the way you sleep on those big planes, not really resting and getting your neck all stiff. I don't think the sun could have been quite up. We had begun our descent into the Sault airport.

My seat was at the leading edge of the right wing. Those big fan-jet motors make quite a whine. I've been a pilot long enough to learn to listen.

It quit! The whole aircraft just kind of sagged in the air. You wake up fast then. The ventilation stopped, then came on again but sounded different. I don't have backup power on the chopper, but I knew that change.

You don't log a couple thousand hours in the air without learning to listen and feel. You get to know air-currents, dirty fuel, an out-of-balance prop. There's a thousand little things you get to know. But this wasn't my machine.

We kind of hung there for a second. Then we seemed to drop out of the sky. If the motors were still working I'd have hardly noticed. But with them making no noise...

Someone was snoring, maybe three rows back. The stewardess had been pushing a trolley with drinks. She stumbled when the plane began going down. A cup of coffee tipped and spattered. We weren't quite in free-fall, but the drops seemed awful slow making it to the floor. You'd think somebody had opened a tap and drained all the blood from her face. Even whites, with their fish-belly colour, are never *that* white. But her voice didn't shake at all. She stayed all professional as she told us to fasten our seat belts.

She left the cart right there in the way, probably *not* the professional thing to do, then got herself forward to the little galley where she picked up the phone. Her hand was waving circles like she was signalling someone to hurry up and answer. Then she stuck her head through into the cockpit.

I unlocked my seat-belt and headed forward. I pushed the cart in front of me. This was no little glitch. We were losing altitude fast. I could feel the pressure building in my ears. I told the stewardess to get the cart locked down. Her mouth was working but she didn't know what to say. I was giving orders like I was the captain.

The pilot and first-officer were working down a checklist. I could hear static on the radio and the Mayday call going out. Gauges are different than in the chopper, but I found the altimeter. We'd already dropped below 6,000 metres.

This is beautiful country. I love this country when the helicopter is working or when I'm on the ground with a rifle in hand. When you're up in the air and something goes wrong though, it's all stone teeth below, in one big, hungry mouth.

I asked how I could lower the landing gear. The pilot never took his hands off the controls. He nodded in the direction of a plate set into the floor behind the first officer's chair.

I was starting to sweat it. These guys were pros. They were scared but doing everything right. Those motors weren't coming back on. We had less than a minute of air-time left.

"I'm a helicopter pilot" I told them. "You've got backups for the backups in these birds. "How the heck can you lose both engines?"

"We can't!" The pilot spat the words. "There's just no possible way. Damn it! We don't have airtime to make it to the Sault. Not a thing under us but rocks and ice."

Switches kept clicking, almost silent curses kept sounding. It was worse than if they'd been yelling them.

"It's the computer. They just refitted this girl." The first engineer's voice broke. "It's supposed to eliminate human error. Instead ... "

I think I was dripping sweat. If I hadn't already known something of how to lower the landing gear manually, I'd have been skunked. Somebody who never learned English must have written the instructions. I heard the tonal alarm as the plane passed through 3,000 metres. Time was running out fast.

I got the nose wheel down and locked.

"Give me all the right pedal you can," the pilot's voice spoke. "That stretch of highway is our only chance. We've got to come around another 40 degrees." He shut up for a second and concentrated. "That transport's going to come over the hill just about the time we touch down. Think he'll have the guts to lay his rig on its side?

"Forget the radio! Too late to do us any good. If you're any good at praying now would be a good time.

"Where's Karen? She should be prepping for an emergency landing."

"She already was," I broke into the conversation again.

"Thirty seconds! You got those wheels down?"

"What you make our ground-speed, Captain?"

"At least 300. Probably higher. Can't count on brakes and we have no reverse thrusters. Hope they grow soft maples here."

"Ten seconds."

A clunk sounded below as the main wheels dropped. A ripping sound from the belly of the aircraft had me wanting to scream. I fought the lever as I forced the lock in place to hold the wheels. Branches slapped against the bottom of the plane. Wheels tearing leaves from trees add a noise I never want to hear again in this life or any other. Tires screamed against pavement. We hit hard and I hit the floor.

"Everything you've got into the flaps! We've got to slow this thing down," the pilot shouted. "There's that rig. Hope he's got his head screwed on right."

I got up behind the co-pilot. The brakes should have been shoving me through the windshield, but they didn't seem to be doing much. The right wing tip whipped branches across a strip of grass. The left wing stretched across the median and shoulder of the divided highway. Two approaching cars could have passed under the wings, but I don't guess they'd ever seen an aircraft on the highway coming from the wrong direction at 300 clicks. One car rolled while the other skidded and bounced along the ditch before plowing into trees.

That transport driver was a pro. You could see the thing belching smoke as he down-shifted. And he must have come as close to locking up the wheels as possible with any control left, 'cause his brakes were smoking too. He took the right-hand ditch—his right hand—as we got closer, somehow keeping all his wheels under him. But the ditch wasn't deep enough.

You never want to hear the scream of tortured metal when an airplane wing makes like a can opener on a transport trailer. Never saw a movie that made it sound real—or maybe you just hear it different when you're there.

That lifted our left wing and had the right wing chewing gravel. We started rocking like a drunk, overstuffed goose.

We were losing steam when two cars came side by side over the hill, with one of those big pickups tail-gaiting the car in the left lane, just itching for a chance to pass.

The car on the right moved onto the shoulder, slowing fast, then took the ditch. The left one locked the bakes. It went into a skid, sliding half sideways. The pickup rammed it.

I've been in some tight situations where a couple seconds get stretched an hour long. This was one of those times. I think the car was on its second roll when it went under our wing. The pickup did a real fancy cartwheel, the kind they try for in movies. Seemed like it was slow motion.

It's weird, the things that burn into your brain at a time like that. The pickup was all shiny and waxed as the leading edge of our left wing cut the box clear of the cab. The driver had his mouth as wide open as it would go. Looked like he was cheering on a roller-coaster ride.

We had been climbing a long hill and losing speed all the way. But now the highway cut through the rock itself and the grass border narrowed. I couldn't believe the beating those wings took and stayed with the plane. Would have been better if they broke off and we could leave them behind, 'cause that's where the fuel tanks are.

Another transport crawled over the top just as we ground to a stop. His four-way flashers were warning of his slow climb. We were close enough to see him yank on the cord and get his air-horn screaming. He got stopped about two metres from our nose and stared up at the three of us in the cockpit. He had one of those faces that tell you a lot even if you're deaf. We could read his lips as he grabbed his CB mike.

"This is south-bound *Wacko Willy* with a load of hamburg still on the hoof. Stop all traffic comin' up this hill! There's a bird come down to roost. It's gonna be hotter'n hell here in a couple seconds. I'm backing up so's my rig don't burn. There were two motorboats a half-mile behind. You guys reading me?"

Black smoke rolled from the stack as he began to creep backwards. In the cockpit, we had other things to do. I asked if the doors would open and the emergency slides work.

"Depends how much damage has been done," the captain answered me. "Let's get out of here. That trucker had one thing right. It's going to be hotter than hell in here awful fast."

"Captain. That was good flying." I had to tell him that.

The stewardess, Karen I think she was, banged the door open from the passenger cabin. We could see three emergency exits open and people moving like they had just woke up from a long drunk.

I hollered at them. "Don't stand like you're waiting in line for the theatre, people. You fellows who are strong. Get yourselves down the slides and help at the bottom. You're slowing things down and endangering lives." Then I remembered this wasn't my bird. "Sorry Captain. I'll try to keep my mouth shut now."

"It's what needed to be said. Now, take your own advice and get down that ramp. I want someone on the outside with sense enough to see what needs done. Go!"

I went, flying off the end of the ramp that hung almost two metres above the pavement. I wrenched my knee and bruised both hands. My feet felt like I'd jumped barefoot into a fire.

Breaking the fall of full-grown bodies coming off the end of a slide is no child's play. I think I broke some ribs. I had come down the front left ramp, just back of the cockpit. The ramp spit me out almost under the nose of the plane.

Most of the fuel had been drained from the left tanks when the pickup had torn into the wing. The right side seemed to have more than enough left.

The highway had narrowed into a cut through the rock. The northbound lane had pulled away. Dirty snow lay deep along the south shoulder. The north side was pretty much bare.

The trucker stood beside me, cursing as he stared at the little extinguisher in his hand. The heat was already forcing us back.

It was a nightmare. I helped a couple people limp away, but one poor sucker sat on the shoulder of the highway, his leg twisted all wrong. He screamed curses at me, the crew, and everybody else. I couldn't get back to him in time. When a section of the burning wing collapsed, he died screaming curses at God.

The fire kept us separated into two groups. People were either so shell-shocked they just sat and stared at nothing, or they went all hyper and hysterical. I did what I could to calm things down. The trucker had a first-aid kit, but there were more cuts and bruises and burns than I knew how to deal with. I never did see what happened to the drivers of those cars. I was pretty sure I didn't need to look for the pickup driver.

As soon as there was a bit of a break I looked for the captain but couldn't find him. I found the first officer, hands burned, but otherwise okay. "I thought Jim was right behind me when I took the ramp." He told me, almost sobbing. "We were both almost too late." His raspy voice, singed hair and scorched uniform fit his words too well.

"He was a brave man, and a good pilot." I'm not the crying type, but I wasn't sure I could trust my voice to say more just then.

"But what good did it do him to stay behind?" the first officer asked. "It didn't save a single extra life."

If you know an answer to that one, you're a whole lot smarter than me.

It was late afternoon on April 5th when I got home. Skin still pretty red but bruising almost healed. The light switch didn't work. The fridge hadn't run for days. The furnace and the stove were dead. Even my answering machine had as much life as a belly-up fish.

I'd helped people after the blizzard on the 3rd, snaring a couple of rabbits and getting enough food to keep them alive, barely. A tractor-trailer had carried most of them back to Sudbury. I scrounged a ride to Sault Ste. Marie, then walked most of the way home from there.

I got the bushing replaced on the helicopter. Good thing it was still in my jacket pocket. It hurt my side, climbing up there to fix it. I didn't have much fuel, so just started the chopper long enough to check for vibration in the prop before I cut the engine again.

I hauled up my net from the river. Three good sized fish were spoiled, too long dead in the net. I'd have thrown the one little one back, but I'd eaten almost nothing for the last day. I built a fire out on the rock and fried it. I could have eaten three that size, but it was something.

I tramped over to the Trading Post where Don Jensen just stared at me. "Keep your money in your pocket, Deerfoot." He spat on the ground and swore. "Banks gone under. They've gone through the ice an' they got the whole damn town harnessed to the sleigh behind them." He kicked at the ground. "Where you been?"

There was nothing for me to say, so I didn't.

"You bring fresh meat, stuff Indians used to be good for, an' I'll trade with you. Fur is past prime, so no sense starting now. But you might as well use your money for rolling smokes. If you got a bank card, the best you can do is file the edges and cut your wrists, unless you want to cut the bank manager's throat first. Then you'd be doing something useful before you died."

I turned and walked away.

"I'm talkin' to you, boy." Don hollered at me like I was a dog. "Don't you turn your back on me. And don't come round here looking for no handouts, boy." His voice got all high and squeaky.

It's weird. Almost no whites use the word "Indian" any more, but it got resurrected when that computer virus killed other things off.

At Charlie's Pub and Café, a wood stove threw smoky heat. Oil lamps hung from the ceiling. Two small clusters of men sat at tables, smoking. They stared at me like a pack of half-starved dogs.

"I thought we had laws about smoking inside," I told Charlie as the cigar stink reached me. "It was one of the few smart things the government's ever done."

"Still playing the white-man's game, Sam? Ashamed to have some colour to your skin?" The man who spoke had a cruel face, a broken nose and fresh bruising from a recent fight. He pushed back from the table and stood, thrusting out his chest. "Mr. High an' Mighty white man. Gonna enforce the smoking ban? Here, then. Use this. You can trim the ashes off my ce-gar—if you're man enough." He made an exaggerated bow, then whipped out a knife and threw it. I leaned to the side as the blade hit and quivered in the wall behind me. Smart people shouldn't miss if they're gonna throw knives at me.

"White as a gutted fish." He kept blathering. "Ain't got the guts to be a real man and not enough smarts to say a word." He hunched down as he moved toward me. Three drinking buddies all scraped their chairs as they got up to watch the show.

The man charged. No sport to it at all. I just sidestepped and planted my fist in his gut. He went down like a heart-shot bull moose.

I turned and yanked the knife out of the wall. My ribs about killed me, but I wasn't paying attention to them. He was sort of half rising, but my knee thumped his head and slammed it into the floor. Lucky for him too, 'cause the knife came down where his neck would have been and stabbed into the floor. I pulled it out and sawed at his neck with it. Why anybody'd carry a knife that dull I'll never know, but I got it deep enough that he didn't move he was so scared. I told the rest of them to come on if they wanted a fight. I'd take this dog's head off then I'd take them one at a time or all together. Not too smart of me, against the three of them, but I told them if they didn't want a fight to get the hell out, 'cause the longer they waited, the deeper I'd shove the blade. There was one of those long seconds while they all waited for each other to make the first move. But they hadn't got into the hard liquor yet, so they weren't so brave as they thought. There was a pounding of boots as they all headed out the door. I could smell that the guy under me had pissed himself. I got my knee off him, then dragged him back and forth to mop up his own puddle with his clothes before I hauled him to the door and dumped him out. I told him then, that "red skin on a skunk's carcass don't make an Indian. A half-drunk bulldog looking for a fight don't make an Indian. You've got to be a man, first! You're proud of your red skin. Good! So wear it like a man." Then I left him there in his own blood and piss.

I picked up a handful of snow and wiped the knife blade clean, then rubbed it dry on my pants. In my house I slapped it down on the counter, then stared at it. I got memories you don't want to know about and it brought too many of them back.

It took me two hours to put together a complete outfit. Then I dumped most of it out and took only what I needed for a couple days hunting. I had committed no crime so I wasn't going to run and make it look like I had. I left a note on the counter saying I'd gone hunting.

Two days later I had a dressed deer across my shoulders when I found Don Jensen at the Trading Post. I asked him how much fuel it would buy me.

He just stared at me for a bit and then drew a breath and mumbled "About 40 litres, I suppose. It'll fill two jugs."

That sounded pretty steep but I said I'd take it, with a couple tins of creamed corn and a bag of flour added.

He started to grumble, then said. "You're one stubborn old Indian. I'll get the corn. Flours too much. Let me unlock the smoke-house."

A bit later I had the fuel tank in the chopper half full. The next morning I decided to risk your cooking.

A WOMAN'S TOUCH

Roland Handson
Tuesday, April 7

*D*ust covered everything in the warehouse, bringing little change to the rusted hulk of the barge. I saw no sign of forced entry. I examined the massive beam and the winches at the sea-door, wondering how we could open it.

"Sam," I was closer than I liked to crying. "You've had a first-hand taste of the horror. There is so much hurting out there. I want to pack up and run but I can't. With the chopper we can bring bodies out nobody else can reach. Just maybe, we might still save a life or two, though it's probably too late for that by now."

Sam's voice held weary amusement. "You wouldn't be the crazy guy I've almost come to believe has real Red-Man's blood in his veins if you could walk away from this. But didn't that Jesus guy you follow say, *Let the dead bury their own dead?*"

I looked quizzically at Sam.

"Yeah. I've been reading the book you gave me." Sam looked like a kid caught with his hand in the cookie jar. "This Jesus character was either the dumbest guy who ever lived, or he was the smartest. He was crazy, like you are. He'd stick his head into some snake's nest and never back up an inch while all the religious big-shots tried to bite it off. He played that bunch of smart-asses for suckers. Sure wish I could believe that resurrection story.

"You know. You're a whole lot like him."

"Sam," I choked on that one. "If I had a million dollars and could pay for compliments, I couldn't ask for a better one than you just gave me."

"I tell you you're crazy as a guy they nail to a hunk of wood and you take it as a compliment. I'm going to throw out that book of insults and buy a new one.

"There's a cargo net and 200 metres of rope in the chopper. I'll try not to spill my breakfast down your neck if you get into too much of a mess. I saw the colour of your face when those crows left the body in that high-rise. I almost wanted a barf-bag too. I'm glad I'll be the one flying. You sure you want to do this?"

"Want? What's that got to do with anything? I want to be able to live with myself when we get home."

"You think you can live with what you're gonna see? You think you're gonna close your eyes at night and not remember?" Sam stared moodily at me. "I wish to God you could be right."

Through the endless hours of that day and the two weeks following, I wept, vomited, and slid my hands under bodies half frozen, beginning to decay, often burned, and almost always partly eaten by rats and crows. Carrying them to a patio, I would signal Sam, load them into the net and take them to one of the mass burial sights.

The body count had passed 2000. Countless more were still buried in the rubble.

Using the helicopter, we concentrated on the upper floors of high-rise apartments and office buildings.

Fuel for the helicopter was pumped from any of several tanker trucks touring the streets, keeping the rescuers at work. No one asked for pay.

Six million people still lived in the greater Toronto area. Some things were back on. The computer virus was easy to beat once people knew what they were looking for. But so much had been wrecked in the mob mentality that what might have taken weeks of rebuilding would now need years. Gangs worked the streets and alleys too. More than once I picked up a body that was still warm, blood pooling around it. More than once Sam pulled me out of some alley as a gang closed in on me. I almost wanted to fight them. Dying right now didn't seem too bad a prospect. It was living that scared me.

Without electricity, water, or sewage, disease swept in repeating waves across the city. Cooking fires burned in streets and alleys. Concrete and steel high-rises, supposedly fireproof, became their own little corner of hell as cooking fires caught something flammable and raced with it. Suicide, disease, and out-of-control fires added to the death-toll. Fuel dwindled. The pay-loaders ground to a halt. Bodies lay exposed. Rats became bolder.

A few old CB Radios still worked. Desperate for an energy source, I tried over and over in lulls during the rescue effort to persuade a trucker to pick up the nuclear furnaces still stored in Owen Sound. They could save lives. They could provide sterilized water and hot showers.

I thought often of the *EAGLE* hidden in the French River area. For all I knew, the computers on it were also corrupted.

A cube van had been abandoned where it ran out of gas. The roll-up back door had been broken open by looters. When nothing of value remained to be stolen, garbage was thrown in. I had scrounged gasoline in little bits—a cupful here, a couple of litres there. I had managed to fill a 20-litre container but thought I needed at least double that before I dared attempt the trip.

I had no keys. The steering wheel was locked. I thought I could find a way to break the lock on the steering wheel. I didn't know yet then, that *The Virus* had messed up most automotive computers. I figured if I blew the thing up trying to hot-wire it, I wouldn't lose much. Still, the possibility of an energy source seemed worth the effort.

I had accumulated half a second jug of gas when I learned that the storage facility in Owen Sound had been looted and burned. The furnaces would have survived that, but you'd have to get through the rubble to reach them, and with the packing cases likely gone, getting a forklift under them might prove impossible. I gave up my hopes and poured my dwindling strength into the rescue effort in Toronto.

Bone aching weariness plagued the hours of darkness when the helicopter sat at rest. We fished in the polluted waters, considering ourselves more fortunate than most of the city's population. Sometimes, as we deliberately put off the moment of entering the barge, we shared details of our lives.

"You ever been in love, Sam?" I questioned one night.

He stared at me a long time, then shook his head. "You mean the movie kind, where you're in bed before you think to ask each other's name, or you mean the growing old together kind?"

"I guess I hadn't thought of it that way," I admitted. "Maybe the growing old kind."

"It's a good way to think about it," Sam said. "You get itching to jump in the sack with somebody, ask yourself if you can see yourself waking up beside her when you're both 60?"

"60? Gosh!" I chortled. "Well that just might cure AIDS."

Sam stared at the scar on his right hand moodily. "It might at that." He mumbled the words.

"I always figured there was a story behind that scar," I said quietly. "I've got time to listen if you have time to share."

After a long moment Sam sighed and stared bleakly at me. "It's dangerous to ever let yourself think you're in love," he informed me. "I'm not sure she even knew I was alive. I was about your age. She was the wrong colour. Her hair was so blond it looked like honey and hung way down her back." He sighed again. "Her brother was always flashing money. He had slept with half the girls on the reserve and bragged about it. But he'd had a couple drinks too many when somebody talked about me having an eye for his sister." Sam's fist clenched and unclenched. "This scar is from the broken bottle he tried to shove in my face." Sam was silent for a long time, gazing at the small fire.

"Why, Roland? Why was it okay for him to sleep with all the Indian girls, but I couldn't look at his sister?" Too exhausted for anger, a deep gnawing pain seemed to cry from behind the questions.

"I put him down. When he got up, I put him down again. He didn't get up that time. He spent two days in the hospital. I spent four months looking through bars from the wrong side."

The silence stretched long before I spoke softly. "There are times I'm not proud to be white, Sam. Us Canadians. We look down our noses at the Americans and their prejudice against the Blacks. But we can't see that our own noses are just as snotty." I groaned. "This hell we're in the middle of, somebody, probably a bored high school computer hacker wrote the program, created the virus. It's somebody's joke."

I stood stiffly, stretched and bent. "I can't go on much longer, Sam." I stood for another long moment, then spoke with a sigh. "The bed-bugs are lonesome in there. Guess I'll turn in."

At the door, I stopped and half turned. "I can sit for hours with a book and be content. I've read about jail and seen movies but I can't quite grasp what it must be like on the inside. What kind of hell must it have been for you?"

We worked for two more days. But truckers were being killed. With fuel no longer available, the helicopter finally sat at rest. Lethargy crept in when the endless hours of gut-wrenching toil ground to a halt.

Cold rain pushed us inside the warehouse with its mingled stink of oil, rust, and stale water. "I think this place needs a woman's touch. I think my life needs a woman's touch," I exclaimed weakly.

"You! Looking for a woman? I don't believe it." Sam's voice held a spark of tired interest.

A bleak smile crept across my face. "I've been less than proud of myself at times, Sam, and for sure my thoughts. The way some of those girls dress..." I heaved myself to my feet and paced heavily. "I've hungered, Sam. I've hungered till I thought I would go crazy." I sighed and sat down. Sam stared wordlessly at the smoky lantern.

I spoke again. "I wish God had made me blind, or made girls less—I don't know—less girly, I guess."

Physical and emotional exhaustion finally broke me. Meagre food supplies dwindled. The helicopter was grounded, perhaps an hour's fuel remaining.

Sam came in with a fish caught and cleaned outside the warehouse. He found me sitting on the floor, staring blankly across the drab room. Choking out the words I told him, "I can't go on, Sam. We're not helping anymore. While I thought we were helping I could face it. Now, we're just two more bodies, eating food somebody else needs. Not much more alive than some I've scraped into bags."

Sam's shoulders slumped. Without saying anything, he dropped the fish in a rusted pan and headed to the fire built on the pavement outside the warehouse. Ten minutes later I stumbled out the door. I watched Sam at the fire for a long moment, then approached.

"I'm sorry, Sam. It was my idea to stay. I'm not man enough for any more of this. I'm not man enough for anything right now. We'll park the chopper on the barge. If we can't get up the locks at the Welland Canal, we'll take what supplies we can and leave the rusty old tub. Either way, it's time to leave."

"D'you think you were Superman?" Weariness slurred Sam's words. "You've hauled out more'n 80 bodies. I lost count about then. You've helped every living person you could. You didn't have to stay, but you did. You didn't have to help, but you did. I'm proud I was with you, had a bit of a part."

"A *bit* of a part Sam? Could I have gotten any of those bodies out without you at the controls? When I was hanging in that net with a decaying body, vomiting my guts out, wishing you'd dash my brains against a wall, and praying I could go on for one more day, who was at the other end of that rope? There's not one bit of anything good I've done that you're not part of."

CHAPTER FIFTEEN

UPWIND FROM MYSELF

Friday, April 24

The old diesel engine on the barge coughed and snorted, then belched foul fumes into the enclosed building. I cast off the lines and backed the ungainly stern tight against the sea-door, then cut the engine. Raw diesel fumes burned my lungs and eyes. Picking up bolts and bits of broken concrete, I hurled them at windows, shattering them, letting in a meagre measure of air. Sam brought the acetylene torch he usually carried in the helicopter.

With no electricity and no possibility of obtaining a generator, my plan was simple. Cut the locks and the hydraulics that secured the door, then force them open by backing the barge through them. The structural damage would be minimal. My only concern was protecting the propeller and rudder of the boat.

A winch on either side of the barge answered the need. With a cable from each winch wrapped around the beam that spanned and secured the double doors, Sam cut the beam in the centre. Starting up the engine again, I shifted the barge five metres forward. The battery gave barely sufficient cranking power to bring the power plant into reluctant life. In spite of the fumes, I was afraid to shut it off. I didn't know if the nausea or the burning eyes were worse.

"Get out of here, Sam." I gasped. "No sense both of us being sicker than dogs."

With a rag over my mouth and my nose and eyes streaming, I rushed back to the winches and strained against the rusty metal. Screaming like some demented creature in its death agony, the cable wound in. When the beam was high enough, I swung the 12-metre length of steel and lay it on the deck, with three metres hanging over the back.

Before finishing the job on the opposite side of the boat, I had hung over the edge and vomited. Grabbing one of the coils of stiff tarry rope, I made a dozen awkward loops around a cleat and the end of the steel beam, giving at least some resistance to sliding on the deck. Trying to knot the thick braid was beyond my skill. I ran the slack to a second cleat, took a loop, and brought it back. After doing the same on the other side, a quick detour to the side left me gasping and wiping my face on my sleeve as I pulled on the clutch.

The big screw on the old boat turned reluctantly. The boat trembled and backed slowly. The screech of metal against metal sounded as the beams bumped against the door. Resistance of the water made the task exasperatingly slow.

One of the beams slid a few centimetres on the floor. The crack between doors widened. A screech of rusty metal echoed in the enclosure. The engine rumbled with a lower, smoother growl. The exhaust showed less colour, though I wondered if the air was simply so thick the fumes were less visible.

The doors spread to a metre. A visible front of clean air cut a swath through the murk. My eyes burned and ran. The spread of the doors stretched to three metres. One of the beams slid sideways, chewing its way across the face of the door with a demented squeal. The boat rocked. The second beam slid sideways. The doors reached six metres. Both beams slipped clear.

The rear corners of the boat struck against the angled doors, forcing them still farther back. With a grinding squeal that seemed to go on forever, I finally emerged into clear air. The dirty brown smog we had seen on approaching the city now seemed to be the sweetest of air.

Pushing the clutch in, I stopped the screw. Grabbing a bucket, I tossed it over the side on a light rope, then pulled it up, dripping. I plunged my hands into the murky water and splashed it over my face, trying to force myself to keep my eyes open as I did so.

Uncertain at the controls, I started with the screw turning too slowly, not giving steerageway. When the blunt toboggan nose crunched against a small scow moored among a tangle of wreckage, a stream of curses met me. Giving the boat more throttle, I found I had control. That didn't come soon enough to prevent a bottle from smashing through the cabin window.

Unseen wreckage dragged and screeched underneath, but the barge rode high with little weight on her. Someone waved and shouted from a small shanty that had the sign of the harbourmaster on it. I was amazed someone still claimed that authority. When I failed to stop, a handgun appeared. Ducking down, I gave the boat more throttle. A shell shattered more shards of glass from the window the bottle had already broken. A second shot smacked against the rusty steel wall. Raising myself to peer ahead, I spun the wheel rapidly as the narrow band of open water between Toronto Island and the man-made harbour approached. The ungainly squat mass responded sluggishly.

It was a big power-plant on a craft carrying little weight. I gave it more throttle. The motor had been overhauled. The screw was almost a metre in diameter and the guy at the controls had no experience. Black smoke poured from the stack. The engine noise rose from a growl to an enraged snarl. The barge lumbered forward like a startled draft horse. The stern slued hard to the right. I had too much rudder angle for the amount of power being fed to the screw.

Spinning the wheel back, I over-reacted. With a wailing screech the blunt bow ground against concrete. She was a stout, if ugly, little tub. Although she left a rusty streak for several metres along the concrete embankment, she charged for open water like a fat sow turned out of the barn.

A lingering sense of nausea plagued me. My eyes continued to burn. I reduced throttle, turning the wheel slightly to pass between two moored buoys.

Clear of the breakwater now, one-metre waves of cold grey water slapped against the side of the barge. The wallowing caused my uneasy stomach to churn.

"Oh God. Haven't I been sick enough?" The words spilled out in a whispered groan. I realized I sounded like a whining kid.

"I don't know why You put up with me, God. I hope whatever I'm accomplishing is worth it." I mused silently for a moment. "I want to say thanks.

"What I said to Sam..." I paused for a moment, startled that I was talking to God like this, "Yeah, I'm mad! Yeah, I want answers! You don't have to give them to me. You're big enough to squash me like a bug and not answer to anybody for it. But I'm still fool enough to ask.

"Oh God. How many?" The words became a groan. "Thousands in Toronto alone. Their bodies rotting. Rats chewing on the corpses. And that's just one city..." The grief, the sickness, became too great. My prayer died into a wordless cry of anguish.

The throb of helicopter blades penetrated my consciousness. I reduced throttle, maintaining just enough to keep steerageway. The helicopter held pace, settling slowly onto the deck.

It took Sam 15 minutes to scrounge sufficient ropes to tie the helicopter down. I had flushed my eyes and gained control of myself before Sam entered the wheelhouse. With the barge on a south bearing, heading towards the Welland Canal, I increased throttle.

"I feel guilty about leaving, Sam. All those people, sick, starving. Not even water to flush toilets. We can't do any more. But there are several million people who deserve a way out as much as we do. Why, Sam? What makes us special? Why should we escape?

"I want to forget it. I want to pretend I never smelled the stink of death. I want to go back to my hideout in the north, pretend this hell was just some insane writer's nightmare on paper, a horror story somebody hoped would make them rich.

"Do you have any idea how many times I've screamed at God? But God didn't do it. Some computer hacker did it. It's all a joke, Sam. So why aren't we laughing?

"Do you suppose the kid cares? He's got no power for his computer now. That's probably the only thing that bothers him.

"Why don't you just throw me over-board and shut me up, Sam? It gave some poor fish an awful belly ache when Jonah was running away, but it saved the sailors.

"I wish to God throwing me over-board could save somebody!"

The crossing to the Welland Canal took four hours as the old boat plowed through the waves. At the first lock, we were greeted incredulously. "You figure we've got some magic touch? We don't have electricity. The only things still work around here is stuff somebody dragged out of the junkyard. Now get out of this waterway before that heap of scrap sinks. Someday real boats will want to travel here again."

Sam looked at me, shrugged, and pointed at the controls. The slight current bore us backwards down the canal a short distance until I clumsily turned the boat.

There seemed no point in staying on the south side of the lake. We aimed for Etobicoke, west of Toronto. We spent the crossing time transferring much of the small treasure buried under bags and boxes of used clothes. The stock purchased from two jewelry stores crowded the helicopter uncomfortably, yet took surprisingly little room to house what in better days would have been valued at more than a million.

Nondescript boxes carried labels: Kitchen, Computer & Electronics, Bedroom, Linen. The hope was that anyone looking in the helicopter would think someone's household contents, mostly useless without electricity but still hoarded, made up the load.

The fuel gauge on the barge dropped dangerously low. We kept a diamond ring, a set of pearl earrings, and two gold chains separate from the rest. When the barge thumped against the wharf along the Woodlawn Petroleum Company's dock, late in the afternoon, I held them in my hand as an armed security worker approached.

"You can't tie up here. This is private property." He cradled a shotgun and wore a holstered hand-gun as well. He kept the muzzle of the shotgun down, but his finger fondled the trigger.

"We don't want to stay," I replied. "We'd like to buy fuel. We're prepared to pay... with gold."

The muzzle of the shot-gun rose. "I'll take that, thank you. You move real slow and toss it onto the shore. Then you get that scrap heap away from this dock."

"Not... So... Fast!" Sam spoke the words slow and hard.

The guard made a startled turn, his gun wavering and the aim moving away from me. I dived for a spot behind a steel bulkhead.

"We have a business proposition to make," Sam continued. "Obviously, you're not a businessman." There was a pause, then, "You might want to put that thing down before somebody gets hurt."

I couldn't see from my place of shelter, but I heard the dull clatter faintly above the barge's engine as the gun was dropped onto the concrete.

"The hand-gun too," Sam continued. "Leave it in the holster. Take off the whole belt. It's better for your health if you don't make me nervous."

There were other unidentifiable sounds before Sam spoke again. "Okay. Now, who here has authority to sell to us?" Sam's voice sounded matter-of-fact, as if talking over the sights of a shotgun was an everyday occurrence.

I don't much like people pointing guns at me. With Sam covering the guard, I moved under the aim of his gun and grabbed both the shot-gun and the handgun. It was a cheap shot, but I turned back and buried my fist in the guy's gut. The breath went out of him in a rush. He slumped to the ground, sucking air with a strangled squeak.

"We understand each other now?" I questioned. "Who can sell us fuel?"

"There's – nobody – else – here." The man gasped the words out. "They pay me – a bit to guard – the place. I can't sell. None of the pumps – work."

"What kind of fuel is in what tanks? We want a couple jugs of diesel and some aviation fuel."

"I told you – I can't sell." His voice became a whine. "I don't even know, man."

"You and me are going for a little walk," I told the guard.

"I'm telling the truth, man." His voice was panicked. "I swear to God. Hey, I'd give you the fuel if I could."

"Yeah, I noticed," I snorted. I picked up the holster and buckled the belt around me. The guard had quite a belly, so the thing sagged. With a snort of disgust I unclasped the holster and grabbed the hand-gun. I don't know much about guns but this was a revolver, with a shell in each chamber. I stuffed it into the back of my pants and dropped the belt and holster onto the dock again.

Sam passed fuel jugs across to me. It was a bit of a clumsy move because he kept the shot-gun levelled at the guard's gut. I set two jugs to one side of the guard, careful to never get between him and Sam's aim. "Carry those, and come with me," I ordered. Looking around the area, I saw a cluster of pipes and valves behind a locked chain-link fence. I clumsily worked the action on the gun, chambering a shell. A shot broke the padlock.

"Think about the sparks when you do that," I heard Sam call from the boat.

I entered the compound, angry at Sam for questioning me. Each valve was labelled and locked. Gritting my teeth I fired a second shot to break the lock on the shed.

"Damn fool! You know where you're standing? You want to blow up half the city?" Sam wasn't quite shouting, but almost.

"Yeah," I burst out. "I know where I'm standing. I also know sometimes the only reason anything gets done is 'cause somebody's stupid enough to do it."

Inside the door numbered keys hung on a piece of pegboard. I removed the key for valve number six. Stomping back outside, I fought with the rusted padlock. A wheel the size of a car steering-wheel turned the valve on the huge pipe. A faint gurgle sounded. Walking to the pumping station, I opened the hand valve on the hose. Only a few drops flowed. I slumped to the ground, suddenly embarrassed and ashamed. "Sorry, Sam," I muttered, knowing that wasn't good enough.

I forced myself back to my feet, then studied the length of pipe. A two-centimetre steel pipe thrust upright from each main line. A stubby cylinder near the top might have been to trap air. A discharge pipe turned and tipped down again, with a valve above the open end.

Back in the shed, I found a length of heavy rubber hose. It was too large to fit snugly over the pipe, but I could make do with it. Black electrical tape hung in neat rolls from a section of pegboard wall.

Sliding the hose over the discharge end of the pipe, I used most of a roll of tape securing it. With the guard holding the hose, I opened the valve. Gravity did the rest.

We probably spilled two litres from the oversized hose while filling the four jugs. The guard walked ahead of me, each of us carrying two jugs back to the barge.

We got a few hours running time for the barge, then did the same thing for aviation fuel, filling the helicopter tank and ending with four full jugs.

I stared at the guard for a long moment. "For your sake, I won't leave your boss to wonder about your honesty." I told him. "There's a city going to hell just beyond these tanks. Rescue workers were desperate for fuel. Lives could have been saved, might still be saved, with something as small as a smoky fire in a five-gallon pail. But you've been hired to guard the tanks. That tells me more than I want to know. Still, I'll not steal.

"Twelve jugs of fuel, diesel and aviation. That makes, what? About 250 litres? At $3.00 that comes to $750. The gold chains are each worth $165. The earrings are about $95 for the set. The diamond ring is the real prize. The price tag on it said $1100. Even with your guns thrown in, you're getting close to double for everything." I snorted. "Dad thought there'd be people shot at the pumps when gas hit two dollars. People squawked a lot but just kept driving. Now, when lives could be saved, they crank the price higher. Makes you proud, doesn't it?" I could hear the bitterness in my voice.

"Your boss might be a little more understanding if he finds payment in a visible place." A full roll of electrical tape bound the man's wrists tightly together. I pushed the guard down onto the floor, lying on his side, then lashed him at the ankles and wrists to pipes. I set the jewelry on top of a metal plate a couple paces away. "There's too much stretch to this stuff so it won't hold you long. But if you're smart you won't try to pocket the jewelry and run. I'm guessing your boss might not be the forgiving kind."

The barge moved away from the dock, trailing slowly westward along the shoreline. Two hours later we tied up alongside a small boathouse. An overgrown trail led up through the bush to a house with windows broken out. It had an abandoned look about it.

Sam had juggled parcels until he managed to squeeze three of the fuel jugs into the helicopter. There was barely room for the two of us.

"All those supplies." I stared moodily into the hold of the barge. "The lights, the pipes. I sure hate to leave it behind."

"What'd you buy it all for?" Sam asked. "One guy living out in the sticks. It makes no sense to me."

"You remember that story you told me about the fish-thing coming out of the water, sheltering people from a storm? Well, I'm guessing those people might find things pretty cold and dark without this stuff." I fell silent as Sam stared at me blankly.

"You're looking for even more reasons to think I'm completely crazy. I can't make sense in my own head, Sam, so I don't know how to explain it to you."

We locked the covers to the hold, little as that would do to stop looting. We slept on the barge one more time, rose with the dawn, and several hours later the helicopter set down in my valley. The ice was gone except for the south shoreline. Sam hovered the helicopter with the struts against the shore as I jumped out. By the time the propellor noise had stilled, I was back with the canoe.

"Who gets to the tub first, Sam? I guess I'm not quite liberated enough yet to bath together." I sighed deeply as I opened the door of the cabin. "It feels good to be home."

Rummaging on a shelf, I found clean underwear, jeans, and a shirt, and handed them to Sam. "These will be small but they're clean. I'll scare up some food. You go ahead and have a soak. If my cooking kills you at least I can bury a clean corpse."

"After what we've eaten the last three weeks? Guess I'll take a chance. Do you smell it?"

"What?" I asked.

"The air. The trees. The rocks. The water. All of it."

"You're going to be a poet if you're not careful." I paused and breathed deeply. "I'm smelling too much of me. But if I manage to get upwind from myself, ah, it smells like heaven. And hey! Thanks!"

"Thanks for what? Smelling like a dead skunk?"

"You're being too humble, Sam. A skunk wouldn't have a chance beside you. But really, thanks for putting up with me. Thanks for not throwing me overboard when I deserved it. Thanks for all you did to help out in Toronto. Thanks for being a friend, Sam, to a 'damn fool,' I think you called me." I fell silent.

Sam grinned and closed the door with a solid thump.

An hour later we ate a simple meal of bannock, rice and dried venison. A fresh pot of strong coffee, complete with a tin of hoarded evaporated milk, and a can of peaches for dessert made it a feast. I had a quick scrub off as Sam tended the bannock. Skin glowed pink from vigorous scrubbing. We lingered long over the meal, drinking too much coffee.

Finally, reluctantly, I pushed back from the table. "Guess I'll see what's left under the mud on those clothes out there. I've got more to change into, but I'll have to starve you a while longer to fit you into my pants."

"I suppose that leaves me with the dishes. With all that hot water you have coming out of a rock out there, how come there isn't any in the cabin?"

"Well, Sam. I was supposed to be roughing it when I came out here. I figured when I got the hot tub I'd have myself spoiled rotten and not get any work done. You know, it's funny nobody ever found that hot-spring before."

"Yeah, now you mention it, it is funny." Sam snorted. "There's a big hump of rock out there nobody noticed before either. I could have sworn I set a package there heavy enough to drag the chopper out of the sky. But all there is now is rock. Strange how the snow melts off it." Sam grumbled good-naturedly. "Ah well. I guess if a guy can have a hot bath, he'd better not complain too much about boiling water to wash dishes. I just wish we'd had the pot on an hour ago. It'd be ready now."

"Give a man five minutes in a hot tub and he thinks he should have champagne and caviar, with maid service too." I shook my head. "People just don't know how to fend for themselves these days. Such a shame."

I stood at the sink, lifted a raised knot free, and drew the tubing out of the hole. Turning the valve, I produced a stream that began to steam after a few seconds. With an exaggerated bow to Sam I said: "We try hard to keep our customers happy, Sir. Is there anything else you require?"

Sam shook his head and grinned. "Why'd you go to all the work of hiding it?"

"I'm just a strange bird, Sam. And I like surprises. I've read too many stories. I'm always looking for surprise endings.

"An uncle came up with the heat source. He died in an accident. But more and more I don't think it was an accident. With next to no visitors in a valley under a curse, a hot-spring isn't too long a shot to explain. And I like hot baths. It seemed like hot water in the cabin was more likely to raise questions. So, for an extra half day's work, the hot water's here, but out of sight. It seemed to make sense at the time."

With the helicopter unloaded and the jewelry moved into the storage cave I filled a box and handed it to Sam. "Buy all the fuel you can. It's not going to get any easier to come by. And I want you to bring all those supplies back from the barge. I've rented a place from Essar Steel Algoma. It's on Whitefish Bay."

"It's too much," Sam protested, opening a tiny case from the contents of the box and staring at a gold ring.

"It's too little." I groped for words. "You've been a friend. There's no price to put on that. Besides..." I grinned. "I want the use of that egg-beater a bit longer. And since the computer muck-up I feel another sermon brewing."

"God help me!" Sam burst out. "Get me another box then."

"The jewelry has buying power. It's not good for anything else. I didn't buy it for anything else."

"You knew this was coming. How?" Sam questioned.

"I thought something was coming." I paused for a moment. "I don't know what was God leading and what was me running away and hiding from life. Now I've got hot water in an isolated valley with enough food stored up that when some wild character flies in I can feed him. It really looks like God has set me up to rescue millions, doesn't it?"

It took Sam three trips to bring most of the supplies back from the barge. By the third trip he had drawn the attention of looters and not much remained to salvage. The supplies crowded the rented warehouse on Whitefish Bay.

After learning Sam had made the final delivery, I headed for the cave.

Chapter Sixteen

Only Fools

*I*t took me an hour the next morning to reach the cave entrance. Again, I carried the rifle. Again, I left it inside the tunnel descending from the entrance gallery. I made swift progress this time, reaching the bottom of the shaft quickly. Taking the second, nearly horizontal chamber, angling towards the north, I entered unexplored territory. I used the mobile LiDAR mapping system to track things, probably relying too much on the technology considering the scope of the recent computer muck-up. I followed a small stream that soon forced me down to a belly-crawl. It descended into a pond, shallow at one end.

Light is deceptive in caves. The reflection off the water makes depth hard to judge. One moment I was less than knee deep, the next moment over my head with a pack weighing me down. Three steps forward had my head above water again, but my confidence dashed. *You gotta be a special kind of fool to do this even in a group. Is there a word for idiots who try to do it alone? There must be a padded cell somewhere with my name on it.*

But fools don't give up easy. I was soaked and cold, but I dragged myself up the tunnel beyond the water. I could almost stand straight for most of it until it crossed a hump and descended into water again. I tested each footfall as I descended up to my neck. I ducked my face under the water to get a look ahead. I'd stirred up a bit of silt but could still see the bottom. That didn't fit cave-diving stories I had read. But this was bare rock with almost no sand or mud. I unfastened the clasps on my pack and shrugged it off. Dragging it behind me was a pain. But at least that way it wouldn't hold me on the bottom. The ceiling dipped until it offered just a glimpse of airspace above the water surface. "You come up in a panic and you bash your head," I muttered to myself. "Knock yourself senseless here and you end your caving career real fast."

Senseless? My mind mocked. *Don't you have to start with at least a bit of sense before you can lose it?*

It must have been ten metres across the water, trying to keep my nose and mouth above the surface, my helmet bumping the ceiling at times. Just once my head went under.

A quick climb led to another belly-crawl and then a plunge into a deep hole. Without the pack I could have crossed it in one push and glide. But the pack was dragging me down so I dropped it. A cloud of silt muddied this water as the pack disappeared from sight. It wasn't that big a deal, but I suddenly felt hungry with everything I had brought sealed in the pack somewhere below me.

The water cleared surprisingly fast, though it remained cloudy. The hole seemed to reach back beneath a hump of rock. As far as I could see from my position it was still descending steeply. I could not see the pack.

I let myself back into the water, stirring it as little as possible. The hole was no more than three metres across. As I drifted toward the centre, with my face and light underwater, the pack showed itself down four metres and under the overhanging hump of rock. Not a good place for a blind dive. You could be almost sure of bumping against the overhang while coming up. Since you were going to stir up all that soup, you'd be blind, with three wrong directions and one right one to choose from. The only way with some measure of safety was to leave the light at the surface, shining down toward the backpack.

I always thought I did okay swimming in a pool, but there is something different about doing it down in a hole in the ground. And hardly any pools take you down four metres or more. So you really never know what your ears can stand.

I would have to work by feel as soon I had stirred up the soup. The coil of rope on the outside of the pack had to be detached, then an end found and tied. The rest of it would float. Then I'd have to come up slow so I didn't smash against the rock. Enough light should show through the murk as soon as I cleared the bottom to show me which way to go.

In the few moments it took me to fix the light in place, my courage (or stupidity) almost failed. But I wasn't ready to give it up without a try. I clung to the side for a moment, breathing deeply, shivering, then ducked my face and kicked my way down.

Almost from the moment I reached the pack the cloud rose off the bottom and swirled around me. I closed my eyes against the grey-brown blindness, fighting panic as I fumbled with the rope. I felt one of the clasps release, then groped for an end as coils of rope seemed to writhe around me like snakes. Feeling short of air already I grabbed a coil and shoved it through one of the shoulder straps, twisting and fumbling to form some type of knot. Then I forced myself to let go of everything and allow my own buoyancy to raise me toward the surface again. I fought against the urge to scream as a coil of rope brushed against my neck, then my back bumped against rock. Opening my eyes now, I could see the light slanting down towards me, so pushed slightly down from the rock and then pulled for the top. It seemed to take forever before I broke surface, gasping and gulping air.

I grabbed a coil of rope and thrust across to the other side. Finding an underwater ledge I could stand on, I began pulling in the rope until I finally felt the weight of the pack. It bumped against the rock hump but swung out and beyond it without difficulty. I then climbed clear of the water and dragged the rope and pack up after me.

After I had coiled the rope and attached it again to my pack, I opened one of the waterproof pockets and downed a couple fistfuls of trail-mix, followed by a drink of water. I went over a hump of dry rock then and found myself facing a shaft. I marked the entrance with one of my popsicle sticks and then found a place to anchor the rope and lowered myself down. After reaching the bottom of the shaft, the tunnel began to twist and drop in a series of steep one- and two-metre steps. Easily navigated, a bit of loose rubble demanded caution. After descending 12 metres, the steps gave way to a smooth 50° incline, with little to grip. 26 metres of the rope, still attached inside the shaft had been bunched at the bottom. I also carried three more rolls of 100 metres each. It was a simple matter to toss the coil down the slope, clip into the rappelling harness, and descend smoothly, feeling backwards with each step. The slope ended abruptly, twisting and angling back toward the cliff-face. Where the direction changed, my feet reached into emptiness.

The cold was getting to me even though I was working hard and sometimes sweating. I had to lower myself over a ledge and hang from the rope until I found footing again. Another nine metres of steep drop brought me to a gentler slope where I could walk upright. Stooping occasionally to avoid low humps in the ceiling I continued to go deeper. A switchback turned the tunnel abruptly to the east. Water seeped from fissures in the roof and walls. Pools formed in the floor but fissures drained the overflow away. Low hanging humps forced me down on my belly at times, while seconds later I could stand and stretch without reaching the ceiling. The floor dipped and rose in the same tortured form, forcing me to put my face into the water at times to proceed. Holes through the fissured rock showed chambers on the other side. With my pack off I wriggled through.

Once I became wedged underwater. I fought against panic, forced myself to release my breath, collapsing my chest, then pushed backwards. A surge of adrenaline drew me forward a few centimetres, then back with a mighty thrust. My body shifted and slithered free. My face came clear of the water. I gulped air like a drowning man.

An hour later, hammer and chisel had widened one of the many small openings to 35 centimetres. Crawling through, I drew my pack behind me, then settled, a muddy, wet mess, at the base of a rock to rest. I ate a bit, then pulled out my journal. Finding a dry shelf of rock of convenient height, I used my pack as a cushion, leaned against it, and with a shaky hand, wrote:

Friday, May 29

The large caves I enjoy. There is a thrill, a sense of discovery. But wallowing on my belly through black water cold as the inside of a grave doesn't fit my idea of fun. I'm not sure why I keep going. Almost drowned an hour ago, stuck in a hollow, my face underwater. Maybe I'm just too stupid to be scared.

Every once in a while, I see something that seems to say: "Men have been here before." If you ask me to point to specific examples, I can't. That bothers me. But I feel like I'm called to go deeper.

"Called." That's a word Dad would have used. He wouldn't have been able to tell you what he meant, and I can't either.

If it was Indigenous people who were down here before me, and what bit of logic my brain can find in all this says it could only have been Indigenous, they were probably near naked, slimmer than me, and could have slipped through holes I can't manage. If all they wore were breechcloths at this temperature, they were tougher than I am.

I keep thinking of what is going on outside. I almost wish the Rapture was the explanation, although if it was and I'm still here, I'm in big trouble. But from what I've heard and read it doesn't fit.

It seems like time is running out. Time for what? I really can't say. But I feel driven.

I'm 237 metres above sea level, which puts me 32 metres above Lake Superior.

Through ten minutes of alternate crawling and walking, the folds in the rock took me up and down with little overall change in elevation. The sensation of damp air and open space seemed like a breath of spring after an endless winter. Turning a corner in the tunnel, my light reached into a large chamber. Water lapped four metres below me with just the faintest ripple.

My light was inadequate for the size of the chamber. I guessed it at six metres to the farther side and 30 metres to either end. Water covered almost the entire floor. A thin stream flowed from a crack three metres below me, splashing softly into the large reservoir. Switching my lamp to ultraviolet for a few seconds, scattered bits of amethyst gleamed softly with a cool purple and white sparkle. A narrow ledge worked down the face of the wall to join a two-metre strip of black gravel at the water's edge. As I leaned out the opening, my lights showed drawings on the wall above the ledge.

A cracked earthenware bowl rested in a shallow recess in the tunnel wall just short of the entrance to the chamber. Of unglazed clay, the bowl itself was not remarkable. A piece of bone supported some black twisted fibre. Fed through a hole bored in the bone, it intrigued me. I was sure it was a lamp. I guessed the wick was twisted flax. It might have been any kind of fibre. I knew the Inuit used somewhat similar lamps burning whale oil but had never heard of other First Nations people using them. I wished I had studied archeology. I didn't touch the lamp but took several pictures of it.

As I moved along the narrow ledge I found figures carved into the face of the rock wall. Slight splashes told me my light was stirring a response in the water. Remembering the large fish with its spines and teeth, I wasn't sure I wanted to be that close to the edge. However, the drawings and carvings continued along the shoreline.

A huge carved fish, jaws gaping, guarded a rift in the rock. I paused for a bit, surveyed the small enclosed lake, then shone my lights into the opening. The glitter of amethyst reflected light back to me.

The floor of the opening started a metre up the rock wall. Shaped like a lopsided egg, the hole reached almost two metres high by one wide. It ascended for a metre, then levelled out.

Dipping and rising, the tunnel meandered in a northeasterly direction with a gradual gain in elevation. In places I could stand freely. Sometimes I stooped. Sometimes I crawled. For three hours I saw little change, but my clothes had dried and I had warmed up. Where a swelling of the passage gave the illusion of space, I stopped for a brief rest. Drinking from my canteen and eating a few bites, I took a moment to carefully examine the walls. They were granite, with rusty streaks. A green patina over small nodules suggested copper. The compass was erratic, so there was probably other metal as well. I pressed on. My watch showed 4:32 p.m.

A twist in the chamber led to a long slow descent that I followed for most of an hour. Fine dry dust choked me. Weird, because from any research I'd done, dry dust is pretty rare underground. The descent abruptly changed to a tough climb. At the bottom of the descent, my instruments had shown me at 14 metres above the surface level of Lake-Superior. The climb levelled out at 31 metres above. As near as I could figure, I was five kilometres northeast of the cave entrance. Several gold streaks gleamed dully against my lights. And yes, I was fool enough to wonder if it was real gold. It didn't seem to flake away like fool's gold did but I couldn't break a big enough piece off the wall to hammer on it and see if it was soft. Twice, in sandy spots, I found the prints of naked human feet. Dust from untold years had dulled the prints but failed to hide them.

Running horizontal again, twisting back and forth, but tending in a northerly direction, the tunnel opened into a large chamber that fell away in a gentle slope to the north. From where I stood, I could see six tunnel openings. I marked the entrance before moving into the chamber.

Granite, rose quartz, and amethyst made this chamber something special. A stone hammer, several arrowheads, and a spear lay neatly on a rock shelf. The stiff and brittle remains of a leather bag sat inside one of the tunnel entrances. Two arrows and a clay pot sat beside it. Assuming the tools marked the entrance to the tunnel I should follow, I entered. It angled back to the southeast, rising gently. Twisting due east, it abruptly turned almost straight up, narrowing to a knife slit I could just slide through. A difficult six-metre climb brought me into another small chamber.

A trickle of water fed out of a crack half way up the south face. Sediment spread across two-thirds of the floor. Fractures bore the water away.

Several small pebbles littered the floor. Some showed a slight trail where they had rolled down the slope of the sediment bed. The telltale green yielded to the tapping of a hammer. The malleable metal spread and flattened. Not gold, but probably more useful. I had done enough research to know copper nuggets were even more rare than gold in its pure form, so wasn't sure if I believe what my senses tried to tell me.

No other openings would allow anything bigger than a rabbit. I lowered myself down the narrow passage again. At the entrance to the larger chamber, I gently spread the cracking pieces of dry leather from the bag I had earlier photographed. Stone arrowheads, lumps of hard stone, and nodules with a green patina showed.

Footprints could be seen in places on the chamber floor. Most of them were almost obscured by fine dust. Although the edges were poorly defined, I could make out three sets. One seemed somehow misshapen, with short dragging steps.

I had now spent many hours hunting. I had learned to tell if an animal was fresh or tired, whether it was running scared or leisurely. I had a distinct mental image of an exhausted old man supported by two friends, shuffling with his last remaining strength. That any man could fit the image, having negotiated the passage I had come down seemed as crazy as me being down here.

CHAPTER SEVENTEEN

STANDING IN THE FIRE

For the moment, I left the other openings unexplored. Instead, I followed the chamber as it descended slowly. Forming a lazy S-bend, the gallery at its widest spread five and a half metres. I could hear muted thunder, distant and subdued. It grew in volume as I followed the bend from north to east. The angle of descent became steeper. Two of the tunnels fed small streams of water into the chamber. It formed a gentle brook, narrowing and burbling as it dashed light-heartedly downward.

Finding a knob of rock to which I could secure a rope, I attached myself to the rappelling harness and moved carefully downward. After a three-metre vertical drop and a twist back to the north, I could feel mist blowing in my face. The thunder became deep and resonant. I could feel a tremor through my feet. A broken stairway of granite slabs took me down another five metres. The tiny stream splashed and sprayed as it broke over each small fall. An abrupt turn to the right, facing me almost due east again, brought me face to face with one of those things so cool there's no words for it. I thought of the book Dad had almost forced me to read. I had never admitted it to him, but I re-read it a couple of times. *Hind's Feet On High Places* has somebody named "Much Afraid" who describes a waterfall. It was my favourite part of a book already old before Dad was born. I'm probably stealing her words when I try to describe this one, although she was describing a waterfall out in full sunlight.

Spilling over a crest of rock way above, a long curve of purple caught and cast back my light. As it fell, the water seemed to suck up air and light, then separate into crystal droplets, dancing all the way down. It surged around the rocks, leaping, spinning, whirling and shouting with excitement. Then in a dizzying circle, taking another breath-taking plunge, it danced out of sight, into the very heart of the rock.

For a moment the wild excitement infected me. I wanted to jump in and abandon myself to such a wild plunge. I took picture after picture but knew somehow that much of what I was experiencing could not be seen or felt by another. The feeling was like coming home, being welcomed with loving arms. *That's a strange thought. How many years since there'd been a hug when I came home? Not since Mom got sick.*

I sat against the side of the chamber, gazed around me, then took out my journal. For long moments I held pen over paper. Finally I put it away. Dad was the writer, not me. He'd have found some way to put on paper what he was seeing and feeling. I was just too full, if that was the right word.

The faintest outlines of a drawing remained on the rock wall. It seemed to disappear behind the waterfall. I took repeated pictures with different colour filters, knowing some details might show up in the pictures that my eyes could not see. Although my digital camera was far behind technology at the time *The Virus* activated, some sense of the vaguely familiar kept me clicking the shutter.

My mind reached back to the legend Sam had told. Words that had shook me up then rang clear in my memory now.

The legend tells of a cave, old even at the time of this event. A painting on the wall shows a man. Beside the man, a creature comes out of the water. Many people shelter under the wings from a wild storm.

The reasons have been forgotten for unnumbered years, but the shamans teach that when the man is purified in the whirlpool, the lovers will show him a world so new that Michabo has not yet painted the sky blue or let an eagle's feather fall to the ground. They teach that the serpent still lurks in the dark waters and hates all sons of Edáyíné Nezqi.

My watch showed 7:21 p.m. I had breakfasted at 5:45 that morning. I ate a simple meal of dried venison, trail-mix, and a cup of instant coffee, heated over a tiny camp-stove. The chill was starting to penetrate my clothes again as I sat near the whirlpool.

With supper behind I removed a small spool of cable. Fitting a lens on one end, I attached the other to the adapter on the camera. Feeding the cable through the eyelets of a fishing rod I had carried collapsed in my pack, I lowered the lens as close as possible to the centre of the whirlpool. The strong tug of the water quickly drew line off the spool.

With the camera lying on the ground, the screen toward me, I watched the swirling images as the lens descended. At six metres down, repeated images of grey rock swept by, followed by white water. Dizziness threatened as I watched the whirling patterns on the tiny screen. A metre deeper, the whirling slowed, although the image jiggled constantly. As far as the light could penetrate, foam swirled in a deep pool. A slab of granite just beyond the lens was polished smooth. A dozen centimetres deeper, the lens lay still on the bottom, angled back toward the surface, showing nothing but frothing water.

I took many pictures but doubted I had captured much noteworthy. The one significant fact was that calm water lay seven metres down. A great deal of air was being carried down by the whirlpool. Seven metres was a survivable distance, one way. I didn't want to guess what it would do to my ears with the water pounding so hard. I also didn't try to guess how a guy might come back through it.

I reeled the lens back in. Then, as I knelt to anchor the tiny generator for my rechargeable batteries, a strange reflection seemed to come from behind the waterfall. Securing the rope through my rappelling harness, I felt my way against the slick wall behind the waterfall. Like a heavy rainfall the spray quickly soaked my clothing, yet after three metres the back wall receded. It reminded me of going under Niagara Falls.

The chamber before me sloped up toward the south, with a ceiling too low to allow me to stand. It was the drawings though, that caught my full attention.

I had to creep forward before the chamber opened sufficiently for me to see it all. Wiping the spray from my eyes I gazed at the picture spoken of in the legend. Rain struck the *EAGLE*. I couldn't call it anything else. Lightning split the sky. Two people, not the *many* of the legend as I had heard it, sheltered under the wings. To the left a hunter faced a deer with spear ready to throw. Lower down three figures stood together in a black and red base. On the chalky yellow surface the drawings showed flat and two dimensional, yet carried the stark realism of so much ancient art.[7]

I was no expert but the closeness of the legend to the reality made me wonder if not so many generations as supposed had passed since someone had gazed on these drawings. I took repeated pictures, then finally slipped back through the mist, spread my bedroll, stripped my wet clothes off, and lay wearily down. It took me a long time to warm up before I fell asleep.

Almost before I knew it, my alarm told me morning had come. In the endless darkness, there were no clues of time. The bats did not come this far into the cave. I washed my face and hands in the biting cold of the water. Breakfast, like supper, was dried venison and trail-mix. For an hour, I wrote in my journal. Then, leaving what supplies I could, I headed back to the surface.

My lights showed a narrow side chamber I had missed earlier. The dust seemed heavier here than in other places. If any footprints went into it, they were covered. I followed it for about a hundred metres, finding it descended gently as it twisted in a broad spiral. The dust grew steadily deeper and each footfall raised a puff. A break-down finally blocked me so I turned and went back to the main chamber.

---

[7] *See Appendix A, Image 6*

For long, weary hours I worked my way upwards. A flurry of bats passed me shortly before I reached the entrance to the cavern. Dusk was settling into night when I regained the rifle and moved into fresh outside air.

Muscles ached as I made breakfast and washed dishes the next morning. I listened to sporadic voices on the ham radio. Chaos had increased if that was possible. Looting, riot, and rape had become the norm. People bartered for what they could not steal, killed for what they could neither steal nor barter for. Cash was worth next to nothing, though people still got killed for it.

A couple of newspapers had found a way to roll presses. A radio station was back on the air, dramatizing the horror.

Sleep in my own bed was sweet. But an overwhelming sense of pain weighed on me. In the morning I stirred up the fire and set the coffee pot on to boil. After breakfast dishes were cleared, I inserted the memory card from my camera into the computer.

By 11 a.m. I had viewed more than 500 images. I sorted them in sequence. I put a caption with the time and estimated depth for each photograph underneath it. The drawing behind the waterfall, so easily identified as a picture of the *EAGLE*, absorbed me.

Tuesday June 9

As a slow morning crept toward noon, I began to sort and pack supplies. Dehydrated foods were ideal for spelunking. What a neat word that was. But dehydrated foods had crazy price tags even before the computer crash. Outfitters stores here at the back end of nowhere didn't carry much for caving either. I went with what I had. The afternoon saw two round trips to the entrance chamber. Securely rolled into 15-kilogram bundles, wrapped and waterproofed, I lowered them on rope to the bottom of the vertical shaft. At the bottom, a quick hard jerk slipped a loop out of the binding, releasing the rope. The second bundle snagged part way down. Trying to release it, the rope disengaged. I could hear the bundle bouncing and slapping against rock. Returning to the cabin, I prepared a third bundle. This one contained carefully protected fragile items. I prepared and ate a simple meal, then went to bed.

My watch showed 5:30 a.m. as I walked out the door. My pack this time was slightly less than 12 kilograms. Supplies for a lengthy underground stay were already at the bottom of the shaft. At the last second I shoved a container of pepper into the pack. Dried meat becomes tiresome after a while. I carried the notebook computer, extra batteries, a diving dry-suit, and other stuff. Mid-morning saw me at the bottom of the shaft, already feeling the strain. I took time for a cup of coffee and snack before going on.

Almost six kilometres of rugged tunnel lay between the whirlpool and me. Some of that had to be navigated on my belly while pushing a pack ahead of myself. Three round trips meant 36 kilometres. I wouldn't do it in one day.

It took five exhausting hours with the first pack. A hurried lunch and five hours later, I had returned for the second pack. I rested for an hour, jotted down some ideas in my journal, then slept. In the early morning I started out again. My legs felt like rubber when I reached the bottom of the shaft for the second time. I rolled out my bedroll and fell into it. Seven hours sleep and an unexciting meal let me face the new day with courage again. By 6 a.m. I was on my way.

Thursday, June 11

Carrying only 12 kilograms this time, I moved faster where there was room to stand upright. I finally reached the whirlpool at 11:00 a.m. After resting for an hour and eating another boring meal, I opened one pack. Carrying a cordless drill, anchors, and coils of rope, I moved cautiously around the whirlpool. The water had hollowed a bowl-shaped depression. Polished smooth and sloping slightly, the narrow edge was treacherous.

Drilling into minute fissures, I set anchors and tied myself as I moved farther around. By 4 p.m. I had 20 anchors set into the stone, each with an advertised test strength of 540 kilograms.

It took a number of trials before I spanned the central eddy of the whirlpool with six lengths of sturdy rope. Attached to four anchors, I plaited the bottom ropes together into one exceptionally strong one, then tied it off to anchors on the opposite side of the whirlpool. I did the same with the upper ropes, plaiting two together.

With a flimsy looking suspended bridge spanning the whirlpool, I gripped the top rope while walking on the bottom one. I moved out over the ravenous throat.

I lowered a heavy rock into the water, tied securely to 12 metres of rope. The suction pulled so strongly for a few seconds that I could hardly hold it. Then it passed through the throat and descended smoothly. The rope itself gave the current little to grip. I could feel the rock strike bottom. Marking the spot on the rope, I drew the rock back in, again fighting against the pull for the last metre. When measured, the depth showed 8.8 metres from the bottom of my rope bridge to the bottom of the whirlpool.

Longing to go deeper, I knew I was too tired. I took another look at the drawings in the chamber behind the waterfall, lingering for a half hour. Then, leaving everything possible in preparation for the next push, I turned back. At 11 p.m. I spread my bedroll at the bottom of the vertical shaft.

Friday, June 12

I still felt tired when I started out early the next morning. I sank into the chair in front of a cold hearth in the cabin at 1:00 p.m. Hunger and exhaustion competed, but I had made a dozen poor meals. After a short rest, hunger won.

A couple days later I left a note on the table:

Monday June 15

Hi Sam,

I've got some pictures I want to show you but haven't got them printed yet. It will be easier to show you on the computer.

You keep reminding me how crazy I am. So if I haven't made it back by the 30th, don't you be crazy too and get yourself in trouble trying to find me.

Roland

Fifteen days? What fairy-tales have you been reading? You can't eat enough calories when you're caving—even if you could carry that much.

With two lazy days behind me, I again stared with wonder at the whirlpool. It took two hours to plait together an eight-metre rope ladder. Every knot had to be tested and double tested. I hung two 20-kilogram rocks from the bottom. Plaited loops lay loosely over the bridge base rope and were tied securely back onto themselves. Attaching a rope to my own waist and securing a loop to the upper bridge rope, I hauled the clumsy ladder with its 40 kilograms of rock to the centre of the bridge. There I simply dumped it into the water, allowing it to unroll as the current took it down. The quick jerk almost pulled the bottom rope from beneath my feet.

The ladder caught much more of the force of the whirlpool. But the rocks, sitting solidly on the floor, stretched the ropes tight. Vibrating like the strings on a colossal guitar, the ladder showed no tendency to wind upon itself, though I was sure it had already done so as it descended.

Tuesday June 16

I sealed each pouch, then sent it down the whirlpool on 15-metre lengths of rope. I stripped in the cold air and donned my diving suit. I tried to eliminate anything extra that might catch the force of the water. I dipped the full-face shield in the water before putting it on, then secured it so tightly it made my head ache. I pulled the gloves on, then walked awkwardly sideways onto the bridge.

Drawing a sharp breath, I stepped down. As my feet entered the water, it seemed as if I was simply stepping into cold, coloured air. The foam had no substance. By the time my knees were wet though, I could feel a strong tug drawing me downward. As my shoulders entered the foam, it took all my strength to hold on. Yet, I could already feel the pull lessening at my feet.

With deliberate movements I took a deep breath and lowered myself one slow step at a time. A hurricane of icy water sought to tear me from the ladder. I held myself in close, making sure of each hand and foothold before I relinquished the grip the other hand or foot had on the ladder. At 16 rungs down, I no longer felt as if I were being physically torn from the ladder. But I was running out of air fast.

Close to the bottom, the current tried to sweep me to the east. Hanging onto the rope, I turned my lights to scan the polished bowl. Fine bubbles defined the current, sweeping in wide circles. Several pebbles, probably fragments from the rocks I had used to weight my rope and the ladder, tumbled awkwardly. The pressure on my ears felt like my head was ready to split.

Following the ropes from my packs, I allowed the current to carry me as I released my hold on the ladder. Brief moments later I broke surface in a spacious chamber. After a few minutes of drifting my feet touched bottom four metres from the tethered packages.

Water streamed from my suit and stained the sand dark grey. A wide sweeping curve formed my landing spot. Near the back, it appeared as though a reverse eddy had cut a second smaller chamber.

Wading back into the water I caught the ropes tethering the packs and dragged them to shore. Quickly checking the camera and computer, I found they had made the plunge without damage.

The ceiling here made an inverted bowl. It reached six metres high and spanned ten metres. A few splashes of purple hinted at amethyst. With ultraviolet light, a seam of limestone gleamed softly, while the amethyst came alive with an inner glow.

Water covered three-quarters of the floor. Foam boiled up at one end. The rock formation hid the whirlpool, sealing off most of its thunder. A quickening current showed at the opposite end where an abrupt narrowing carried the water flow around a curve and out of sight.

I stripped out of my diving suit, then dressed in more comfortable clothes. Walking the shoreline, two sets of footprints startled me. They *had* somehow been this deep.

The sand reached back only a metre or so. Grey rock rose from the floor, even as the ceiling bent down to meet it.

Charcoal etchings on the floor showed three scenes with a massive fish. The first showed two men pulling the fish from the water. The second showed the body of the fish opened. One of the men, perhaps a priest or shaman, seemed to be holding the heart raised in both hands. The third figure showed the heart of the fish, set on the chest of a man lying on a table. All three had the startling realism of so much ancient art.

As I moved on into the chamber, the sculpting work of water showed. Amethyst studded the walls with crystalline brilliance. The most striking feature was a broken pillar of granite. The top hung suspended as if it had descended like some massive piston. A pedestal rose off the floor, about three metres in diameter. Three stone columns rose from the pedestal. I estimated the centre figure at two metres tall, the outside figures at almost three.

I stood for long moments and stared. Blinking back tears I hurried to my packs and started blindly digging for my camera before I remembered I was carrying it on a strap around my neck.

I took many pictures, examining the formation from all angles. Rose quartz, amethyst, and black basalt gave back my light with an eerie living fire. The words Sam had used to relate the legend still resonated in my memory.

"... A maiden's voice mingled with the spirit song. She sang so beautiful the smoke forgot to rise. She ran to the rock. She stood in the fire, unburned, caught the hand of each of the men who loved her and lifted her voice to Edáyíné Nezqi.

"She sang of the joy and pain that she should be so loved. She asked the Spirit to take the three of them to the place beyond coupling and beyond parting.

"Thunder shouted again. The rocks shook and broke. The bay boiled. The fire flared up and surrounded the three. The rock they stood on sank. The maiden and her lovers sang, until they were seen no more."

If these stone columns weren't the three lovers, then the foolishness that had gotten me this far had obviously fried my brains. I would have bet a whole lot that the story of the rock sinking came from people seeing this rock formation rather than from any memory of actual lovers standing in the fire and sinking, but I liked the legend lots better than my wise, grown-up interpretation of it.

Reluctantly tearing my gaze away from the central feature, I looked long at a huge slab of fallen granite. As if cut from a quarry, a flat table rose a metre from the floor. The underside was rounded, curving in to touch the floor along a narrow band, adding to the illusion of a table.

A trickle of water spilled from a rent in the wall and filled a clear pool that bordered the slab on two sides. A blackened ring marked the floor in a precise circle.

A body lay on the stone slab. I had no training, but the worn, broken teeth gave an image of an old man. The right femur showed a discoloured line across it and a misshapen roughness that spoke of an improperly set break healing slowly, painfully. A few wisps of hair still clung to the scalp, as well as parchment thin remains of skin. Some of the tough, calloused skin of the hands and the soles of the feet was still visible as well, desiccated and a deep red-bronze. The man's right hand lay across his breast, grasping three copper plates. Two plates had fallen to the stone slab beside him. One could be seen in the clear water. All appeared to be covered with figures and drawings.

A spear with shaft of hammered copper and point of obsidian still had a keen edge. A clay pot sat beside the table. A black residue inside showed several small lumps. Without touching it, I took pictures. Minute figures covered the unglazed clay.

The body was not a war-like figure in spite of the spear and arrows. The spear looked too heavy to be an effective weapon in the hands of any but a giant, and this was no giant. It seemed more like a sceptre, although from what I remembered from the history high school teachers managed to make boring, sceptres were a kind of old-world symbolism and didn't belong in a burial outside of Europe and Asia.

I saw no masks, no idols, nothing to suggest religious rites. Nothing of added adornment altered the chamber. Yet a more majestic resting place would have been difficult to imagine. He was obviously someone of great status, at least in the eyes of those who laid his body here.

A little alcove off the small cave sheltered pointed stone tools beside a rough, unfinished copper plate and a cluster of copper nodules. A scattering of tiny curls of green gave the floor a strange colour.

Further exploration showed a narrow passage closed off by a break-down. A body lay trapped at the base of the rubble. One leg twisted at a crazy angle. A boulder trapped the other one. Broken fingers told the story of a desperate effort to clear the rubble. For a long moment I stared at the death-agony written in the floor of the passage.

It had to be the other end of the break-down I had found previously. Most likely, I supposed, the other man was buried somewhere under all that rock. I had seen a lot of dead bodies in Toronto but they are still creepy things to find.

I returned to the main burial chamber and examined the copper plates. One of them showed a crude drawing of the *EAGLE* coming out of the water. I couldn't even pretend any longer that the pictures were not of the *EAGLE*. The ancient drama was a snare and I was the rabbit—caught.

One plate showed three people standing in a fire, embracing, while water closed over their heads. I recognized it instantly from the legend Sam had repeated. Although flat and two-dimensional, it pictured the stone figures only a few metres from where I sat.

A third plate seemed to be a map. The burial chamber with just a hint of the stone figures showed. Below that, the minute outlines of the *EAGLE* rested in another cavern. What might have been a waterfall joined the two. Details were lacking. I was alone with my meagre understanding of ancient Indigenous culture. Under a mountain of rock, six kilometres northeast of the cabin, I would have to draw my own conclusions.

The other three plates were typical ancient art, hunting scenes executed in bold strokes of a sharp blade across the soft metal. A treasure in the truest sense, if they carried a message, I did not know how to read it.

Laying the plates on the ground, I took close-up pictures of each one, then a picture of the cluster. Almost reluctantly, I prepared to leave the burial chamber.

CHAPTER EIGHTEEN

GOING DEEPER

*B*ack at the water's edge I walked as far to the northeast as the narrowing shoreline would allow. Where the chamber narrowed into a falling tunnel again, the ripples became foam. No thunder sounded here, but the rushing of water brought its own rich melody.

Going back to my pack, I brought the coil of fibre-optic-cable, the notebook computer and the specialized lens. Interfacing the cable, the camera, and the computer, I fed the cable into the swift water.

The computer screen brought back a jumbled image that leaped and whirled like a class five rapid. The beauty of the computer was that it recorded still images at about five a second, even while the screen displayed the foaming chaos. Few of the images would be worth saving, but what my eyes could not pick out in the mad dance, the computer recorded, flash-frozen on disk. The computer also recorded pressure, temperature, and time, coding the information at the bottom of each image.

With 38 metres of cable out, the images calmed. Few details could be seen, but a widening of the channel became evident. Securing the cable and shutting off the light, I reviewed the passage down.

Most of the images showed nothing but surging water. A few glimpses of polished rock showed through streams of bubbles.

I had taken one-and-a-half hours examining a passage the lens had covered in eight minutes. Letting the lens drift with the current, I now waited a further ten minutes before the images began to show significant movement again. The computer seemed to indicate bubbles rising gently with the flow of water.

A vertical plunge added another 11 metres of depth before the lens found calm water again. Then a twisting rapids and another fall gained seven metres. I had 94 metres of cable out now; 56 metres remained on the spool. A shelf on which a man might rest became visible in the small cone the focus of my lens could see.

I sent one of my packs down on a rope. Knowing my lens was at the end of 94 metres of rope, I watched for the brightly coloured package to appear on the screen.

Wednesday, June 17

I prepared as good a meal as possible with the supplies I had, slept well, then reviewed the computer images once again. Calling myself a suicidal maniac and other, less flattering names, I changed back into my diving suit and bundled up the packs. I kept the tiny generator out. I lowered the packs on ropes measured to approach the ledge my camera had viewed. I tethered the generator to my boot by a half metre of cable. It was a pear-sized lump that looked suspiciously like a grenade, with a propeller inside a wire guard. I set it to recharge my headlamp battery even as I descended. With the ropes clipped through the rappelling harness I had donned over my diving suit, I stepped into the water and allowed the current to carry me down.

If exploring a cave alone is stupid, cave-diving alone is suicidal. But I'm nothing if not stubborn. Besides, I wasn't doing true cave-diving. These were sumps you could pass through on a single breath. A nagging voice in the back of my mind murmured that a fibre-optic cable with a finger-tip size lens wasn't the best authority on how far a guy could go on a single breath. But I wouldn't be this far underground if I hadn't become skilled at ignoring that voice.

Letting the harness take virtually all the strain, I kept my camera ready as I examined the walls where the current swept me close enough to see them. I could almost always keep my face in little air-pockets. As the current swirled around me, strong but manageable, it was pulling air-pockets along the way.

Fifteen minutes brought me to the widening of the channel where I had first stopped the fibre-optic cable. I breathed deeply as I allowed myself to drift slowly. The rock was surprisingly dark in this chamber. I wondered if it was volcanic. Not for the first time, I wished I was a geologist.

As the current picked up at the farther end and the ceiling lowered, I faced another sump, longer and deeper this time. There is a point of no return where you don't have enough air to go back but don't know what lies ahead. I had passed that before a gentle rise faced me. Clawing for the surface, my head slammed hard into a knob descending from the roof of the channel. My helmet protected my skull, but I felt the jar down my back. Disoriented for a few seconds and now desperate for air, I forced myself to be still and allow the current to move me forward. My back scraped along the tunnel roof, polished smooth by running water.

A deep sadness engulfed me. It wasn't supposed to end this way. *I'm sorry, Sam.* I spoke the words in my mind. *Don't—please don't try to find me. You're still needed up there.*

"And you're not?" The question sounded startlingly close, though I was sure it hadn't actually been spoken aloud. "Wasn't there a call? Don't you have a purpose?"

A call? I could feel consciousness fading, but the question demanded an answer, gave me a focus for a second or two longer. How do you tell between a "call" and a crazy imagination on overdrive? "Oh God, I'm sorry."

The inevitable happened as I knew it must. My breath went out in a great blast, followed by a desperate sucking in. Pain hit my chest with fists of iron. Then I was somehow gasping, gagging, coughing, dull rock ten centimetres above my head, but my mouth just clear of the surface.

There are times when a guy needs to stop and pray. I'm pretty sure that's true even for people who think they don't believe in God. My feet barely touched the floor and the slightest dip forward put my face under water again. I couldn't tell how far I had to go before I could find a place to rest. For a couple of moments I wasn't even sure which direction I should be going, but the current soon got at least that much through to my muddled brain.

I had somehow got hold of the rope again. It floated at the surface but stretched down-stream. With one hand keeping a grip on the rope I worked my way along the channel, the thin air space just allowing me to catch regular breaths. The ceiling dipped to the surface repeatedly, but almost never below it, letting me move as little as one metre at a time if I chose.

There's something wrong with a guy who doesn't have enough sense to be scared of something before he does it, then starts to shake and tremble after he's got away with it. Somebody should rewire his brain. I could hardly control the trembling by the time the chamber rose enough to let me get clear of the water. With the little generator still tethered to my ankle I dragged myself up. I sat there, huddled up and shaking.

"Well, God…" My teeth chattered as I tried to pray, although the diving suit had kept me surprisingly warm. "Don't know who said it, but we're supposed to try things only God can bail us out on. I guess this fits." I drew a long shuddering breath. "But Proverbs has a bunch of verses about not trying to straighten out a fool, 'cause it won't work. I seem to fit there too." I stared around the long, narrow chamber with water rushing across most of its floor, my light casting wild shadows as I turned my head. "Thanks again for keeping me alive."

I sat for long moments, but it took less nerve to go forward. My fingers still trembled as I forced myself back into the water again. A shallow dip followed by a gentle rise faced me, the flow of water doing all the work. A short vertical plunge, then a long rapid, brought me to another brief calm. Moving almost level now, strange gulping noises sounded at irregular intervals. Rising to the surface, lifting my face into small air pockets, I saw huge bubbles being slowly pushed by the current. Distorted by the pull of the water, they would bend and stretch, then break away to roll along the stone ceiling with a strange animal-like gurgling. For 10 minutes I moved easily, holding my breath for the few seconds from bubble to bubble. Then the current began to pick up again. Twisting rapids guided me swiftly down.

Slowing my descent with the rappelling rope, I still moved quickly. A vertical drop plunged me into the relative calm where my camera had shown a resting place. Gauges showed me 14 metres above Lake Superior surface, while almost 90 metres of rope fed deeper.

Opening a zipper in my suit, I removed a package of the ever-present trail mix and ate several handfuls. The cold was beginning to penetrate the insulation of my diving suit. I needed to keep moving unless I could get out of the water and change my clothes. Sealing the zipper again, I allowed myself to drift with the current until a strong undertow and swirling ripples warned me of another plunge.

The churning current didn't quite make a full whirlpool, but the pull of the rope, tight above and below me, held me against the wall as I reached the lip down which the water plunged.

"Do I do it again, God?" I could hardly hear my own voice above the sound of the water. "I can't stop here, but I've got to go in blind. Are You really leading me, or am I just plain stupid?"

I gripped hard against the rappelling harness, gulped a great breath of air, then let myself down fast, water surging around me. My feet smacked against a polished stone floor. A flurry of bubbles swirled outward in all directions. Ropes, barely visible through the bubbles, trailed off in three directions, all rising in a gentle curve. I followed one and surfaced in a chamber where my gauges showed me one metre above Lake Superior surface.

I found myself in a jagged circular dome. I guessed it at 100 metres across and 30 metres high. Foam boiled up around me, but a wall of rock totally concealed the waterfall.

Ducking my face below the surface and shining my light downward, I could see the floor dropping into inky blackness from where the waterfall had spit me out. I could not guess the depth. But a moving grey shadow suggested it might be time to move.

Taking care not to splash, I swam toward a narrow gravel beach. An upwelling of water alerted me. Turning my light downward, I saw eyes and huge jaws approaching. I had no weapons. The creature was in its own element. I was not.

In a split-second, thoughtless reaction, I held the camera button down. The strobe-light effect of the camera when the button was held down allowed for rapid sequence pictures. It drained the battery swiftly so I rarely used it. Now, coupled with light from my headlamp striking the eyes of a creature bred in the darkness of the cavern, it must have brought stabbing pain.

In that endless instant of frozen time, I saw pupils dilate, then constrict. Jaws clamped shut. I heard the clashing of rows of teeth. A mighty tail whipped. The creature turned and was gone. I spun in the roiling water, gasping and sputtering when I regained the surface. I didn't need urging to hurry to the shore.

A six-metre strip of naked rock bordered the steep wall of the chamber. Checking my compass, I found I was facing almost due north. I unhooked the small generator attached to my boot and laid it on bare rock.

I had let go of the rope when the fish came at me, but it floated bright and yellow just a couple metres out. The rock at the edge plunged so quickly that I had to swim, but was back on shore within seconds. My gaze searched for the other ropes as I pulled this one in. I could not see them. I dragged the pack a pace above what looked like a high-water mark before I opened it.

With my notebook computer, a number of instruments and a limited quantity of clothing and food I could function for a time even if the other packages were lost.

Already cold, I stripped out of the diving suit, then crouched at the water's edge for a frigid, splashing bath. Even there visions of great, gaping jaws added to my haste. Towelling myself dry, I shivered as I pulled on clean long underwear, jeans, and a shirt. I longed for a cup of coffee but the small camp stove was in another pack. Once again, I made a meal of dried venison and trail-mix. With food in my belly and warm clothing I soon stopped shivering.

I thought I could glimpse something yellow just below the surface near the far shore, although the storm of rising bubbles made it hard to be sure.

I walked the shoreline of this nearly round cavern. Several narrow passages led off from the sides. An easy half hour walk made a circuit of the lake. The rock shelf narrowed to almost nothing in places and widened to ten metres in others. Opposite the spot where I had left the water there was no shore. A slab of grey rock reached down into foaming water.

Sand filled several depressions in the wider areas. A few white and purple shells lay half buried. Dark purple and black shells of periwinkles gave a coarse texture to otherwise polished rock. They seemed to congregate along fissures where a different colour of rock showed.

The rock did not allow me a glimpse of the rope from the other side of the lake. I saw no outlet either. Several times the water welled up close to the shore where I walked.

As I returned to the first pack I searched for a fist-sized rock with cracks or grooves that would allow me to tie it into a loop of rope. Because I had tried to separate things so every pack had key survival items in it, I had fishhooks with me. But the collapsible rod was in one of the other packs. Still, I should be able to find a way to snag the rope, if that is what I was seeing.

It took a dozen throws, but I finally did snag the elusive yellow strand. Caught on something it refused to pull clear, so I walked the circumference of the lake again, trying from different angles. It was not until making almost the full circuit that I succeeded, and only then that I was sure it was a rope I had hooked.

A half hour later I had two packs together. Carrying supplies to where sand offered a more comfortable bed, I spread out a blanket. Most of my bedding was in the third pack. It was only 4:30, but I felt physically and emotionally drained.

Sleep did not come quickly. I was well dressed but the cold seeped up from beneath me. In the impenetrable darkness when I shut off my lights, the murmur of bubbles rising and bursting sounded like a monster's breath. The slight vibration from the nearby waterfall, surging down the tight throat of rock, seemed like the heartbeat of some primeval beast.

I dreamed of great jaws and gnashing teeth. Huge vacant eyes exploded before my lights. The fragments turned into slavering fangs, grinning in anticipation. I woke drenched with sweat. With a dry chuckle at my own foolishness, I sat up, grabbed my journal, and began to write.

Thursday, June 18

I wish I was the main character in one of Dad's books. Main characters are a special breed. They are experts in a half dozen disciplines. They carry the wisdom of an 80 year old in the body of an 18 year old. They have experienced great victories through great trials, have learned all the most important things. They can pick up a rock and tell you what the mineral composition is, what geological epoch it came from, where it fits in the evolutionary timetable (even if they don't believe in evolution – though that's something they're usually scared to admit). They know how it came to be deposited where their hand found it. They can look at a bone fragment and tell you instantly what animal it was from, giving the full Latin name, whether the animal was young or mature, how it died, and what the environment was like at the time it lived. A main character could have looked into the eyes of that monster fish and known how to defeat it.

Unfortunately I'm just me. I'm stupid enough to be in some hole way underground. I've done all the things that smart people don't do. Somehow, I've got away with it – for now.

Monday, June 22

On my computer I plotted the phases of the moon. One more of the many things I did not pretend to understand was the way it affected fishing. But not understanding was different from not respecting. I supposed it was an interaction of tidal forces and light. Only one of those factors could work down here. Under so much rock, even that was doubtful. The poorest time for fishing over the next several days should be from four to seven this morning. I had to enter the water, find the rope, and retrieve the other pack. Without it I only had sufficient supplies for two more days. That wouldn't even get me back to the surface.

I wished I had one of those armour suits that people almost as crazy as me wear while they try to film sharks in a feeding frenzy. I filled four small plastic bags with water and added half a teaspoon of pepper to each. I sealed the bags, then tied them to my waist and trailed them out around me on lengths of fishing line. Two of them had a small pocket of air added to float just above me. I stepped into the water. *It's a strange day when you add the spices before you enter the beast's dining room,* I mused darkly. *But you forgot the salt.* I sincerely hoped the computer was right and no fish would be hungry for the next couple of hours.

The camera strobe-light seemed to be my most effective weapon. I allowed the bags of pepper to trail around me as I swam toward the waterfall. As the turbulence built up, it would be impossible to feel the rush of water if the creature approached. *I sure hope that stuff has enough fire to make the beast decide I'm not fit to eat.* I paused at the face of the rock, drawing deep breaths into my lungs.

A sudden tug and snap charged my already tense body with adrenaline. I spun, the camera already flashing. But I could see nothing.

I had no choice but to go on. I willed myself to slow my breathing, filling and emptying my lungs several times. With the dizziness of hyperventilation threatening, I lowered my face into the water and swam down along the face of rock. I had gone four metres down through a storm of rising bubbles before the rock face curled back and let me move directly under the waterfall. My lights showed little but white foam against a black background. I followed the ropes I had already retrieved. They were still anchored way up the tunnel.

Hand over hand I went up the rope. As the channel narrowed, the driving force of falling water became more powerful. A pocket of air surprised me. Exhaling, I found I could not inhale. It was a low-pressure cup formed by falling water curling over a bump in the wall. More a vacuum than a pocket, it had tricked me. The mistake could easily prove fatal.

Relinquishing my hold, I allowed the water to plunge me to the bottom again. With a swift look around I allowed the pressure of falling water to overcome my buoyancy. The rope I sought was only three metres away, stretching the opposite direction from the other two.

Desperate for air, I thrust clear of the floor. 15 seconds later my head broke the surface.

Swimming slowly back to the face of the rock my chest heaved several times as I breathed deeply. With lungs full, I swam down again. Pushing against the current I moved into the down-flow from the waterfall. At the bottom, I looked again for the rope. Through the storm of bubbles, it was difficult to see but the brilliant yellow finally reflected my light back to me.

I crouched down, then thrust upward, reaching. The current swept me past my target point before it began to lessen. I gripped the rope two metres beyond where I had aimed. I attached a strand of heavy fishing line with a stiff hook pressed into the rope, then began a swift hand-over-hand pull against the current.

When the force of the waterfall was thrusting almost straight down on me again, I was nearing my limits for holding my breath. I released my hold on the rope while allowing the fishing line to play out easily. I let the water force me to the bottom. I thrust off and struck out for the surface.

Fifteen minutes later, with a slow steady pull, I had drawn the rope as far as the placement of the hook would allow. Securing it so I would not lose what I had gained, I entered the water again. Sliding one hand along the fishing line, I reached the rope in 30 seconds. It was just where the rock face curled back toward the waterfall. Bracing my legs against the rock, I pulled hand over hand on the rope until the need for air forced me to the surface. With a loop over my shoulder, I swam up to where a few lazy coils floated. Scrambling onto the shore, I continued to draw on the rope. It came slowly against strong resistance. Then, caught in the turbulence of the waterfall, it was hurled out towards me. With a sigh, I backed onto the dry rock and slowly coiled the rope, drawing the third pack with it.

At 5:42 a.m. I entered the water one more time. With a wire trailing from my tiny generator, I carried it to the lip of rock where the surging current from the waterfall flowed. Playing with the positioning for a few seconds until it was spinning rapidly, I attached it. I trailed a wire as I returned to shore, then thankfully stripped off the diving suit and dressed.

With the generator recharging battery packs and allowing for uninterrupted light, I turned my attention to a welcome cup of coffee. While it brewed, I checked a number of fishing lures. I attached a small, luminous worm, hoping for an eating size fish, not bragging rights.

This was supposed to be the poorest time for fishing according to phases of the moon. But now that I was no longer the bait it seemed worth a try. I watched with wonder as several small fish flitted toward the worm, glowing as it sank.

On only the second cast, a jerk that was almost too much for the collapsible rod I had brought started me on a 10-minute battle. My arms and shoulders ached before I brought this one to the edge. It was a deep grey-green, slightly iridescent, with bony spines forming a jagged saw-tooth back. I thought it was the same kind as the one in the upper lake. Nearly a metre long and weighing 10 or 12 kilograms, this was more fish than I was looking for. As I reached to grasp it by the gill slits, the gasping mouth opened and snapped shut, narrowly missing me. I shook my head with wonder and respect. I would have released it, but those powerful jaws and wicked teeth made sticking my hand inside the mouth to remove the hook very uninviting.

Laying my knife against my left hand where it gripped the gill slits, I paused for a second, then thrust up and forward, seeking the brain. The struggle lasted for 15 seconds. I grasped the knife handle with both hands, pinning the fish to the ground. The tail whipped. The teeth gnashed. In its dying seconds, the fish fought with astonishing strength.

I took several pictures, then scratched out a rough sketch.[8] It was difficult to compare with the gaping jaws I had stared into when I had entered the lake. But even at this size you wanted full body armour.

I gutted and cleaned the fish, carefully preserving the jelly-like oil from the swim bladder. I fried the largest fillet I could fit on my small camp stove.

After eating my fill, I cut the remaining meat in thin strips and laid it on the cold rock. I had no ability to smoke it or preserve it in any way. I knew much of the meat would inevitably be wasted. It seemed too noble a creature to end its life as rotting strips on a rock.

By Sunday morning, June 28th, I had thoroughly explored the cavern, including many small recesses and tunnels running off in different directions. The LiDAR system had mapped it. The remaining strips of fish stunk. I peeled them off the rock and tossed them into the water. A flurry of activity testified that the over-ripe state did not deter at least some of the fish in this lake.

With my supplies again bundled and tied flat against my chest, I entered the water when the computer again said fishing would be poorest.

I knew this first stint would stretch me to my absolute limits, but I'd been practicing holding my breath and running, though I could only take a dozen paces in either direction. I'd been ten days down here now. If there's a Hall of Fame for idiots, somebody should be nominating me.

Climbing against vertically falling water was incredibly difficult. Three times I found small air pockets. I would tie off to the rope and rest

---

8 *See Appendix A, Image 7*

my hands for a few moments. Then I would fill my lungs again and climb hard and fast, knowing I couldn't keep this up for long. It was only moments, but my hands, arms, shoulders and chest all ached when my head cleared the water as it started the final plunge into the lake. I couldn't rest yet, there was another two metres of steeply falling water before a level shelf where I could anchor my feet.

My whole body trembled when I got there. My fingers felt like claws. I could not fully open them. The muscles in my arms quivered.

I tried to rest, but the floor here was polished smooth and the pull of the current threatened to sweep my feet out from under me.

My fingers could not gain a purchase on the rope to advance farther so I clumsily gripped with my arms and wrists, and slowly gained a bit at a time. After a few more metres the tunnel levelled out. It remained narrow and swift, with no place I could get out of the water. Tying myself off with fingers that seemed unable to do the simplest task proved a struggle, but I could finally trust myself fully to the rope and give muscles a much needed break. Fifteen minutes rest saw me able to fully flex and open my fingers again. The discomfort of the current pulling me against the rope had become a motivation to move.

A fairly gentle but steady slope led upwards to the next major obstacle, a short squeeze against surging water.

Food was dangerously low when I stood in the burial chamber 22 hours later. My physical exhaustion was well into the danger level, especially with the climb still ahead. I slept, but dreamed of monster fish and waterfalls and woke sweating and gasping for breath.

I ate my remaining food, left all possible supplies below the whirlpool and then tackled the short, but wild climb against the force of the water. The trembling weakness of my arms and legs as I emerged at the top of my rope ladder disgusted me. I had thought I was stronger than this. Six hours later I staggered from the entrance hole, the darkness of a northern Ontario night seemed brilliant after several days underground.

CHAPTER NINETEEN

THE LEGEND RE-TOLD

Tuesday, June 30

Properly seasoned meat plus bannock cooked in bacon grease, all followed by a hot bath seemed unimaginable luxury. Listening on the ham radio, I caught up on the situation outside.

Cooking fires continued to burn in back alleys. Improvised stoves had been built. Lines outside soup kitchens remained long. A few places had electricity again.

Hospitals, stripped of most of their sophisticated diagnostic and treatment tools, had found ways to provide basic care.

Fewer and fewer vehicles rolled the streets. Fuel rationing sought to stretch the meagre supplies where local leaders held nominal authority.

There were things working, computers that functioned and areas where technology still did what it had always done, but in little pockets.

Leaders, some good, some bad, had emerged. But with the media crippled, no single individual had gained control. I heard one name repeated several times. *Nassir Felipe*. Something in me reacted with vague disquiet.

I finally turned off the radio. With a sigh, I stretched out on my bunk. The next thing I knew, brilliant sunlight poured though the cabin window, but the chill had wakened me. I'd slept through the afternoon and night and the fire had gone out.

I puttered for a couple hours, muscles aching at even little tasks. A good meal, followed by time spent reading, found me yawning widely in the early afternoon. The days in the cave had taken more out of me than I had realized. I went to bed early and slept soundly. I woke to a moaning wind and dull sky in the early morning. My arms and shoulders remained stiff.

The thumping of helicopter blades broke through a keening wind about noon. A weary smile marked Sam's face as he stepped down. Waves slapped the canoe, rocking it dangerously. "You've been away awhile. No smoke last couple of times I've flown over." He settled into the canoe and glanced around the valley. "Wish I had a place like this where I could hide." He spoke loudly over the sighing wind and slapping water. "Are they ever going to put this world back together again?"

"I guess it depends on who *they* are," I answered. We maneuvered the canoe around the helicopter, fishing out the ropes anchored to the rock. With the struts firmly tied down, I spoke again.

"I kind of like this valley just the way it was before man's interfering hands made too many changes. Why don't you stay? There's more than enough room."

"And put up with you and your preaching?" Sam asked, half mocking.

"Well," I responded. "There's the storage cave. Nothing left of the cabin that used to be there, but lots of room inside."

"Think I'll pass," Sam told me. "Holes in the rock might suit you okay. That where you've been? I want to see the sky."

The canoe wallowed uneasily in the rough water, spray wetting both of us. "You're pretty long in the face today, Sam," I observed as I paddled. "Must be you miss my cooking."

"Ha! That's what scares me. Kind of like looking forward to a firing squad. You know, if you turned this tub a little to the right, we might make it to shore without drowning." Spray washed over the side.

I clapped Sam on the back, rolling the canoe sluggishly. A wave spilled over the side. "I know it's only June, but you were due for a bath." I dipped the paddle deeply, swung the canoe around and guided it deftly to the shore.

The wind moaned and wailed. Scudding clouds raced across a grey sky. "Do you always bring such weather with you?" I asked.

A rabbit roasted in the oven. I had started sourdough bread in the early morning. The yeasty smell filled the cabin. While a pot of rice cooked, I shaped a loaf and then prepared a salad of wild greens. A pot of coffee simmered at the back of the stove, adding its pungent richness to the sweet air.

Sam sniffed appreciatively. "It almost smells like a man could eat and survive," he said.

"Don't trust your nose, Sam. It's led you into trouble more than once before this. Now if you'd move your brown hide, I could put this food on the table."

Sam growled back. "I like my brown hide. I've seen you with your shirt off. You're the colour of a real man on your face, neck and arms. The rest of you's the colour of a fish's belly. So what's that make you? One-quarter of a man?"

Over the meal, Sam chatted about happenings outside. "Our people are going back to the old ways. Many of the younger ones have little experience hunting, but they're learning fast. There've been a couple knife fights, a couple shootings, but alcohol has dried up. Government cheques have stopped. A rifle in hand puts some back-bone into these young bucks who have sat too long with a pack of cards and a bottle." Sam paused while he chewed a piece of meat off a leg bone. "You know what, Roland? It's good." The wind wailed around the cabin. The glass rattled in the window. A gust of smoke and ashes blew in from a downdraft at the fireplace.

"It STINKS!" Sam's voice exploded, then dropped again. "It shouldn't take this to make men of First-Nations people. But all the white-man's garbage has been taken away. We have to be Indian again. And it's good!" he snorted. "This computer virus has made hell in every city, but it's been hell for the us ever since white-men came. You know what? I hope they never get it fixed." Rain spattered against the windows.

Sam's voice became low, reflective, sad. "You found me swilling beer in the corner of a café. I had worked hard to be part of the white-man's world. I was ashamed to be Indian. I thought it was a curse. White men would pretend they didn't see the colour of my skin, but they couldn't see past it. A college degree, a helicopter license, owning my own business, it all meant nothing. I was still a shiftless, drunken, good-for-nothing Indian.

"I'd had two beers when you found me. I'd taken an hour to drink them because I had no money." Sam spoke through clenched teeth. "Charlie and his big mouth. I wasn't drunk. I wanted to put a knife in his gut and yours! Instead I took your money, flew you in here. I almost wanted to believe in the serpent. I'd already seen what the mudslide could do. I planned to celebrate with my bills paid and a full bottle of whiskey." A long sigh escaped him. Light, then shadow played across the window as a break in the clouds let a flash of sunlight knife through. "It's strange. I learned that under that fish-belly skin of a half-grown kid was more of a man than can be easily found on the reserve. That made me hate you. Still makes me hate you sometimes. A real man and a... a friend should have a few more years behind him and real red-man's blood in his veins." A pulsing flash lit up the room. The crash and receding rumble of thunder cut across Sam's voice.

We felt trembling through the floor. Cups on the shelf vibrated. A swelling rumble, like a huge cat purring outside the door, blended with the drumming of rain on the roof. The smells of wet wood and baking bread mingled. The trembling grew to a throbbing vibration. Lightning flashed again. Thunder echoed and reechoed. Loud, but almost lost in the other storm noises, waves broke against the rocks. The vibration stilled.

Sam spoke in a hushed whisper. "The mud slide! Or is it the Serpent?" His voice was barely audible over the drumming rain and crackle of the fire. "It's been years since I've felt it, years since I've been this close." He bit his bottom lip, then went on. "Every drop of blood in me remembers the legend, the curse and the promise. What does it mean?"

I stared at the smoke swirling in the fireplace. "The legend fascinates me, Sam. There's something about that mudslide... It's dangerous to give a guy with too much imagination a legend to chew on. It's even more dangerous when you let him see bits and pieces of the reality.

"I think I'm too much like Dad. He was a writer. They're a strange breed, Sam. I'm doing more of it all the time, though I can't imagine any publisher paying for my work." I pushed back my chair and paced in the small cabin. "We try to convince ourselves we're creative. But you look at our heroes and villains and it's like we're walking through a hall of mirrors at some fair. We don't go to psychiatrists because we're always spilling our guts on paper. Our villains have all our faults, plus the ones we'd have if we dared. Our heroes have all our strengths, plus the ones we'd have if we had the guts. Good and bad, they are a picture of us, bigger than life, more exciting than life.

"We make good soldiers, policemen, firefighters, not because we're braver than most, but because we've read and written so many stories and in the last chapter the good guy always wins. Of course, we are the good guys. We think we're invulnerable.

"We don't really believe that in our heads. We're not quite that dumb. But in our gut we believe it, act as if it was true.

"We like to call it courage. Lack of sense might be more accurate." I mused for a while, then continued. "I've been underground, Sam. You wouldn't believe what I've seen. I need to learn more about the legend. I'd like to talk to some of the elders of your people."

Heavy driving rain continued to fall. Distant thunder grumbled. Gusts shook the door and rattled the window.

Four hours later the helicopter beat its way across a grey sky. Ten minutes into the flight, Sam pointed out a doe with two half grown fawns bedded down in a small clearing. "You would do the old man honour if you took a gift," he shouted. "My rifle is behind you. Shoot the doe. The fawns are weaned."

"I don't have treaty rights. I'm the colour of a fish's belly, remember. It's out of season for me." I shouted back over the roar of the helicopter. "Besides, I hate to kill a doe when the fawns are still running with her."

"I'm not talking about the doe or the fawns," Sam responded. "I'm talking about coming to an elder like he is an elder. He probably won't remember the last time it ever happened. Most of the old ways are forgotten. But it's never a mistake to show respect."

"But shooting from the chopper isn't hunting. Won't that cheapen the gift? If I show no respect for the deer, can the meat show respect to the old man?"

"I think you're more First Nations than I am," Sam muttered, a slow grin splitting his face. Raising his voice again he shouted. "You're wearing your knife. Jump! It's not quite the old way, but if you're looking for honour..." His voice trailed away.

I stared at him, astonished, then grinned and nodded. It's a good thing I didn't have more time to think. I swung the door back as the helicopter dipped toward the small clearing. The doe rose uncertainly. The fawns danced nervously.

"Either you're insane or I am." The words escaped as a rush of adrenaline surged through my body in the second before I plunged the last four metres. The doe sprang on coiled steel springs. My breath went out in a grunt as I slammed into the fragile looking animal, smashing it to the ground. An arm grasped the slender neck, gripping fiercely as I fought to drag air into my lungs. The deer struggled to its feet. I slid around under the brisket, my right hand groping for the knife on my belt. Pain exploded through my chest and side as I sucked a lungful of air. A sharp hoof caught my shin. My hand gripped the cool wood of the knife handle as the deer flung itself sideways, trying desperately to break free from me. Twisting my wrist awkwardly to bring the cutting edge of the blade against the throat, scant centimetres from my left upper arm, I slashed hard, then released my hold.

Four sharp hooves pummelled my body as the deer leaped clear of me. Vaguely conscious of the knife in my hand, I rolled painfully over onto my stomach, then dragged myself to my hands and knees. With eyes closed and head slumped toward the ground, I drew several long painful breaths, then forced myself to my feet.

Staggering a little, I followed the blood trail. The knife had done its work. The doe had made three great jumps before collapsing. Her eyes were already beginning to film over as I approached.

I knelt and laid my hand on the side of the deer's head. A shudder went through the animal. *One thing about killing the First Nations way,* I mused silently, *you can't hide from the death of the animal.* I spoke softly. "I hope there was more honour in that than it felt like. If I was Indigenous, I would ask your pardon for killing you. I would thank you for feeding those I love." I paused as I drew in a shuddering breath. "I'm not Indigenous, but I still ask your pardon. I ask the God who created you for pardon."

I vaguely sensed Sam's approach. I don't know how he got the chopper on the ground so fast. "Remind me to think before I listen to you next time, Sam." A worn smile played across my face as I rose painfully to my feet.

With Sam's help, it took 20 minutes to dress the deer and load it in the helicopter. With no water close to wash with, we wiped ourselves clean with grass as well as possible.

Sam sat with his hand on the ignition switch. Without looking at me, he spoke softly. "Under the old ways there would be a naming ceremony. Shamans would come together. The story would be told. Every bruise on your body would be celebrated. The words I heard you whisper as you knelt by that deer would not be lost for ten generations."

The big motor came to roaring life. I leaned back in my seat, the ache in my side radiating out through my body. A great weariness weighed on me. I heard Sam's words as if from a far distance. The smell of blood filled my nostrils. Clear eyes, fading, glazing, filled my vision. A fly buzzed around my head, lighting on my left arm and flitting away over and over.

Sam set the helicopter down on a shingled beach near an old, weathered cabin. I stripped off my shirt and splashed cold water over my face and chest. Gasping and sputtering, I flushed blood and grime away. I thrust my shirt into the water and scrubbed it vigorously, taking most of the bloodstains and hair out of it, then pulled it over my head again.

A brown weathered face with squinting eyes peered out the door of an old cabin. I guessed the cabin at a century. The man at the door looked like he might be grandfather to the builder.

"Mingnen." Sam spoke loudly. "Have you got room for fresh meat?" A broad smile cracked the ancient lines as the old man looked at the deer I carried.

"I brought you a crazy man. He's got old ideas for a young buck with white man's blood. He wouldn't shoot this deer from the helicopter. He thought that would dishonour the deer and you." Sam grinned broadly. "That knife on his belt... He was dragging his heels under the deer's belly before he managed to get it into its throat. It's a story that deserves telling the old way.

"You've heard about the crazy white-man living in the Snake Pit valley." Sam continued. "This is him. Name is Roland Handson. Roland, this is Mingnen Kiona." Sam turned his attention back to the old man. "He wanted to talk with someone older and smarter than me. After jumping out of the helicopter, I figure he needs all the smarts he can get."

Water dripped off me as the old man invited us inside. "Don'tcha worry none 'bout water. Been worse on this 'ere floor.

"Sam took me up once in that flyin' conterr-raption of his'n. Never thought huntin' from up there was fair-like t'animals. But if'n ya gots to jump out an' cut their throats, I spect that evens t'odds considerable. Hardly never heard of no white mans who cared two licks 'bout being fair t'animals." The cracked voice rose in wonder at the end. "I spect ya gots Red Man's blood in youse somewheres."

The old man fumbled at the stove for a moment. "Yeah'll have a coffee." It was a statement, not a question. "Ain't got no beer. Never travels well back to these parts. The bottles're always empty afore I makes it home. Cain't figure that." His voice cackled with brittle laughter. Setting the pot on the stove, he turned to Sam. "Got any baccy young feller?" he asked.

"I've got a little bit, Grandfather." Sam pulled a pack from his breast pocket. "Roland's been trying to cure me of all my bad habits and get me converted both. But I still like a puff now and then. He might have some real man's blood in him somewhere. I've wondered that myself. But he's sure enough a full-blooded preacher man."

After contentedly drawing on the cigarette for a long moment, the old man spoke up. "Ya say something 'bout a snake pit? Reminds me of a story I heard as a young pup. Course t'was told in the old tongue, round a fire, with smoke in yer eyes." He puffed appreciatively. "Smoke wasn't t'kind to rot yer gizzard like this, though we liked our baccy then too.

"Seems there was this valley. Ever time it rained the mud would go down like a snake on hot bear's grease. But it never filled the valley."

Sam caught my eye with a grin, then settled back in his chair to listen. I too tried to make myself comfortable.

"Story was old afore my Grandfather's Grandfather could tell a rabbit's track from a bear's. That serpent's trail is older than the memory of my people, but it never gets past a ring of rock ya sees under the water. Did I already tell ya that?" Without waiting for a response he went on.

"It was a place strong medicine was made. Two warriors was addled with the same maid. It weren't their way to kill one another, 'cause they both honoured the strength and courage of t'other. They weren't like white mens, no more'n some red folks neither. They tested their skill hunt'n the bear and the moose. They cut the ice and brought the purple fire rock from the deeps. They asked the Turtle and the Hawk to show 'em. They prayed to Michabo and to Edáyíné Nezqi. They didn't know he was the white man's Manito, cause there weren't no white man's then. They sung their spirit song on a rock that shadowed Snake Pit from Morning-Sun. They got the most strongest shamans from all the tribes. The smoke from their fire drifted across Snake Pit.

"Thunder shouted from a clear sky. There weren't no storm clouds.

"A maid's voice mingled with the spirit song. She sung so wonderful the smoke forgot ta rise. She run ta the rock. Her hair was black as a raven's wing. Morning-Sun near fell outta the sky fer a closer look at her.

She stood in the fire—unburned—caught the hand of each of the men what loved her and lifted her voice ta Edáyíné Nezqi.

"In a strange tongue she sung of the joy and pain that she should be so loved. She asked the Manito ta take the three of them ta the place beyond coupling an' beyond parting."

The old man chuckled. "Fer a woman like that I might stand in the fire too. But she'd probably take one look at my wrinkled old face and die of fright. Now, where was I? Oh ya.

"Thunder shouted again. The rocks broke apart like egg shells. The bay boiled like stew on a white-man's fire what was too big an' hot. (That weren't the way my grandfather told it.) The fire flared up an' surrounded the three lovers. The rock they stood on sunk. The maid an' her lovers sung —till they wasn't seen no more.

"Some of our people still say ya can hear the maid sing on a windy day. Some still say it was their love was the strength of the curse. A love great as theirs may receive the same reward. A selfish or shameful love will find a god-awful death an' grave. Animals in the shadowlands will fear an' hate the hunter. The bow will break. The arrow an' spear won't fly true. Wood will be wet an' flint won't light a fire. Hunger an' disgrace will walk with the hunter always.

"Seems there's somewhat more ta the story, though how it fits I never could tell.

"They tell of a cave. A painting on the wall using charcoal, chalk, an' blood shows a man. Beside the man, a critter's coming outta the water. Many people shelter under the wings from a wild blow.

"The reason's been forgot for unnumbered winters, but the shamans teach that when the man is purified in the whirlpool the lovers will show him a world so new that Michabo ain't yet painted the sky blue or let a eagle's feather fall. They tell that the serpent still hides in the dark waters an' hates all sons of Edáyíné Nezqi." He paused for a long moment.

"I believed it once. So I did. But I's a old man now an' the world's changed. Shamans get their vision outta a brown bottle now, stead of fasting an' going alone into the wilderness. White man's bought us for a stinking brown bottle—an' we was stupid 'nough ta take the price.

"Was better in my Grandfather's day. I wouldn't have lived so long then. Wouldn't have seed our people lose their pride. I'd of died out on the trail, with a rifle in my hands—way a man otta die. 'stead, till just a bit ago I gets my cheque every month. Don't matter if I'm a man or not.

"I'm First Nations! Times I'm shamed ta say it. Same as you should be shamed ta be a white man. Still, these ears itch ta hear the old stories even if I can't make myself believe them no more." The voice, weathered and cracked as the face, fell silent.

I leaned forward in my chair, wincing at the pain in my side. "Father. Do I dare to call you father when there isn't a drop of First Nations blood in my veins? Have you ever seen a picture of the creature coming out of the water? Do you have any idea what it looks like?" The earnestness in my voice seemed to grip the man.

"Well, now you ask, I misremember that I ever did. Still, seems there's a picture stuck atween these old leather ears. An' it's not like any fish you ever saw, leastwise in these parts. Shaped weird it is, with a tail at the point and the head making a bump across the big flat front. Now as ta why I got that picture in this thick old skull, I couldn't tell if you lit a fire under me an' put a gun ta me both."

There was a long spell of thoughtful silence. The old man rocked slowly in his straight-backed wooden chair. I chewed on my lip, frowning. Sam waited with a hunter's sure patience.

Slowly, hesitantly, I reached for the notebook computer. I unlatched and opened it, reached for the switch, then stopped. I turned to Sam and then the old man, searching their eyes. A sigh escaped, somehow combining decision, resignation, and relief. I punched the switch.

Sam's posture didn't change, but his eyes came suddenly fully alive. Like a hunter with game in sight, he sat poised. The old man watched with idle curiosity.

"I want to show you something." I spoke into the quietness. "I told Sam I had been underground. I've got some pictures—from inside a cave.

"A bear led me to the cave. Well, 'led' is probably the wrong word.

He'd just come out of hibernation and wasn't in a good mood. First time I met him I didn't have the rifle with me. I got back to the cabin, but he'd set his sights on a fish-fry. When he shoved his hairy mug through the window, I answered with buckshot.

"The next day he was stalking me. Four shots with the rifle, as near misses as I could make, and he finally got the message. He high-tailed it straight up the ridge. I haven't seen him since.

"I followed his back-trail." A picture on the computer screen showed the rent in the rock face, then I advanced to the mat of black hair within the chamber.

"As soon as I could I explored deeper." I showed a quick sequence of the shaft and the fish in the first enclosed lake I had found. "That fellow scared me half to death. I broke the bulb on my lamp when I jumped back. Nearly broke my neck at the same time. It was so stiff and sore I had a time making it home.

"I messed up my hands pretty good when I jumped back from that monster. The gravel was awful sharp. While they healed, I went to Toronto to take care of some things. I got back in time to learn about this computer virus that has made such a mess. It was a while before I got underground again."

Pictures showed the passage to the whirlpool. "The legend talked about the man 'being purified in the whirlpool,'" I spoke again. "I can't help wondering if this is the one it means." I returned to the image of the whirlpool taken from above. "The legend spoke of a drawing." I paused for a moment. "There's a chamber behind the waterfall." I then brought up images of the drawings.

The old man's laughter cackled: "An' I said I didn't believe. More fool me."

"These are taken below the whirlpool," I said. The image then switched to footprints. I allowed the pictures to tell their own story. Both men had more experience hunting than I did. Then I showed the carvings in the sloped floor.

The picture of the stone figures brought breathless silence. I waited for a moment, then showed several views of the same rock formation.

"The addled lovers. So they's real too." The voice, abnormally high, cracked in a hoarse whisper. "An' if they ain't standing in the fire, it sure enough looks hotter'n hell."

I continued, showing the burial slab. A close-up showed the fracture in the leg-bone. I also showed the copper plates and the weapons. When a close-up showed the worn teeth, the old man found his voice.

"He went there ta die. He knew his time had come an' that was where he wanted ta be. But how could he manage? He had ta get through the whirlpool." His voice died into mutterings.

"I think these next pictures will answer your questions, Father." I spoke the word this time with almost no awareness. "I don't think he came down the whirlpool." I showed the body at the rubble from the cave-in.

"Hell of a way to die, that is," the old man muttered.

"I didn't think I could feel much more after the rescue work in Toronto," I confessed. "But that guy got to me. His companion must still be under there. I found the other end of the cave-in. Break-down is the word they use in caving books."

During the long silence they each sipped their coffee, then I clicked on the computer once again. "I'm not sure how significant the rest of this is," I said. "But you've seen this much. You might as well see it all." A series of pictures took them down rapids and waterfalls, and suddenly had them staring into the maw of a great fish. "Now if I could make somebody believe that one, I'd be doing something." I said with a grin. "That old boy was hungry and I was on the menu. Guess the flash must have been like an explosion inside his head. If you'd lived forever in absolute darkness, can you imagine how your eyes would hurt if somebody fired off a camera right in your face?" I shook my head, grinning. "He came at me once more when I had to go into the water. Man! He was a big brute! I had filled plastic bags with water and added pepper. Had them tied around my waist with fishing line. They were trailing out five metres or so. Well, one of those lines snapped. I had hoped the pepper would make him decide I wasn't fit to eat. It seemed to work."

I was silent for a moment, then pulled the clearest image of the huge fish from the bottom cavern and split the screen, showing the picture of the *EAGLE* etched on copper. "Is this the creature the legend talks about?" I asked, pointing to the fish.

For the first time in a half hour Sam spoke. "The only shelter that beast offered was inside its gut. Only thing I know close to that size would be a sturgeon, but it's not right. The jaw's blunter and full of teeth. And it looks to be the biggest one I've heard of. It's nothing like the picture. It doesn't fit the legend, not that part of it." He paused. "But one look at the business end of those jaws and a man could make a convincing snake story. I never quite believed in *The Great Serpent*, but now I wonder..."

I looked at the old man. He simply nodded in agreement with Sam's conclusion.

Blanking out the image of the fish, I brought up a picture of the *EAGLE*. Sam sat forward like a lightening bolt had struck him.

"What's...? That's no painting, Indigenous or otherwise." He fell silent, staring.

"I call it the *EAGLE*. It's a bit like an eagle ray, a kind of fish." I spoke with quiet earnestness. "It's hidden right now in a little cave. It's been there for over a year. It's time I brought it out if the computers on it haven't been fried. I think there is another way into that cavern. It will be somewhere on the bottom of Lake Superior. With the *EAGLE,* I can find it. With the *EAGLE,* I can bring people to where they will be safe.

"I didn't know about the legend till Sam told me when he flew me into the valley the first time. Legends get my brain going in weird circles—or give one more proof I'm a nutcase. I'm not sure which. I couldn't help making the connection, the creature coming out of the water sheltering people, and the *EAGLE*. I had already built the *EAGLE*. I was looking for a place obscure enough that I could shelter people there.

"I've got the deed for that valley. With every bank belly up I don't know what the paper's worth, even though it says it's mine. But it doesn't belong to me."

Abruptly I fell silent, then continued more slowly.

"Father, you saw the pictures of the plates. They don't belong in a white guy's hands. They should go to your people but I need the value of them. They could buy fuel for Sam's chopper. They could buy food for people who are starving. They could buy somebody not looking too close while a locked door gets opened and people sneak out. They can also get people killed. White-men go insane over anything they can call a treasure. Do you have any ideas?"

"Well sir, I misremember that a white-man ever spoke ta me like I was an elder of his own people before. I don't carry so much weight 'mong the leaders no more. They figure there's nothin' but air 'tween these old ears. They're probably right. But if I was ta put a word into the right ears, they'd listen if they could feel the weight o' one o' them plates. If t'was rightly First Nations treasure they'd pay a million for it."

The old man cackled. "What colour bum wipe you like best? The blue ones with the five on them, or the hunnerds? They're the colour of a deer in spring." His chuckle died away. "Actually we can get you more of what you needs than most white mens. We ain't forgot ever'thin' our grandfathers taught us. Even a dry old tree like me can still teach a young buck some things 'bout huntin'. An' if Sam's telling it straight—and I'm look'n at the bruising on yer face an' the hair stuck ta yer shirt what's all bloody—ya gots most as good a right ta Indian treasure as any man with red skin 'round these parts."

CHAPTER FIFTEEN

RETURN OF THE EAGLE

Saturday, July 4

The helicopter beat its way along the backwater of the French River. Both Sam and I scanned the area for observers. A couple of small fishing boats worked the main river. Three canoes laboured upstream on the Bad River Channel. The backwater itself looked empty.

Sam nosed the helicopter in where a shelf of rock offered a step for me. With the struts nudging the rock, he hovered while I threw a pack out, then jumped. The change in weight caused the helicopter to lift. Sam drew up and away.

I waved, then turned quickly to my task.

Five minutes later I slipped into the water. I submerged and swam to the rock hump that held the cave entrance. I searched again for any observers, then crept into the crevice in the rock and worked my way down the crack until I reached water. From there I swam to the craft. I entered through the upper hatch and activated the furnace. The craft began to hum. Gurgles and thumps sounded as trapped air bubbles in the pipes of the nuclear furnace expanded differently from the water itself.

Twelve minutes after leaving the helicopter, I spoke into the radio: "Thanks for the use of the egg beater. It looks like the cake will turn out okay."

Sam's voice came back. "I'd invite myself for a piece, but since the computer muck-up I can't get life-insurance for your cooking."

"Good hunting, old man. I'll look you up when I can." My voice fell silent again.

"Roger." Sam replied.

I inspected the *EAGLE* inside and out. Periwinkles had cemented themselves onto the lower wing surface. I scraped them away.

I bumped the sides twice as I sat at the controls after so long, lowering the *EAGLE* and then gingerly rising out of the trench with jagged rock fingers reaching towards me. It had been over a year and I found my ability to read the lateral-line sensors almost totally lost. I moved slow enough, however, that I did no damage except to paint.

I remained just where the trench broke into the wider back-water of the French River, letting darkness settle. Then I rose to the surface and moved as quietly as possible back into Georgian Bay, taking several hours to do so. With deeper water beneath me, I submerged once again as the pale light before sunrise began to penetrate the water. Even in those few hours I found myself feeling with the lateral-line sensors. But I didn't trust my ability to descend visually blind and did not want lights to draw attention to the *EAGLE*.

It felt so small and confining now, yet so freeing to be at the controls. I reluctantly rested the *EAGLE* on the bay floor, prepared a simple meal from old canned foods, then opened the bed, musty after so long unused.

Daylight saw me maneuvering just above the bottom of Georgian Bay, testing my abilities once again, working slowly closer to where the ferry used to cross between the Bruce Peninsula and Manitoulin Island.

With very few provisions inside the *EAGLE*, I fished again, sending out a lure and drawing it back in, clumsily retrieving my catch through the lower access panel.

I made a poor meal. It had been too long since I had cooked in the tiny galley. But I managed to choke it down and went to bed feeling full, if not totally satisfied.

In the *gloaming* (there was one of those words Dad had loved) I brought the *EAGLE* up and took to the air, skimming the surface. My GPS didn't work, no surprise with satellite communications still down. Few if any radar stations would be operating and in the low contrast lighting just after sunset, I would be difficult to see.

Because of the risk of discovery, I had only flown the *EAGLE* twice since the day I had launched it. Ponderous and clumsy in the air, flight wasn't exactly a thrill. Yet, the fact that I *could* fly continued to astonish me. Staying in ground-effect, two metres above the surface, I accelerated. Because ground effect flying used so much less power than free flight, I continued to accelerate. At 230 kilometres per hour, the profile drag created by the bulbous shape of the craft balanced the incredible output of the nuclear furnace. With a full load of fuel water, operating at maximum power, I could go no faster.

I crossed the channel into Lake Huron and after another 42 minutes had flown the length of Manitoulin Island. Angling more to the west, I followed the shoreline of Drummond Island on my right. As I approached Martin Bay at the northwest tip of Lake Huron, I pulled back on the control. The *EAGLE* lost speed slowly as it rose. In a wide sweeping turn to the north, I crossed Interstate 75 in U.S. airspace, then passed over water again at Naomikong Point, in Whitefish Bay. My speed had dropped to 147 kph before I began descending.

Michipicoten Island lay 192 kilometres directly ahead. Accelerating again, I covered the distance in an hour. Drawing close, I slowed and submerged. The eastern horizon was tinged with pink as water closed over the pilot's sphere.

Sunday, July 5

Where the tiny islet protected the inlet to the hunting camp, the *EAGLE* crept into the shadow of jagged rock. The peculiar formation amplified the waves into a frothing maelstrom. I had only rarely dared take the canoe through. Carved by the churning water, I had seen a hint of a hollow that gave a submarine entrance under the protected valley.

I felt quite comfortable with the lateral-line sensors again as I felt my way in, though I moved as slow as I could manage. I maneuvered until I could see the hollow beyond me. It looked like enough room for the *EAGLE* inside, but I had to widen the opening.

It took a while to learn to handle the jack-hammer properly with the manipulator arms, but an hour broke out enough stone for the *EAGLE* to slip through. I used the manipulator arms to brace the craft. Little of the stone hollow reached above water, but a crack opened into the roof a metre above the upper access panel of the *EAGLE*. With the anchorage made doubly sure, I emerged from the hatch and wormed my way into the crack. In a tortured route barely large enough to navigate, it twisted and turned, angling back to the face of the cliff. It reached morning daylight between two massive boulders. From there the trail down along the shoreline was child's play. It gave a better docking spot than I had dared hope for.

It was a Sunday and strange as it sounds, I missed church—missed the music and even the preaching. The rebel in me would have been drawn to the underground church—probably taking stupid risks and putting everybody at risk. *Maybe that's why you're alone at the back end of nowhere,* I mused. At least the risks I took crawling through holes in the ground didn't put other lives on the line. I used to have to brush the dust off my Bible any time I picked it up. Now it showed signs of wear. I took the rest of the day off.

Monday, July 6

I spent two days improving the tunnel. A hammer and chisel can accomplish surprising things in a short time, especially when gravity does most of the work removing the rubble. I placed a thick mat over the *EAGLE* to protect it from falling pieces.

When Sam flew over three days later and saw smoke drifting from the chimney, he set the helicopter down. "So!" he shouted over the slowing blades. "I figured I'd have to dredge the bottom of the big puddle to find your body. Your 'flying submarine' actually got you here." He grinned as he stepped into the rocking canoe.

"Welcome, Sam. Now that I'm not totally at the mercy of a crazy man with a flying eggbeater, I might be able to get along with you. Come for a tour. There's a pot of stew on the stove but it'll improve with a few hours simmering." My paddle dipped softly. The canoe glided across the calm bay. Drawing it up onto the shingling rock near the inlet, I led Sam up to the crack between boulders.

"I should have held back on the grub," I said as I looked critically at his large torso. "Half a man, like you so graciously call me, gets through this hole easier than one and a half."

"Is this that cave you got all the pictures of?" Sam stared suspiciously into the dark crack. "You taking me down for shark bait?"

"I just found this one. The garage door opener doesn't work yet. The installers had a delay." I paused, thinking. "I hadn't thought of bait." I spoke with exaggerated seriousness. "It might work. I wonder what kind of hook I could use? Something the size of an anchor, maybe?"

"Get yourself down there before I nail your scalp to the entrance for a beacon."

"These violent Savages! Another massacre of innocent white folks. I can see the headlines now..." I chuckled as I ducked into the dark entrance. Sam's grunting followed me.

"It's only a little way down," I called back to Sam. "If you get stuck I've got some dynamite back in the storage cave. I wouldn't think it would take more than two or three sticks to open a hole you'd fit through." I stepped onto the *EAGLE* and raised the access panel. By the time Sam had forced his way through the tight squeeze, lights glowed in the small dome above the water surface.

"Looks like a bug somebody stepped on." Sam panted out the words.

"Come on in, Sam. One of these bigger waves is going to soak your feet any minute. I know how bad your socks stink when they get wet."

Sam grunted and lowered himself down the ladder. He stared

apprehensively around as I closed and secured the access panel. Turning back, I spoke appreciatively. "That's your first time through a hole in the rock I think. There's many a brave man can't make themselves do it. Then there's idiots like me who never know when they should be scared. Thanks for coming in, Sam. I really wanted you to see the *EAGLE*, to get a feel for what she can do, where she can go."

I pulled myself into the pilot's sphere. Sam crouched at the entrance peering over my shoulder into the tiny space. The cluster of dials must have looked childish beside the helicopter's. Winking lights and the glowing computer monitor seemed to fill the area.

"How come your computer still works?" Sam asked.

"The computer's an old one. It was cutting edge when I bought it. But it's never been on the Internet. The programming was better than anything I'd used before. I was busy enough finishing the *EAGLE* I never got a chance to see what other toys were out there. I guess *The Virus* was already out there, reproducing itself with all the restraint of a tomcat. I must have just snuck in under the wire.

"I never trusted computers. I got into the habit of backing up stuff, assuming the system was going to fail. It got me thinking how stupid we were to build empires a single microchip could bring down. I talked myself into being afraid of the Internet. I used an old computer just for that. If I had to go online, that was the only computer I used. I never transferred files from that computer, not even with my virus check up to date. Seems like I wasn't far wrong."

The computer screen flashed a checklist. I clicked each item as I scanned dials and instruments. "The computer simplifies life. I'd have trouble living without it."

Power level was approaching maximum. I reduced power, slipped back through the hatch and stripped my outer clothes off.

"Don't look so shocked, Sam. You know the lateral line sensors almost every fish has? This is the closest I could come." Slipping the tape down through my shorts, I fastened it to my legs and side, then quickly dressed again. "There's another set here," I said as I opened a door and pointed to neatly hanging thin strips. "You might want to try it. It took months to learn to read them, but from the very first day they helped. I think you'd find it interesting." I reentered the pilot's sphere, clipped the wire from the lateral line sensors into the instrument panel, then fastened my safety belt.

The craft lurched as the mechanical arm disengaged its anchorage against the rock. I blew enough ballast water to gain neutral buoyancy. Slowly, carefully, I maneuvered through the turbulent waters of the entrance channel.

For an hour we explored along the deepening lake floor. Sam occasionally exclaimed over different features. Then I blew ballast water and took the *EAGLE* to the surface. "I wanted to be well clear of the shore before we did this, Sam," I said. "There are people who would kill for the *EAGLE* and its power-plant." Rocking gently on the surface, I turned the craft slowly in a full circle, searching the water around me. A faint streak marked the shoreline far to the east. My instruments recorded a small aircraft 30 kilometres south. Its slow airspeed suggested a helicopter. I turned northward and fed steam to the jet.

As the craft accelerated, Sam continually turned to stare out each side window. Then we were airborne.

"It really does fly," I heard Sam mutter. "I wouldn't have believed it coming from anybody else. I'm not sure I believe it now."

"What are you griping about back there, Sam?"

"What? Oh nothing... Just thinking out loud."

For 15 minutes, we flew toward the northwest. Sam's eyes turned often to the instruments. The ground speed indicator showed 210 kilometres per hour when the shoreline at Terrace Bay appeared as a brown streak ahead. Elevation showed two metres.

I pushed a button. A soft mechanical rumble sounded, and the whine of wind against some obstruction. I knew Sam would be feeling a slight dragging sensation through his feet. "Just fuelling up, Sam. That's both the beauty and the weakness of this machine. So long as I stay close to water, it'll go just about forever. But it wouldn't be impressed with the Sahara." The muted thunder of the jet increased. A dull *thunk* sounded and the wind-whine stopped. I pulled back on the control stick. The nose rose up, away from the water.

At 354 metres altitude, we began a wide sweeping left turn. The ground-speed indicator showed 142 kilometres per hour. Isle St. Ignace showed on our right. As we continued to turn, a brown smoke-smudge obscured Thunder-Bay. We passed over the northeastern tip of Isle Royale. Fourteen minutes later Keweenaw Point fell behind on our right as we began to descend again, flying almost due east toward Michipicoten Island. As the island drew closer, I again settled into ground effect flight and the *EAGLE* accelerated.

Still eight kilometres out, I brought the craft to a near standstill and submerged. Two hours later I stirred up the embers in the cabin stove, then reheated the stew. Sam sat in contemplative silence.

After we had eaten and washed the dishes, Sam spoke quietly: "You really built that thing? And it really runs on water? You've got hot running water out here in this valley everybody thinks is cursed. There's no fire heating your water. There's no generator roaring in the background. What planet did you say you were from?"

I laughed. "I wonder what planet myself sometimes." I mused silently for a moment. "It was a small thing for me to dream up the *EAGLE*. It was a slightly bigger thing for me to do the math and work it out on paper. To actually make a start on it wasn't real significant. My bedroom was full of projects started." I stopped again, searching for words. "To actually finish the *EAGLE*, to see it in the air, and underwater, working, not sunk... I don't know, Sam. That job's bigger than me. Somebody had His spurs in me for a long time. I can't show you many finished projects. I can't explain how this one got finished, or why it works.

"I can show you the numbers. I can show you the drawings and the specs. But that doesn't translate into a guy like me building a flying submarine that runs on steam jets and leaves no pollution behind." I shook my head, then chuckled. "Every once in a while I amaze myself."

As Sam buckled his safety belt in the helicopter, I stood on the strut, gazing up into the cockpit. "I've got another project for you, Sam, if you can find the time. You know those packing cases we parked at the Trading Store? Can you bring them and drop them in the water just beyond the little island out here? I can pick them up with the *EAGLE* out there."

"Time?" Sam snorted. "I better check my schedule. I think I've had two hours paid flying time since bringing your stuff back from the barge." His big hand gripped mine in a bone-crushing squeeze. "I'll see if I can squeeze you in somewhere. They as heavy as that first one?"

"They're pretty much the same." I stepped down into the canoe as the motor on the helicopter began to whine, then burst into a deep throaty rumble. "Good hunting, old man." I whispered the words as I paddled away from the downdraft as the blades began to spin.

The valley I had grown to love seemed suddenly bleak and empty.

CHAPTER TWENTY-ONE

TO THE CENTRE

Monday, September 21

My search along the lake bottom had gone on for days. I found garbage. I found the wreckage of boats. I even found a house, largely intact, sitting upright. I could see it at 252 metres and couldn't resist taking a closer look.

It may have been carried on a barge that capsized. It may have drifted, buoyed up by air trapped under the roof after the shoreline was undercut during a storm. I almost expected to see smoke drifting from the chimney, mermaids and mermen coming out the doors.

It sat at a strange angle. The remains of a deck leaned over the edge of a rock shelf. The door and deck, leaning and seeming to stare pointedly into the abyss, moved me in an uncanny way.

I called myself a fool but took the craft deeper. The ledge dropped almost vertically for 24 metres. My lights showed granite, sheared off by the mighty power of glaciers eons ago. Seams of softer rock had been gouged deeply from the face of the wall. At another 73 metres depth it abruptly thrust out 89 metres, showing coloured streaks of other rock intermingled with the granite. The out-thrust proved to be merely a bulge, almost like a belly hanging over a belt.

At 331 metres down my lights probed under the bulge. Granite, with streaks of white and rose quartz reflected off the ceiling. I could see no back.

I spent long minutes under the edge of the overhang, turning the craft slowly to search as far as my lights could probe. My sonar indicated 36 metres of water below me, and 64 to the back wall. The vault appeared to run east/west for a kilometre. I wanted the LiDAR system running but the current was just strong enough that I didn't want to leave the controls.

As I moved slowly in, the ceiling lowered gently. The current became noticeably stronger as I approached the back wall. A heady exhilaration filled me. There was now no doubt about it. I had found the mouth of an underground river. More and more, I had to increase power to hold place.

When I entered the actual mouth, the current distorted my vision, but sonar measured the opening at 24 by 8 metres. That gave enough room for the craft, but with bulges of rock coming from the sides or ceiling or floor, it wasn't a place for carelessness.

I cautiously moved forward, holding the *EAGLE* near the middle of the shaft. After 68 metres, the tunnel turned sharply upward. The closer I got to the turn, the more turbulence. Using all my skill, still rusty after so long, I held the *EAGLE* in position for several minutes while I tried to discover a means of safely dealing with the turbulence.

It had already been a long day and my bladder was making insistent demands. I needed full alertness for who knew how many hours. Reducing my power slightly, I let the current draw me backwards. Keeping the *EAGLE'S* nose turned directly into it, I felt my way to the mouth of the river.

I checked and rechecked the exact coordinates of my position, entered them into the computer as well as wrote them into the log. Then I brought the craft out from under the overhang. I moved up the rock face until I reached a level shelf at about 30 metres depth. I settled the craft solidly on the lake floor. After checking instruments one more time, a ritual that had become automatic, I drew myself through the small opening into the second sphere.

Tuesday, September 22

I ate a quick breakfast, spent an hour monkeying with the LiDAR mapping system, then piloted the craft down to the overhang. Checking the coordinates carefully, I passed under the bulge well east of the underground river. I moved slowly along the back face of the overhang, carefully examining features. Granite, white and rose quartz, and the occasional purple gleam of amethyst reflected my lights back. A large fissure opened 300 metres from the east end. It stretched and curved upward at one side like a crooked grin on a huge mouth. Bigger even than the mouth of the underground river almost a kilometre west, it beckoned me. I moved slowly and carefully into it. As I passed beyond the mouth, my instruments could detect an almost imperceptible current.

In the powerfully flowing river farther west, there was no question of finding some blind alley and becoming lost. The question was getting in and back out without being battered to pieces. In the newly found passage, the possibilities of blind leads were all too great. I would have to mark my path before proceeding.

I had equipped the *EAGLE* with an assortment of tools. It was a simple matter to grasp a paint stick in one of the mechanical arms and place a mark on the rock wall of the river channel at specific intervals. Too much like graffiti, I hated defacing the natural beauty, but safety sometimes overrides other things. The popsicle sticks I preferred to use wouldn't stay where I tried to place them.

For several hours, I followed the dormant channel. Sometimes it climbed steeply. Sometimes it ran almost level. A few times, it dipped slightly. I never went more than 100 metres before stopping to mark the walls. Only once did I come upon an alternate route through which the craft could have passed. Each time I stopped to mark the walls, I also checked that the computer was recording what the LiDAR system was mapping. Somehow this didn't seem like a good place to get lost.

I had never fully overcome my distrust of computers. There were many twists and turns, but the channel consistently led me in a northerly direction, ever closer to the surface.

Several times I found myself in large chambers with high ceilings. Once, with 135 metres of water pressure bearing down, I found a vault with a large pocket of trapped air. But the pressure at this depth was still too great for my purposes.

Just beyond that chamber, after a dip and then a sharp rise in the direction of the channel, I passed over a jumble of boulders and loose debris. Spread over the floor, it obstructed much of the channel. There was hardly room to pass through. I moved with increased caution. Several small streams of water burst through openings in the rubble and made the task of piloting much more difficult.

As soon as I passed the rubble I found the channel dramatically reduced in size. It barely allowed the craft to maneuver. It led me almost straight up for 91 metres. A couple of narrow spots took several minutes of maneuvering to wiggle the *Eagle* through. Then once again it meandered off in a gentle slope, working toward the north.

At 7.9 kilometres inland from the Lake Superior shoreline, I was almost 12 kilometres from my point of entry. Because of the twisting, meandering channel, I had traveled 28 kilometres when the channel widened out under a vaulted ceiling. The craft broke the water's surface into a pocket of trapped air. As I moved forward, I found the water increasingly shallow until I could go no farther.

I plotted my position to within a kilometre of the cavern in which the great fish had attacked me. When I broke surface at the same depth, but in a different cavern, a thrill of excitement coursed down my spine.

There had been no measurable current since passing through the rubble-strewn section. I blew ballast tanks, lightening the craft, and then moved it part way up onto a smooth, pebbled shelf. I could not see over the rock in front of me, but the ceiling stretched beyond what my lights could reveal.

My instruments indicated an air temperature of 9.8°C. Nitrogen registered at a normal 77.95%. Oxygen showed slightly lower at 19.05%. Carbon dioxide and methane were both significantly higher than above ground, at 0.65% and 0.004% respectively. Argon, normally the 3rd most plentiful gas, registered at a normal 0.95%. Minute amounts of several other gasses made up the remaining 0.07%. My instruments detected trace amounts of the deadly poison, hydrogen sulphide.

Methane and hydrogen sulphide were the worrisome ones, although methane could be multiplied another 250 times before it reached the one percent threshold of coal-mining safety standards.

With no perceivable air movement I worried about stratification in the still air. I moved the craft back into deeper water. Turning 180 degrees, I carefully manipulated ballast to lower the front end as steeply as possible in the water. With the manipulator arms acting as anchors, I brought the jet up to full power.

It was uncomfortable, but the blast of steam stirred up a great pocket of trapped air that may have been undisturbed for hundreds or even thousands of years.

For ten minutes I held that position. I felt dizzy when I finally reduced power, readjusted ballast, and righted the craft. Remaining low in the water, I once again tested the air quality and composition. The carbon dioxide concentration had dropped to 0.61%. Methane concentration had risen to 0.006%. Hydrogen sulphide could no longer be detected.

I again blew the ballast tanks, brought the craft up onto the pebbled shelf, then set it firmly on solid rock with the top half of the pilot's sphere clear of the water. In the cold air, steam from the *EAGLE* had filled the chamber with fog. I could see almost nothing.

After another quick check of instruments I pulled myself through to the second sphere. It had been over 11 hours since I had taken to deep water. I hadn't been aware of how hard I had been gripping the controls, but my hands felt strangely weak.

I knew I should eat before leaving the craft but so much effort had led to this moment. I quickly stripped and pulled on heavy thermal underwear, then well insulated outer clothing. Donning a miner's hat and chest waders, with a pair of sturdy walking shoes draped over my shoulder, I opened the upper hatch.

I lay the equipment I wished to take with me on the surface of the craft, went back in and slipped the nine-millimetre handgun into a pocket. I loaded six cartridges, checked and double checked that the hammer was down. I couldn't help thinking I had read too many weird adventure stories. Still, the memory of great gaping jaws moved me quickly from the shallow water.

Comfortable with rifles and shotguns, handguns seemed foreign and deadly to me. The gun came from the confrontation with the fuel plant security guard. I would never have purchased it—couldn't have legally. Sam had probably taught me more than needed but I'd never taken a firearms safety course.

Three metres of wading brought me to a rock ridge that rose above the water level. The ceiling looked like another 20 metres above that. The chamber appeared about 80 wide. I climbed the sloping rock, polished smooth by running water over who knows how many years. It showed evidence of recent water in small hollows still half full.

As far back as my lights could reach, the chamber seemed to widen to 150 metres. The fog, just beginning to thin, gave a ghostly feeling to the air. Above the ridge, a lake, a metre higher in level than where I had beached the *EAGLE*, covered much of the floor of the chamber. Along the south side of the lake, a beach, a blend of pebbles, sand, and scoured rock, rose smoothly out of the water and reached back under the lowering ceiling.

I stripped off the hip waders, then turned and looked back to where the craft lay in shallow water. Its lights, far more powerful than my miner's lamp, cast a glow that reached far into the recesses of the cavern, still shrouded with fog.

Logic said this had to be part of the same cave complex I had entered earlier. But it was so much larger that logic battled with what my senses told me.

A splash startled me. Turning, I saw ripples widening on the surface of the lake. Where my light played on the water a fluid movement betrayed a good sized fish.

I laughed as I realized that even as I turned, my hand had thrust into my pocket and closed around the gun. It would have required only a small flight of fancy at that moment if Professor Hardwigg from Jules Vern's, *Journey to the Center of the Earth*, as well as Henry & Hans had appeared, lighting their way with a Ruhmkorff coil. My laughter sounded loud, almost profane in the cathedral like stillness. I became silent again, thinking that something the size of a rocket launcher would make facing that huge fish a lot more comfortable than the little popgun I carried.

Over the next hour I explored the shoreline. A high water mark showed a metre above the present water level along the shoreline. At that height, it would have overflowed into the channel I had brought the craft up. I found bits of wooden flotsam, usually little more than splinters. So I was sure this lake was fed from the surface. Several times fish jumped, the splash startling me.

The chamber varied considerably in width. At the eastern end of the lake white froth bubbled up. A visible current carried it west, apparently stirring the entire lake. I could go no farther.

It seemed reasonable to assume the froth came from the same waterfall that had spit me almost into the jaws of a monster fish.

I turned back, this time exploring close to the outer extremity of the chamber where the ceiling and floor of the rift came together. Much of the time I walked on firmly packed sand, faintly marking with my footprints. At one point I found a large basin carved out of the floor, almost 12 metres across and four deep. Half full of water, it had no visible source or outlet. A massive cone descended from the ceiling above it, so it seemed likely that some time in the distant past massive water-flow had created a whirlpool here and most likely rolling stones had carved the basin. Two smaller basins flanked the large one.

My walk had been a slow exploration. The cold air had chilled me. I walked briskly for the last hundred metres to the rock above the craft. Although chilled, I delayed going back into the confines of the *EAGLE*. My watch showed 2 a.m. It seemed like stars should be shining and the moon reflecting off the lake. Somehow, I could not escape the illusion of being outdoors.

I spent three days in the cavern, exploring, planning. I removed as many provisions as I could spare from the craft and piled them neatly well above the high-water mark. Every bit of space and every kilogram I could possibly gain when I returned would be helpful.

Wednesday, November 11

Entering the craft, I sealed the upper hatch and pulled myself into the pilot's sphere, then made a quick pre-trip inspection. I brought power up to one-third. With ballast blown, the craft lifted off the rock shelf. I moved back into deeper water and submerged, turning 180 degrees. Holding power carefully in check, but at a high enough level to give maneuvering ability, I followed the channel down.

I continually added ballast in small amounts and let the weight do most of the work of the descent. The marks on the rock walls were faint but visible as I moved ever downward. It had taken 11 hours to navigate the channel the first time, although marking and charting my route had lengthened that time. It took two hours and 50 minutes to come back out.

I emerged from the river channel at 331 metres depth. Few boats were on the water this late in the season. The computer virus, activated seven months earlier, had crippled much of the technology. But most of the hardware still existed. Programmers drawing huge wages had been working around the clock. Power-grids were rebuilding. A militant police-state was emerging out of the chaos. I could no longer assume I was invisible. I remained in deep water, moving towards Sault Ste. Marie.

Nine hours later I rested the *EAGLE* on a shelf of rock 183 metres down. I prepared a meal, then gave myself a workout on the treadmill. After a shower and an hour with my journal, I opened a book on the computer and read. I dozed in the afternoon, but set an alarm to wake me at 11:00 p.m.

My computer tried to upgrade when I turned it back on, although it wasn't connected to the Internet, if the Internet even existed still. It had done this several times before but it still took me two hours to get it working right so I could navigate again. I finally got going a bit after 1:00 and surfaced in White Fish Bay at 2:00 a.m. The boathouse I had rented from the Essar Steel Algoma Company served my purposes well. It was a bit of a fool's act to be in there with lights on at night, but with the cavern waiting I couldn't talk myself into delaying for another full day.

Before the sun was up I had the *EAGLE* loaded to capacity and underwater again.

CHAPTER TWENTY-TWO

TO MAKE A BEGINNING

Equipping and provisioning the cave took months. After building the *EAGLE* I thought I could tackle anything, but tents, curtain doors and a few real doors demanded a whole different skill set. Add in a workable kitchen and workable bathrooms and showers. Being something of a tech-nerd didn't prepare me for that. I used pipe for the tent frames. I don't know how many lengths of pipe I cut and threaded (that much I could figure out), but when I tried to put them together they would come out two centimetres long or two centimetres short. That close but wrong, over and over, had me wanting to tear my hair out. "Ha, I'll bet that's why Dad started swearing at the computer. He'd already yanked out all his hair." *Somebody should do a study on male-pattern baldness with that in the equation.*

I brought in the two nuclear furnaces Sam had deposited beyond the entrance to the Smokey Ridge Hunting Camp. He had never got the third one moved. They were miserable things to handle. I had to hold one on top of a wing of the *EAGLE* with the manipulator arms, then blow all the ballast on one side and weight the other side to level out. Because of the weight I couldn't gain neutral buoyancy, so had to rise under steam power all the way. It made it awful dicey going up that underground river. I also had to drop the packing cases and spend hours deepening the channel at a couple places. I stirred up mud with no current to carry it away, so worked half blind much of the time.

After the furnaces were in place, it took many days to move components for two generators to a chosen site high on a rock shelf. Using sections of threaded aluminum pipe to form a tripod, I hung a block and tackle, then hoisted the pieces. There at least, I could shift the tripod enough that it didn't matter if the lengths weren't perfect. Finally, I assembled one of the units and brought it into production. The generator fed a growing web of cables.

With hot water and electricity available, a slow transformation began to take place. I built a simplistic hydroponic unit. PVC pipe formed a grid in seven parallel rows on firmly packed sand. Gluing the joints looked so simple, but a quarter of them leaked after my first attempt. The words that sometimes echoed off those stone walls reminded me too much of the way Dad used to swear at the computer. I'd promised myself I wouldn't ever be like him that way, but... How anybody who could build the *EAGLE* could struggle so much with such basic plumbing baffled me.

I managed a two-centimetre drop for every seven metres of length. I filled the pipe two-thirds full of coarse sand, then drilled four-centimetre holes in the top, spaced 15 centimetres apart. I suspended fluorescent fixtures from a framework. I had a lot of LED's as well, but used the fluorescents first while I experimented and learned. An aquarium pump ran for eight hours a day, cycling a half hour on and an hour off. The lights ran 18 hours a day.

Many times as I worked, an upwelling of water close to the shore showed the presence of the huge fish. If I had to be close to the edge, especially where the shoreline dipped steeply into deep water, I walked cautiously. With more and more light in the cavern, I knew the creature would be adjusting to a different world in which I was visible, even above the surface. It seemed a guarantee that this great cavern joined the one I had entered by way of the waterfall.

The air temperature still stood at 9.8°C, so many of the seeds I planted came up through wet sand, then just kind of sat there for a week or so before they died.

I always thought gardening came naturally, that stuff just grew. Maybe that was true up above where the sun shone. I was way out of my league. It had never occurred to me to download books on a subject that *everybody already knew.* Everybody except me, apparently. Still, within a few short weeks I had more lettuce than I could use.

I built a tent over the hydroponic unit. Even with just the lights, the temperature inside rose several degrees and that seemed to make all the difference. I added peppers and tomatoes, with a scattering of flower seeds among the vegetables. I also started a compost pile.

I lay a hot-water pipe for 400 metres in a shallow ditch dug in the sand. The blisters on my hands shamed me, though there was no one else to see. I'd cut and split so much firewood last winter, then hauled it back to the cabin on a sleigh. It was ten times harder work than anything I was doing now, but I could hardly remember a blister then. I guess I'd built up to it slowly.

The hot-water pipe ran roughly parallel with the lakeshore, five metres back from the high-water mark. I attached a valve every 15 metres, again catching myself swearing over leaks and calling myself a fool because of it. A second pipe ran parallel with the first, 40 metres to the southeast.

I staked the outline for a large tent, then attached pipe to the hot water main. A shallow trench led it to the staked tent site where I installed another valve. Closely spaced parallel loops of pipe lay four centimetres deep in firm sand. The pipe then fed to a return line. I levelled the floor and packed it again. Water fed from the nuclear furnace. Opening the small valve, I activated my first home-heating system. The tent went up with the control valve just inside one corner. By the time my watch showed 8 p.m. gentle warmth radiated from the entire floor. Given my luck so far with plumbing, I kept waiting to see water bubbling up through the floor somewhere.

One nuclear furnace now ran at 60 percent capacity. The second one sat in readiness, not yet activated. After a quick meal and feeling like the need for gloves marked me as a wimp, I dug another trench from the hot water main to the higher of the two small natural depressions in the cave floor. I had to break through two ridges of rock to keep the pipe below the surface. With the pipe in place and the valve on full, fog drifted lazily as hot water filled the hole. By the time I had the pipe buried and the sand packed firmly again, the depression was nearly full. A dark stain of water seepage marked the sand. I dug a second trench, feeding from that depression to the lower one. Dirty brown foam flowed along the trench. Laying a large pipe in the bottom of the trench, I tamped the sand firmly around it.

Tired by this time, I brought a chair, clean clothes, and a towel to the upper, highest temperature pool. A thermometer dipped in the water confirmed the temperature at 41°C. With a sigh of contentment, I eased myself in. A skim of dirty foam clung to the edges but that would clear over the next few days.

When I returned the tent was almost too warm. I closed the valve until I could hear a faint hissing, held the flap open for a few moments to let cool air in, then lay my mat on the floor and slipped between the blankets. I slept deeply and dreamlessly.

Saturday, April 24

In another large chamber, opening off the south side of the main cavern, I contrived an animal shelter. The first section could have held a huge barn. It opened up way bigger beyond that. A stream gurgled out of the opening. Little streams and pools sparkled across the chamber floor. Where it broke into the main cavern, a tiny waterfall spilled over a buildup of sediment. I hung lights and fans from low spots on the ceiling. There didn't seem to be any air movement and I was always afraid of pockets of methane gas.

Excess produce from the hydroponic units accumulated quickly as I experimented with different plantings. I moved the compost pile I had started earlier to a place where chickens could peck through it.

I constructed a hydroponic system directly on the floor. With fluorescent lights supported just above the plantings, and wire mesh bent over the narrow strips, birds and rabbits would feed on what grew through the wire, hopefully without uprooting the plants or damaging the planters. An electric fence wire above the top of the fluorescent fixture should discourage the poultry from roosting on the lights. I planted it with a whole mixture of seeds, then built a tent over top, but left it open for about 15 centimetres at the ground with a couple of higher openings. Chickens and rabbits should be able to go in anywhere. Larger birds like geese and turkeys could go through the higher openings. I hoped later to add sheep or goats to the animal mix. The heat from the florescent lights should warm the tent just enough to help with plant growth, though I also added a hot-water loop buried in the sand of the floor. It was a crude installation but should work.

Across the entrance, I built a wire gateway. My first trip out after completing that project I brought back a wriggling mass of garden worms in a rich, pungent smelling pail of well-rotted manure. Sneaking into someone's barnyard to dig up a pail of manure didn't quite feel like a super-hero stunt, but I sure didn't want to get caught and try to explain. Emptying the bucket onto damp sand in a hollow near the centre of the compost, I took care not to burn the worms by burying them in the heating mass itself. They could burrow into the sand or move into the compost as quickly as conditions suited them.

Five hens and a rooster came in on the next trip. Three does and a crossbred buck, popular meat rabbit breeds, also came in, as well as a drake and three female Muscovy ducks. I hoped for some wild-type turkeys, but couldn't find any. The worms were well established now and the numbers the poultry would eat posed little danger to the population. They had moved down into the sand and were spreading along the bottom layers of the compost. The chickens and ducks would have difficulty even finding them.

The 9.8°C temperature was cool for chickens and ideal for rabbits. It would slowly increase as the main cavern warmed. The compost itself released considerable heat. The birds and rabbits quickly made themselves at home. They were given the run of the full enclosure, not confined to cages, although that would come.

Five more tents, each one a large, double room unit, went up over heated floors during the next couple of weeks. I was finally getting the hang of basic plumbing. I rarely had to redo the same jobs now. The second pool had flushed itself clear, feeding from the first and about eight degrees cooler. It in turn fed into a large shallow pool and from there into the deep stone hollow already half-full of cold water. I added additional heat to the large pool until the temperature reached 22°C.

The swimming pool sized depression took several days to fill. I had more than enough to keep me occupied, so never got too impatient. The lip bordering the low side, closest to the lake, appeared to be slightly above the high-water line. It would only be in times of exceptionally high-water levels the pool would ever be fed. Until my interference, the water looked as still as death.

Channeling the outflow away from the main pool demanded a lot of labour. I was unwilling to tamper with the temperature of the lake itself although long before the task was done I was sorry for my choice. Four day's work cut a drainage channel. Twenty metres had to be chiseled out of the rock. I could dig the other 200 metres through sand. As the tiny, warm stream flowed to the west, I set lights along the way and planted seeds in the damp sand. Depressions formed shallow pools. The stream itself could be stepped across in most places. Only a few of the plants survived. I still didn't know what I was doing but I think it was still a bit too cool. Even those plants gave a sense of visual warmth to the great cavern.

Two additional trips to the outside brought back food staples: wheat, pot barley, rice, dried beans and lentils, coffee, tea, and salt.

I brought seeds of a wide variety of vegetables and herbs. The seeds came mostly from private gardeners who hoarded their supplies. Coffee was especially hard to get hold of.

The buying also proved a challenge. People were suspicious of cash and gave only a fraction of its face value. Jewelry worked but seemed to raise other suspicions.

I built a second hydroponics unit with heating coils in the sand floor. Once enclosed in a plastic tent, the internal temperature quickly rose to 29°C. Peppers and tomatoes thrived. I set out young grapes and planted more flowers. The compost continued to accumulate. The worms multiplied.

Between the hydroponic units in the main chamber, I set boxes for two hives of honeybees. In a fenced-off alcove of the animal shelter, I set a third though I wasn't sure I'd ever have enough flowers there to warrant it.

The next time I took the *EAGLE* outside, I docked it in the warehouse, then walked into Sault Ste. Marie. After finally arranging the purchase of two colonies of bees, it took a diamond ring to gain the use of a beat-up old pick-up truck to carry them back to the warehouse.

I continued to refine the cavern. I built a shower room with easy access to any of the pools. I installed laundry facilities. I still hated the plumbing. I hung more and more lights. The temperature of the entire cave slowly, almost imperceptibly, crept up. It was a vast heat sink. To raise it even one degree required an incredible expenditure in energy.

Sewage system research had not been high on my wish-list. But I had learned enough to devise a septic system with capacity for a small village. The liquid waste fed into a trapped-air pocket six metres deeper in the dormant underground river system that gave the *EAGLE* passage to the cavern. The first two days of work brought pounding headaches in the oxygen-poor air. Wearing an air tank meant for diving made the remaining days of work clumsy as well as hot and sticky. A stream of water fed through a series of five pools. Anaerobic bacteria would break down septic discharge. The drain-pipe, like the overflow from the pool, required chiseling into the rock itself for part of its length. If I understood things right, the series of pools should handle the waste from 100 people plus. Discharging into the dormant river, it could probably multiply that at least ten times before it ever became a pollution issue in the main lake itself.

I turned my attention to perishable food storage. A chamber of almost 1,000 square metres opened off the main living area just south of the kitchens. Cold and dry, it seemed an ideal storage area. A couple of narrow sections provided natural separations where a minimum of construction could install insulated doors. I sprayed foam insulation over the ceiling and the walls, fearing that frost moving very deep into the rock might cause cracks and a possible collapse. Cancer-causing chemicals? Possibly, but my odds of dying of old age had never seemed too high.

I laid out 1,200 metres of small tubing in parallel loops on the floor. The north segment received double the concentration. Seemingly endless trips with the wheelbarrow covered the tubing with sand as well as hiding the spattering of insulation. Beyond where a third narrowing opened into another large chamber, I installed the refrigeration unit. Resting on an insulated pad, surprisingly little noise could be heard, although in the chosen location it would probably never matter.

I built an insulated wall from floor to ceiling in the small cavern. The aluminum framing was light and flimsy and easily transported. The insulation came in pails of liquid chemical. Building and hanging the doors reminded me again of how limited my construction skills were. The ceiling varied from two to five metres in height and the total area looked like it should work for a thousand people rather than the 120 I had planned for. With the reservoir filled with coolant and the circulating pump running, it took hours to bleed the air out of the system.

With the air bled, I pumped several litres of coolant out of the system, creating a partial vacuum, then turned on the compressor. Within minutes, the tube flowing toward the freezer had a skin of frost over it, while the return pipe felt warm to the touch. Before I finished the wall, a thermometer on the floor showed the temperature at -8°C in the main section and -17°C in the deep-freeze section. I hung ceiling fans and lights from the roof of this chamber. I also hung a thermostat set for -21°C.

I turned the compressor off overnight but kept the circulating pump and fans running, drawing any frost out of the floor. In the morning I thoroughly soaked the sand with warm water while raking the floor smooth. With the compressor turned on again, I used the back of the rake to take out the slight furrows. As I worked backwards toward the door, I continued to spray a fine mist over the cooling sand. The result after several hours work was a cement-like non-slip surface, though I had to rough up a couple spots where I'd used too much water.

It took three days before the thermostat started to shut the compressor off occasionally. A week later, with a few supplies inside, looking like crumbs in a giant's kitchen, the compressor was running only a few hours a day.

There remained much to do, but the cavern was ready for people. The air temperature had crept up from 9.4^{o} to 11.2^{o}C in the main chamber. The hydroponic units held at 18° and 28°C, producing far more than I could possibly use. The rabbits thrived. The hens were laying. I enjoyed fried eggs and omelettes, luxuries I had long gone without.

The Muscovy drake always hissed and threatened when I approached but would waddle away in apparent disgust when I ignored it. Flies buzzed lazily around the compost pile. I knew I had introduced them when I brought in the garden-worms, but the ducks kept the numbers low.

Further exploring broke the days of long, weary labour. A cavern that opened off the north side of the main chamber held black, lifeless water behind a crumbling ledge of shale and sandstone. A clammy, stale odour hung heavy in the air, with a hint of sulphur. A slow drip, amplified in the cavity, was the only sound.

A seam of coal formed the floor and northeast wall above the water. Black mud followed a trail of seepage across the floor. I scanned the mud for any signs of life, even as slight as the trail of a worm. I found none. Where a loose flake of coal hung from the wall, I pried it away. The imprint of a fern leaf stood in black relief on the coalface.

My lungs burned slightly. I suspected a higher concentration of methane here than in the main chamber. I had stopped thinking of it as a cavern. It seemed too big for that.

Farther east, a small chamber led into a tunnel that worked in an easterly direction. The air seemed surprisingly fresh. I followed its twisting contours for 200 metres until a 'T' forced a decision. The air movement seemed to come from the left. Striking a match showed smoke trailing behind me down the tunnel I had first traveled. After two steps to the right, the smoke trailed down that channel as well.

The source of air beckoned, but the hours I had allotted to exploration had already passed. I took the right-hand channel, expecting it to bring me back to the main chamber. 150 metres of climbing and descending in a southwesterly direction brought me to a body of cold water. Grey-white rock with streaks of red and blue walled the small chamber in. With my lights off, just the faintest hint of light reached me from reflections off the wall. It proved this did in fact reach back to the main chamber. However, the path ran into a sheer wall of rock that dropped into black depths my light could not penetrate. The water held life. My lights brought a quick stirring in the depths.

It took an hour to retrace my steps. At the 'T' I reluctantly left the east channel unexplored. I moved back along the tunnel heading west.

A brisk walk brought me to the hydroponic units. For several hours I worked diligently, clearing excess produce. I made repeated trips to the compost pile with a full wheelbarrow. The rabbits and poultry converged, searching for tidbits.

I caught a number of rabbits. Releasing nursing does and several young females, I butchered nine. I boxed and froze the skins, unwilling to waste them. I buried the entrails and heads deep in the compost pile. I cooked the meat of two rabbits, then wrapped and froze the others.

After a good night's sleep, a large breakfast, and a shower, I strode toward the *EAGLE*. A strange ambivalence slowed my steps. I turned and stared back at the tents and glowing hydroponic units. *People* would make it a home. *People* would bring life, action, and sound. *People* would bring confusion and conflict.

"I must be the most selfish guy alive," I muttered. "I haven't earned a nickel of what the *EAGLE* cost or what setting this place up cost. I've done all this on Dad's money. Now I don't want to share it." I sighed, turned my back on the lights and warmth and entered the *EAGLE*, heading for the outside.

Now, I would make a beginning ...

ACKNOWLEDGMENTS

Thank you

to Carolyn for continuing to feed me while I followed a dream, for being
my best critic and for still loving me through it all.

to Laurie, *who doesn't read books by male authors,* but honoured my work
with her feedback.

to Bob – for a Notary Public's trained eye.

to Roy – for a Dr. of Ministry's perspective.

to Ed – for a Submarine Captain's input.

to Matthew – for technical advice and mathematical formulas.

to Colin – for a Banker's attention to little details, and a lover of books
grasp of the big picture.

to so many others who encouraged along the way.

Appendix A, Illustrations

Image 1, Popular Science,
December 1977

Image 2, The *EAGLE*

Wingspan 10.7 metres / 35 feet
Length 15.8 metres / 52 feet
Lower Wing area 35.1 square metres / 371 square feet
Max Weight 29,379 kg / 64,752 lbs
Max Thrust 435,164 ft lbs / sec = 791.2 HP

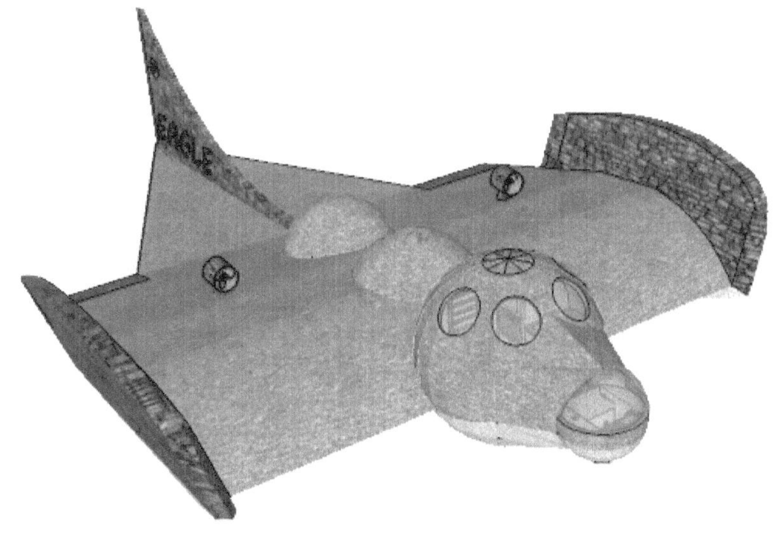

Image 3, Nuclear Furnace

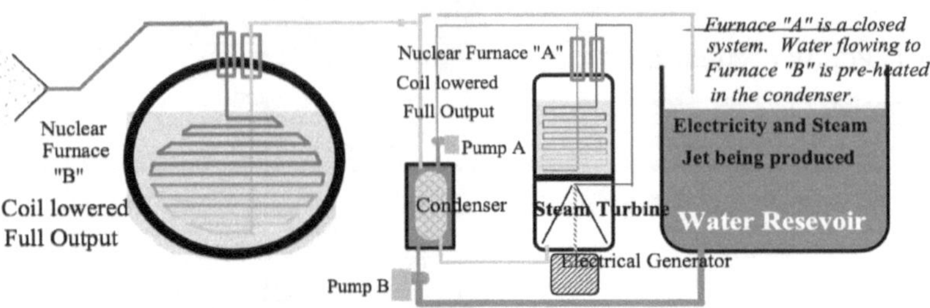

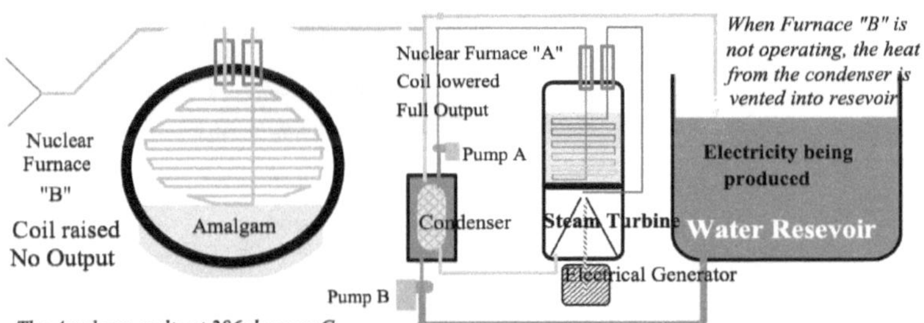

The Amalgam melts at 286 degrees C, allowing the coil to be lowered into it. The mechanism for raising and lowering the coil is not pictured.

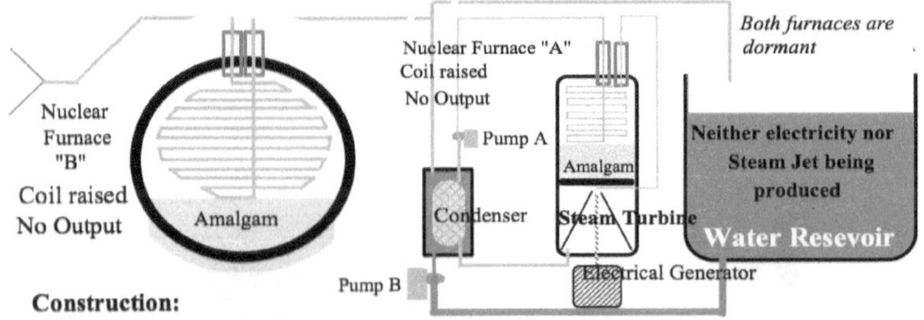

Construction:

1. High temperature steel tubing is bent into a coil. After being etched with acid, paint containing Uranium 293 is applied and baked on at temperatures exceeding 3000 degrees C.
2. An amalgam of murcury, gold and gallium fills the bottom of the chamber.

Operation:

1. Radioactive elements of the paint are inert until immersed in the amalgam. They then increase in temperature, bringing water within the tubing to a boil.
2. Control of heat output is dependent on amount of tubing immersed in amalgam.

For more details see Appendix B.

Image 4, French River Map

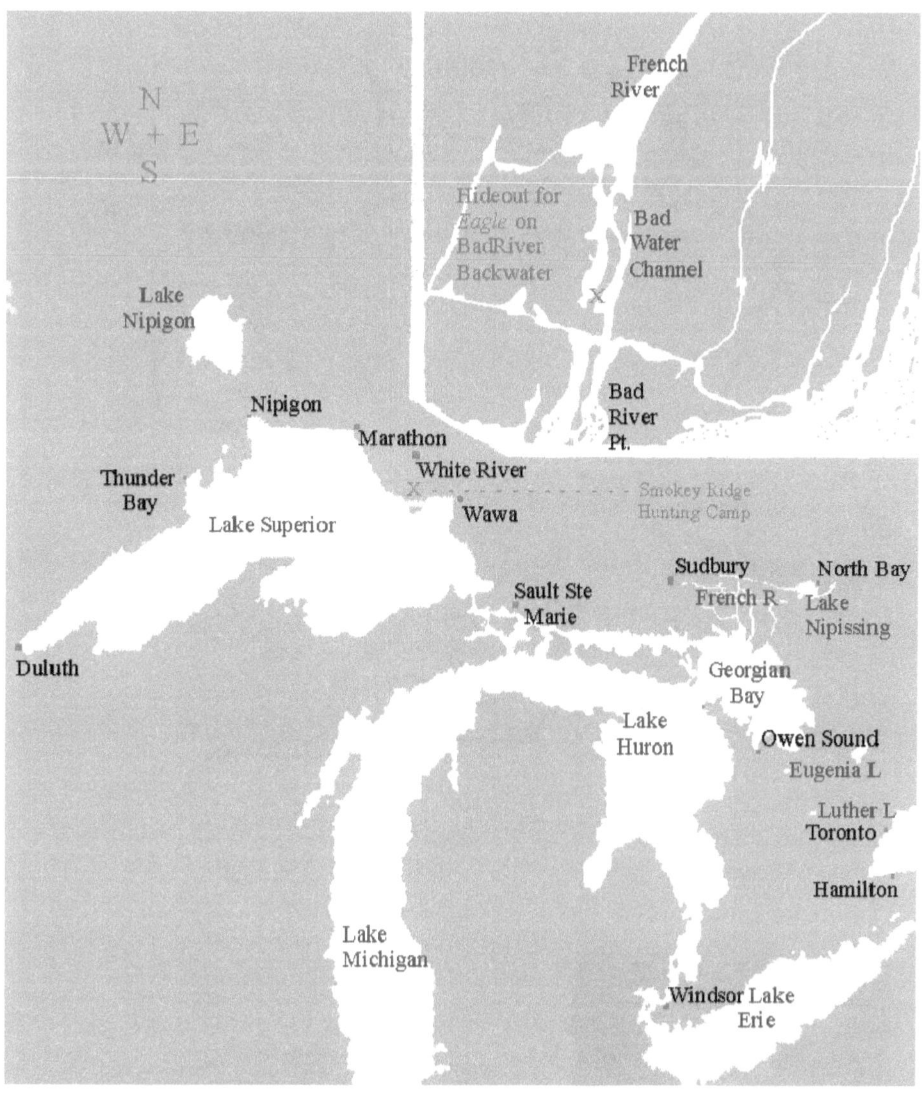

Image 5, Smokey Ridge Hunting Camp

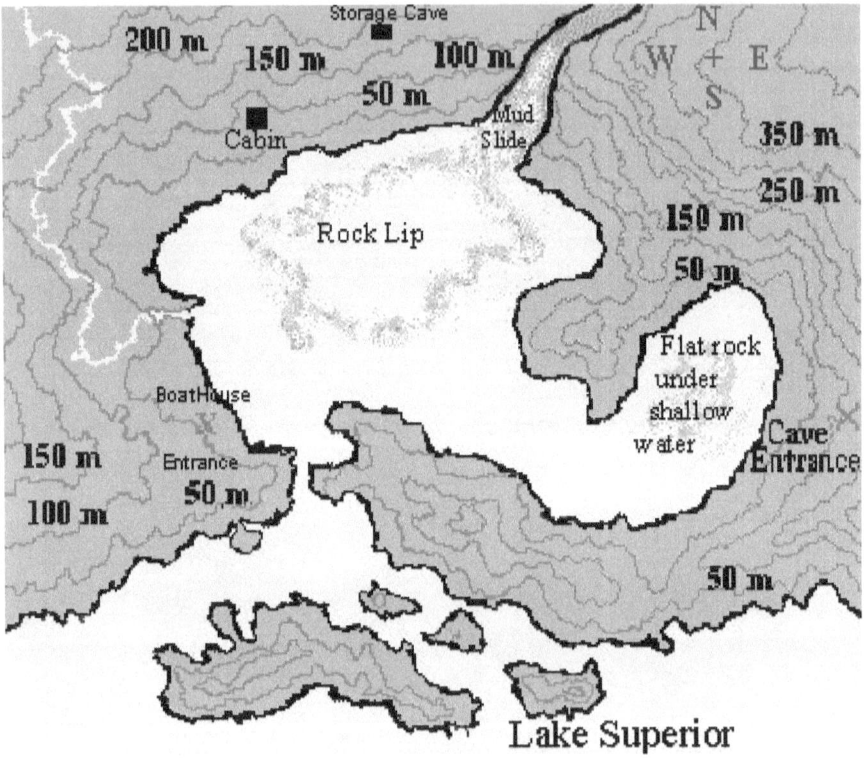

Image 6, Cave Drawings

Image 7, The Fish

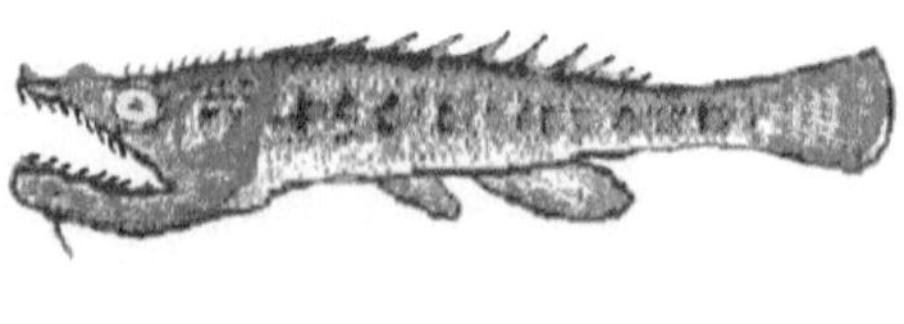

Nuclear Furnace Technical Details

The functioning of the nuclear furnace at its simplest depends on the Uranium isotope coating the coil of pipe, and a solution that activated the isotope.

The solution: an amalgam of mercury, gold and gallium, has a melting point of 286°C. It functions as well when solid. Once the pipe is imbedded in it, the radioactive elements became active. However, temperature control is only possible with the amalgam liquefied, allowing the coil to be raised or lowered, or the amalgam itself to be raised or lowered.

The carrier for Uranium 293: an unrestricted radioactive isotope, Uranium 293 mixes easily with many paints. But few paints adhere to steel alloys without flaking. Even fewer tolerate temperature extremes from 0° to $4,000^{\circ}$C. Acid etching followed by a polymer epoxy coating became the best compromise.

Safety Concerns: the supposed "safety" of the Uranium isotope must be tempered by the reality that it is a radioactive element. It should not be treated complacently. The high temperature at which the furnace functions brings its own special hazards.

Trial and error determined the volume of water that could be boiled, while still keeping the bulk of the amalgam solidified. In the open container, the mercury was a serious hazard if the temperature increased much more.

Advanced Furnace: in a sealed steel sphere, sheathed with ceramics, a mechanical arm raised and lowered the painted coil. The working temperature was regulated at $3,000^{\circ}$C, the internal pressure at 1,500 Kilopascals. (A temperature and pressure combination that would allow normal functioning of the *EAGLE* in deep water, while preventing the amalgam from boiling.) The amalgam stayed fully liquefied, allowing quick adjustments to the positioning of the coil.

The most significant improvement was an expansion chamber with a piston connected to the mechanical arm that raised and lowered the coil. If water-flow was interrupted, steam was restricted, or any other circumstance caused the temperature to climb to dangerous levels, the increased pressure against the piston would lift the coil out of the amalgam, allowing the furnace to cool.

Appendix C, Structural Weights, Contents Weight, Displacement, and Buoyancy in Pounds in Water

	Total Displacement lbs water	Structural Weight in lbs	Contents Weight in lbs	Total Weight in lbs	(Weight) Boyancy in lbs	Comments
1st Sphere	2,956.89	3,848.25	875.01	4,723.26	(1,766.37)	Pilot's Sphere
2nd Sphere	27,819.13	13,576.22	1,599.99	15,176.21	12,642.92	Living Sphere
3rd Sphere	13,702.40	6,218.92	2,400.00	8,618.92	5,083.48	Life Support Sphere
4th Sphere	8,911.41	2,330.77	15,567.01	17,898.78	(8,987.78)	Nuclear Furnace B
Cylinder #1	493.10	232.43	245.00	477.43	15.67	Liquid Oxygen
Cylinder #2	1,459.86	466.17	5,972.00	6,438.17	(4,978.31)	Nuclear Furnace A
Cylinder #3	821.47	362.51	554.00	916.51	(65.04)	Liquid Oxygen
Cylinder #4	711.98	323.79	645.00	968.79	(256.81)	Liquid Oxygen
Cylinder #5	711.98	323.79	645.00	968.79	(256.81)	Liquid Oxygen
Other Structural	567.53	2,528.98	145.00	2,673.98	(2,106.45)	Other Structural
Subtotal 1	**58,155.75**	**30,211.83**	**28,648.01**	**58,859.94**	**(704.09)**	
Propulsion Water Full	5,860.00	0.00	5,860.00	5,860.00	0.00	
Ballast Water	8,125.00	0.00	32.00	32.00	8,093.00	
Subtotal 2	**72,140.75**	**30,211.83**	**34,540.01**	**64,751.84**	**7,388.91**	Minimum weight with no
Ballast Water Full	8,125.00	0.00	8,125.00	8,125.00	0.00	
Subtotal 3	**72,140.75**	**30,211.83**	**42,633.01**	**72,844.84**	**(704.09)**	Maximum weight with no
12 Passengers	0.00	0.00	1,309.99	1,309.99	(1,309.99)	12 Passengers
Subtotal 4	**72,140.75**	**30,211.83**	**35,850.00**	**66,061.83**	**6,078.92**	Minimum weight with 12
Subtotal 5	**72,140.75**	**30,211.83**	**43,943.00**	**74,154.83**	**(2,014.08)**	Maximum weight with 12

About The Author

Books were one of my greatest delights in grade school, high school, and beyond. I devoured the library in the small country school I attended, then practically moved into the much bigger library at the high school. I loved sports, but luring me out of a good book demanded pretty impressive bait. As I grew older, a second passion emerged that led to more than one book being set down too close to aquarium inhabitants who splashed it. I read voraciously, and I wrote, and wrote, and wrote—slowly gaining skill.

Voracious readers don't always become great writers—but they become obsessively unwilling to settle for mediocre writing and impose that on someone else. That is an excellent starting place for quality.

This book had its genesis in the first year of our marriage, sparked by a 1977 *Popular Science* article. It went through multiple rewrites in those first few years. When I became involved with a Writer's Association, it received a complete rewrite EVERY time I learned something new—and there was a great deal to learn. 46 years plus since the first words of this work were hammered out on an old manual typewriter. It should dare to have SOME quality to it by now.

Brian C. Austin

Other Books by Brian C. Austin

Laughter and Tears
(2005) Word Alive Press

Muninn's Keep
(2010) Word Alive Press

Promises and Proclamations from God's Word
(2020) Alanna Rusnak Publishing

THE EMPTY SWING

WHERE EAGLES NEVER FLY BOOK 2

Brian C. Austin

coming later in 2024

www.ingramcontent.com/pod-product-compliance
Lightning Source LLC
Chambersburg PA
CBHW032029310726
48972CB00002B/591